ARRIVED

South Bay Billionaires
Book 1

ASHLEY JACOBS
S. S. RICH

Shelf Indulgences LLC

ISBN 978-1-962441-01-8
ISBN 978-1-962441-00-1 (ebook)

To anyone who daydreams about falling in love with a secret billionaire—this one's for you.

Prologue

Parker

I've watched more than my fair share of people walk away, but watching her do it, for the third time, felt like the worst form of torture.

I knew she was distraught. I knew things hadn't come together the way she wanted them to, but it was heartbreaking all the same.

All I wanted to do was bundle her up in my arms and protect her from the world. Help her discover and achieve every dream she could have. Make a home together, wherever we were, and revel in the safety and comfort of it. Before her, I didn't think love could sustain. I didn't know love could be strong enough to make someone want to stay—even me.

But, with her, I wanted to stay. Oh god, I wanted to. Stay in her orbit, in her heart, at her side. I didn't even realize I had been afraid to let someone in, until she crashed through my defenses and showed me what it meant to be seen, to be cared for. She had opened parts of me I hadn't known were closed, and watching her walk away in that moment sent something sharp straight through the heart of me.

I should've been back in the ballroom with my colleagues,

celebrating the announcement that had just been made. But all I could think about was her–the sound of her laugh, the way her wit answered and challenged my own, the look in her eyes when she fell apart for me–every image that filled my mind was nothing short of perfect.

I had known for a while that she was it for me, that I would do anything for her. I would even give her the space she so clearly needed to process everything that had happened, despite it feeling like I was flaying myself alive.

For now.

Chapter 1

LB

Airports were my happy place. Well, one of them, anyway. For a Southern girl from the Middle of Nowhere, USA, my first plane ride was my ticket to freedom. Going to California and starting college had certainly felt like shedding the shackles of small-town life. Then, before I knew it, I was on a plane every week. But there was still something about that feeling of the world being my oyster that I couldn't shake.

I glanced at my smartwatch and smiled to myself. I had gotten to the airport two hours before boarding, which meant I'd have plenty of time to stop at my favorite cafe and catch up on work before I had to board. Grabbing the handle of my hard-sided carry-on bag from the trunk of my rideshare, I headed into the airport and sized up the security line. I worked for a local venture capital (VC) firm, Price & Livingston Capital, and they covered a couple of security memberships as part of my compensation package. Thank goodness for that, because your girl does *not* like to wait.

It took fifteen minutes to get from the back of the line to Daybreak, the best little breakfast spot in the airport. After ordering my usual–an egg white wrap and a triple soy latte–I grabbed a corner seat right by my gate loading zone and cozied up to an outlet.

That morning, I had already received a pile of emails to respond to, including some related to the startup I was going to Boise, Idaho to court.

A few minutes before they announced the start of the boarding process, my phone vibrated in my pocket. I fished it out and found a text from my boss.

> Mr. Livingston: Make this one count, LB.
> Looking forward to good news.

I closed my eyes briefly and took a deep breath, willing my nerves to settle. He meant well, my boss. Nathaniel Livingston was tough, don't get me wrong, but he was a decent human being. And that just made me want to exceed his expectations more. He'd put a lot of faith in me for this assignment, and I knew what was riding on my success. I'd been working my butt off for the last two years, nonstop. That promotion was mine, and rightfully so, but signing this startup would be the difference between success and failure.

At P&L, your first solo deal was like a pass/fail exam for everything you'd learned up to that point—you either had what it took to be successful in the VC world and got the deal signed, or you didn't. And if you fell into the latter category, your services would no longer be needed at the firm.

For someone who had hung their entire future on succeeding professionally, failure was simply out of the question. I tapped out a quick reply and sent it off.

> Me: You got it, boss! I'll keep you posted.

I sighed and glanced around the boarding area. It had filled up with travelers since I sat down, with nearly every seat taken.

The gate agent called for us to line up, and I joined the passengers slowly congregating by their boarding group. That was my least favorite part of the process—there were always too many people who didn't know the proper boarding etiquette to keep it quick and efficient.

I had nearly reached the gate agent when someone jogged up through the now-empty first-class lane and slipped into the line one person ahead of me. I narrowed my eyes at him for his rudeness, though he was certainly not the only one to have pulled that little stunt. He glanced back over his shoulder as though he could feel my eyes on him.

We locked eyes for a moment, and I blinked slowly. *Holy shit, he is Hot with a capital H.* He quirked a little smile and turned back around as he walked up to the gate agent to get his boarding pass scanned.

He was tall, broad-shouldered, and in the typical finance bro uniform—slacks that looked suspiciously like yoga pants, a tailored, collared shirt, and a rugged vest made by a brand that outfitted hikers, not office workers. In other words, he looked like most of the privileged white boys who grew up around these parts.

I internally rolled my eyes at myself because, *for goodness sake Laura Beth, you have had enough of those boys to last a lifetime.* And I had. The dating pool in this town was seriously homogenous for how massive and diverse the population was. If I had one more cocky asshole offer to help me make it in the business, I think I'd scream.

I blinked back to awareness as I reached the gate agent and offered her my boarding pass. She smiled and nodded, saying, "Thank you, Ms. Calhoun," as I passed.

"Thank you, ma'am," I tossed back over my shoulder. *It takes no effort to be polite, y'all.*

As I entered the plane a few moments later, I noticed

Finance Bro at the very front of business class. He was in arguably the best seat in the section—an aisle, as far forward as you can get without being at the bulkhead. I grumbled internally because I still hadn't gotten enough miles for my status to mean anything. It was annoying.

He looked up as I passed and shot me another of those little smirks as his eyes skated over me from head to toe before meeting mine. I wished it didn't make my tummy flutter, but it did. Damn him and his pretty hazel eyes. Who gave him permission to be so cute? Seriously.

I settled myself into my aisle seat a few rows back, intent on knocking out as much work as possible on the flight. As I sat back up from freeing my laptop from my bag, I glanced over and noticed Finance Bro doing the same. He peeked over his shoulder and caught me looking, and that little smirk turned into a full-on grin. And, you know what, those flutters in my belly turned into mature butterflies because the boy could light a room with that thing. It should be illegal to throw a smile like that around.

It took me a moment to realize I'd just been gawking back at him, but when I did, I shook my head and refocused on the task at hand.

The startup founder I was going to see, Dr. August Gaspar, was notoriously stubborn. A genius in his own right, he was a former pediatrician with a background in biochemistry. Inspired to improve the insurgence of malnutrition he confronted in under-served neighborhoods, he had begun researching agriculture in his spare time. How a man that busy found spare time, I couldn't tell you, but he turned that side hobby into a full-fledged business idea and set out to revolutionize agriculture. His breakthrough could reduce global malnutrition by a significant degree if he got the right investment partners and resources dedicated.

With all that, I knew he would not take any offer from a VC firm lightly. I had my work cut out for me, and ogling handsome strangers would only make it harder. *Focus, Laura Beth. You have a promotion on the line and no pretty face is worth missing the next step in your career.*

Chapter 2

Parker

A irports sucked. There. I said it. We were all thinking it, but I finally just went and said it. They're nothing more than giant waiting rooms. Intersections with traffic lights that drag on and on, keeping us from getting where we want to go.

While I was fortunate enough to afford alternatives to commercial air travel, I often let the firm cover routine commercial flights. Either way, I spent as little time in airports as I feasibly could, and I had gotten the whole thing down to a quick and easy science. With my status and security subscriptions, I could go from the curb to the gate of my preferred airline in roughly fifteen minutes flat. So there was no need to get to the airport more than twenty minutes before boarding.

I stepped out of my ride after a quick thank you to my driver and headed purposefully through the automatic doors, checking my watch as I went. I got through security in ten minutes flat, which meant luck—or was it fate?—was on my side. Maybe that cute little blonde from last week would be on my flight again.

I internally chuckled at myself, because the odds of that were slim to none. But we managed to fly to Boise and back on the same flight last week, so stranger things had certainly happened.

I had left my timing a little tighter than usual, so I walked up to the gate agent during general boarding. All the first- and business-class passengers had already boarded. I flashed her a sheepish smile, and she rolled her eyes at me but didn't stop me as I slipped into line. She shook her head as I reached her to have my boarding pass scanned.

"Cutting it close yet again, Mr. Brooks," she tutted.

"But never too close," I quickly glanced down and read her nametag, "Megan."

She chuckled as I grinned and headed down the gangway. Mentally, I started running through talking points for my meeting tomorrow as I boarded–and I almost missed her because of it. But as I went to claim my preferred seat–first row in business class, on the aisle–a swish of blonde caught my eye.

I looked up, and there she was. The perky blonde from last week's flight, just as I'd hoped. Her eyes widened a bit as she saw me, and I couldn't help the slow smile that crossed my lips. *Ask and ye shall receive, Brooks.*

This time, I gave her a little wave. It wasn't every day I got a second chance to make an impression on a beautiful woman, and she certainly fit the bill. She blinked at me owlishly for a moment, then waved back hesitantly, like she didn't necessarily want to. I figured tossing her a wink was probably a little too suave, so I just turned and settled in for departure.

I wished she was closer so I could strike up a conversation, but I would have to settle for catching glimpses over my shoulder. At least she was a couple of rows closer this time.

During the drink service, I asked if I could send something to another passenger. The flight attendant gave me a look like she had absolutely zero time for any of my shit, and I pulled out my sheepish smile. Her look softened a bit, and I fought back a grin. *Works every time.*

"The girl back there, little blonde in the middle two rows back. Can you give her a snack pack, please? Something with chocolate?" I asked. "Maybe tell her I'd send a drink, but she looks like she's working hard and a snack seemed better?"

The flight attendant outright rolled her eyes. "Technically, there's no rule against it, sir."

"Excellent." I handed over my card. "Thanks so much."

"Mmmhm. You know her?"

"Not yet." I smiled.

She handed my card back and shook her head slowly, a move that reminded me of Megan the gate agent. Honestly, it's a look I had grown used to. I had always had little shame; never had much use for it.

The flight attendant passed the snack pack back to her colleague with a gesture toward the blonde as she mentioned her seat number. I peeked back and watched as Blondie looked up from her laptop in confusion, an adorable little wrinkle appearing between her brows. I wanted to smooth it with my finger. I also wanted to lick it, but I kept that thought to myself for now.

Her eyes suddenly snapped to mine, and I sent another grin her way. She slowly raised one eyebrow and gave me the best "what the actual fuck" face I had ever seen in my life. The girl was fucking talented, that was clear.

I smirked and shrugged, my smile never wavering. She looked down at the snack pack, sitting on her laptop keyboard, and gently opened it up. The businessman next to me cleared his throat, probably because I was encroaching on his space while I peered at Blondie between the seats.

"Can you blame me?" I asked as I glanced up at him briefly.

He made an annoyed grunting noise in response.

"I'll keep it short," I assured him as I peered back through the seats.

She had the chocolate in hand and looked up to meet my eyes as she opened it and took a bite. Her eyes rolled back and there was a happy little smile on her face, and I thought I saw a sigh of contentment pass her lips. Her full, pink lips that I could definitely not imagine sliding over a certain part of my anatomy. Her tongue flicked out to get a smudge of chocolate off her plump bottom lip, and I stifled a groan. I looked back up to her eyes and almost laughed at the mirth I saw there. She one hundred percent knew what that stunt with her tongue was going to do to me. And I couldn't help but appreciate the attitude that came with that little move.

She smiled softly and mouthed, "Thank you."

I nodded back and turned around in my seat. My neighbor huffed a sigh that might have been relief or annoyance. It was hard to tell.

I may not have gotten any closer to closing this deal, but I still felt like I had accomplished something for the day.

Chapter 3

LB

I've always loved traveling, but I couldn't deny I had an extra pep in my step. After catching yet another flight with Finance Bro last week, I was hoping we'd have a three-peat. As much as I didn't need another disaster in my string of dating failures, I was kind of looking forward to what he did next. *I mean, come on, the man gave me chocolate. Can't be mad about that.*

I had noticed he was the last-minute type, which was typical. Those finance and tech bros in the Bay were all the same, rushing around from thing to thing, person to person, life goal to life goal. They certainly weren't taught to take a moment to enjoy the simple things in life, that's for sure. Not that small-town Southern living is all it's cracked up to be, but the life lessons stick with you like glue.

I got up to board, and Finance Bro was still nowhere to be found. It might have been for the best, honestly. The flight was later in the day than usual, because Dr. Gaspar, eccentric as ever, had requested an early morning meeting the next day. He was fully aware of our location and the difficulty of scheduling flights to meet his timetable, but I thought it may have been a bit of a test of our commitment. So, instead of flying in for the day per usual, I would stay overnight in Boise. A few years ago, I would have felt embarrassed about being so excited to spend a night away on my company's dime. However, I had since learned to embrace my inner nerd. *Nothing wrong with celebrating the simple things.*

Whether it was a less full flight or my status had miraculously changed in the last week I would never know, but I ended up in a window seat in the first row of business class. I couldn't help feeling like I had arrived, and I didn't stop the small smile on my face as I got settled. Out of the corner of my eye, I noticed someone moving toward the middle seat beside me.

Just as he was about to sit, the middle-aged man in the sharp suit paused.

"That's my seat," a rich, deep voice called from the aisle.

I glanced up and met Finance Bro's hazel eyes. *You have got to be kidding me, how is his voice so damn attractive?!* I didn't even know voices could be attractive. Sure, anyone could appreciate a deep growl in a romance novel, but have you ever felt your tummy tighten over someone saying something completely mundane? *It's an experience, y'all. A confusing one.*

"Uh, I don't think so," Suit said, still in a half-crouch like he was going to launch into a sprint or pop a squat.

Finance Bro gave him a look that said, clear as day, "Help me out here, buddy", complete with a little eyebrow twitch and a head nod in my direction. Suit peered over at me and his mouth opened in a little "oh" and I swear to all that's good that an actual lightbulb flickered on in his brain.

"Ah." Suit glanced between us quickly. "I see."

"Don't worry," Finance Bro continued, cracking that smile that had been burned into my retinas, "you can take the aisle. Best seat in the house on a normal day."

I couldn't help the incredulous scoff that escaped. *Is this dude for real?* Something told me he had lines for days.

"Uh, s-sure," Suit replied, though he was clearly hesitant. "Okay. But, uh, is that alright with you, miss?"

Miss? Miss!? What am I, twelve!? I worked to keep the scowl off my face—I am a Ms., at least—and gave him a neutral look.

"Bless your heart." I let my full drawl make an appearance (if we're honest, the phrase doesn't work without it). "Sweet of you to ask, but that's just fine."

Suit nodded and stepped out of the row, and Finance Bro slipped into the middle seat. He moved with the efficient grace of a practiced air traveler, and I fought back an eye roll. This guy knew he was smooth, just like every other stereotypical former frat guy in the Bay.

A flicker of apprehension filled my gut. I'd had enough shitty first dates in this town to realize that this flight was about to be fabulous or sheer torture. There would be no in-between.

"Well, well, Blondie," he taunted, giving me a little smile as he finished settling his bag under the seat. "Looks like fate's on my side today."

I scoffed and quirked a brow, something which seemed to make his eyes flare. Or was that a twinkle? *Do eyes twinkle outside of animated movies?! Lord, help me.*

"Is that so, Romeo? You planning to buy me another snack?"

He grinned. "You liked that, hm?"

"Honey, there was chocolate involved. Duh."

He chuckled and ran a hand through his hair gently, ruffling the longish waves without knocking them out of place. Typical male wizardry.

"So, what brings you to Boise?"

Of all the opening lines, he goes with that? The boy is so white bread it hurts. Pity. I arched my brow since he seemed to like that.

14

"Wow." I drew the word out to several syllables, then leaned back and twisted my torso toward him. "You've spent the last how many flights making eyes at me, sending me chocolate, and *that's* how you open the conversation?" I clicked my tongue at him and shook my head. "I'm disappointed, sugar. I expected more."

He blinked at me, and a slow smile spread across his face. "Gotta start somewhere, right?" He tilted his head at me, and the golden retriever energy nearly bowled me over. "How else should I get to know you?"

I shook my head again. "Nope, that's not how this works. See, I think I've got you pegged. You're probably a Stanford graduate, a local Palo Alto boy born and bred. Grew up with everything you ever wanted and used your family connections to get an internship." I paused and narrowed my eyes at him momentarily. "Hell, maybe you even skipped the internship altogether and let yourself just enjoy undergrad, waiting until you graduated to get a junior role."

He looked fascinated and mildly surprised by my tirade. It was clear he was listening to me, though, and he'd hung on every word with a dopey grin still on his face. It was almost like he couldn't believe I was real.

"Your dad is probably friends with your boss or your boss's boss, right?" I continued. There was a flicker of something in his eyes in response to that, a flash of something darker than amusement. I filed it away but continued my assessment. "Your last girlfriend was more of a hookup buddy than a real relationship and you dipped when her feelings started to get a little too real. How am I doing so far?"

"Well enough I'm not sure whether to be impressed or scared. But, please, don't stop."

A little laugh escaped me. "Fair enough. I bet you live in a nice apartment in a central location, have either one roommate or a dog, play some intramural sport on the weekend, and meet the boys at least once a week at the same bar."

I took a breath and sized him up. I'd been watching his reactions and there was a bit of guilt in his expression when I mentioned relationships. It seemed only appropriate to push on that a bit. "I'd bet money that you let girls in enough to keep them interested and get in their pants, but don't believe in love enough to go beyond the surface." The corner of his mouth twitched up, and he blinked, unable to stop his gaze from darting away for a moment. *Busted.*

"And, well, honey—there's not much else to say, is there?" I gave him a wry smile and a shrug. "Met one finance bro in the Bay and you've met them all. I already know you."

"I live alone, actually," he corrected. "No roommate or dog, though I could be persuaded on either with the right offer." The smile was smaller now, but those eyes were still twinkling with amusement. His expression was soft, open. It did things to my insides. "And I play volleyball with the guys when I have time. The rest was close enough."

I nodded, feeling my snarky look soften in response. "See? What else is there to know?"

My voice dipped, and I almost cursed myself for going breathy this early in the conversation. *Get it together, Laura Beth!*

The corner of his mouth twitched up a bit. "My freshman year in college, I fumbled my water bottle before I had to give my first persuasive argument in my speech class. Had to do the whole thing looking like I'd peed my pants," he deadpanned.

I laughed, utterly surprised by the unexpected confession. Maybe there was more to this bro after all. "What? You did not!"

"Swear to God." He raised his right hand like he was taking an oath. "Prof took pity on me and gave me a B anyway, but I couldn't shake the nickname the guys gave me. Being 'P' in college was rough."

I couldn't stop the giggle, because the image of this tall, devastatingly handsome man–who was surely just as attractive in college–being called "Pee" was nothing short of hysterical. "You poor baby." I gave him an exaggerated pouty lip to show how seriously I was taking his humiliation. "They called you Pee?"

He nodded solemnly. "For years. Granted, my name's Parker, so it was close enough that it stuck."

I cracked a deep belly guffaw at his deadpan expression. "Your friends sound like real keepers, Pee."

He groaned and leaned his head back on his seat, eyes closed. "I should never have told you this."

"You really shouldn't have," I agreed with a grin that was not far from diabolical.

He rolled his head on the seat and looked at me. "You gonna put me out of my misery and share something equally humiliating now?"

I gasped and threw my hand up to my chest in indignation. "Sir! I'd never."

He narrowed his eyes at me, teasing. "Come on, Blondie. You gotta give me something."

I shook my head, resolute. "No siree, Bob. It was your choice to go airing your dirty laundry," I said and gave him a pointed look. He groaned in response. "I never asked you to share your shame. A lady doesn't tell such stories during a first meeting."

"A lady, huh?" There was suddenly a heat in his eyes that hit me directly below the belt.

I nodded primly and ignored the tingles. *No time for that, Laura Beth.* "That's right."

"A Southern belle, no less," he smirked. "Tell me, how'd a Southern girl like you end up in the Bay?"

I huffed a chuckle and shook my head slowly. I looked off into the distance for a moment, remembering my journey. "With determination and a hell of a lot of luck."

"Hmm. Something tells me there's more to it than that," he observed, his expression thoughtful. "Tell me about yourself, Blondie. Maybe start with your name?"

I considered him for a moment, trying to read his face. It was open and appeared honest, which was how it had been throughout our conversation. But looks were deceiving, and that didn't mean I had been dealing with the real Parker. And, in my experience, there was more to lose than to gain when it came to romantic relationships. With all that in my head, I'm still not sure why my answer slipped so easily from my lips.

"Laura Beth," I offered, holding my hand out for a shake, "but I go by LB."

He took my hand and his brows hitched a bit when my shake was firm and quick, no-nonsense.

"Nice to meet you, LB."

"Charmed, I'm sure," I drawled. He grinned back at me. Before he could say anything else, I jumped in, because my heart needed me to. My head needed it, too—the part of me driving me relentlessly on to my next achievement. "Let's lay some ground rules, Pee."

He closed his eyes with a look of pure torture on his face and groaned again. "Parker, please. Just Parker."

"Awww," I teased, "you're no fun. Fine. Let's lay some ground rules, Parker. No talk of work—I get enough of that in my life. And this little conversation stays here."

"Wait, no numbers?"

I nodded. "We'll leave it to your friend, Fate."

"Alright, I can live with that," he conceded, though his eyes said otherwise. "No work, and we're going the serendipity route. Very romcom of you."

"Pssh, if only we could be so lucky." I rolled my eyes and promptly changed the subject. "So, you really knew how to pick friends in college, hm?"

He chuckled and nodded. "Yeah, and they all stink. Every last one of them. What is it with dudes?"

I laughed, loudly. "Finally! A guy says it!"

"Oh, fuck, yeah," he agreed enthusiastically. "I'll be the first to admit guys are disgusting. A bunch of guys in one apartment, which was basically my entire college experience, is no one's idea of a good time."

"So why stick with it–with them?"

He got a wistful look. "They're good dudes, under the BO." I wrinkled my nose, and he laughed. "I promise, good dudes. We met freshman year. Somehow I wandered into a party full of computer science majors and they just adopted me."

"Aw! That's adorable. Are they extroverts?" I had adopted my fair share of friends over the years.

"Hell no," he laughed. "I know, usually it's the extroverts doing the adopting, but apparently they get more aggressive in packs. I walked in and they picked me. And now here we are half a decade later, playing volleyball on the regular and sharing way more than four dudes probably should."

"Color me intrigued, sugar," I gave him a suggestive eyebrow waggle. I wasn't exactly getting gay vibes, but I'd been wrong before.

He choked on a laugh, a surprised look on his face. "Oh, god, no, not like that. I see how you went there, but, just—no."

I giggled and nodded. With a reaction like that, I wasn't about to let a perfect opportunity to tease go. "Sure, sure, Pee. Keep telling yourself that."

"Ugh, you!" He reached over and tickled me briefly on the side.

My whole body lit up at the touch, and not just because I'm

ticklish. He bent closer to me to get the right angle, and he was there and gone again in seconds, but our eyes caught and something swelled between us. *Not that, Laura Beth. Don't look down.* I avoided eyeballing his lap and instead swallowed and sat up with a grin, putting distance back between us. But it didn't stop the crackle of electricity arcing from his body to mine.

"Okay, okay," I said, fiercely ignoring the breathiness of my tone. "That was the last time, promise."

Chapter 4

Parker

This girl was going to be the death of me, I swore. She was quick-witted and sassy, which I loved and had rarely gotten from recent dates. And that accent was tying my insides into knots. She was even more fucking gorgeous up close, which didn't seem possible, because I already thought she was a ten. But then she started teasing, laughing, and I realized I was gone on this girl. *Gone*.

When she said we should leave it up to my 'friend' Fate, I wanted to yell. Or kick something. Or both. There was no way in hell I could let this encounter be our last. She was way too much fun to talk to, and the pink in her cheeks, when she laughed or caught my gaze for a beat too long, was going to be my undoing. I wanted to bury my face in the crook of her neck and inhale her like a total creep. I wanted to bury my face in other places, too, but I was doing my best not to think those thoughts because my dick was paying way too much attention to them. He was already *invested*.

She was ribbing me again, but it was like I was having an out-of-body experience. I was present in the conversation with her, but I was also watching it all go down and trying to catalog everything she said, every move she made. And it was fucking weird because I had never gotten involved with girls like this.

LB had pegged me spot on. I don't do relationships. I do benefit-ships. They're great, casual—until they're not, at which point they're over. I didn't go into it with her, because why waste the time we have on a shitty topic, but I don't buy into the idea of "true love". I just don't think people are wired that way.

Love comes in many forms, and most people are going to love far more than just one person in their lifetime. I think suggesting our capacity for love is limited is doing the human heart—and capacity for growth—a gross disservice.

"You still with me, Parker?" LB's voice broke through my thoughts.

"Sorry, got lost in those eyes for a second there." I wasn't lying, either. "What blue even are they? Is that what they mean by cornflower blue? My sister is obsessed with that color."

LB gave me a grin that could buckle my knees if I were standing. "You have a sister? Tell me about her."

"In a minute. Back to your eyes. Cornflower?"

She laughed again, and I wished I could record it without crossing into stalker territory.

"Honestly, honey, I haven't given it much thought," she answered, clearly amused. "My momma always says they're the color of bluebells."

I nodded slowly as I conjured an image of bluebells and compared them to her eyes. "Yeah, yeah. Okay. Bluebells. I like that."

LB was looking at me like I was a little odd and she was a little into it. And, let me tell you, I was there for it. I got lost in those eyes again, but gave myself a little shake. *She's not ready for stalker-level attraction, Brooks. Rein it in.*

"Right, sister. She's my twin."

She gasped. "No way! That's so cool. Do you—"

"No, we don't communicate telepathically or do any of that weird twin shit," I said with a wry grin. "Without fail, that is always the first question people ask."

"Oh, well," she pouted a bit, that bottom lip sticking out just enough to make my cock twitch. "That's anticlimactic."

"Totally agreed," I nodded firmly. "We often complain about our lack of special twin powers. It's not fair if you think about it. All twins should be created equal, and all."

"Oh, yes," she nodded sagely, with a spark of amusement in her bluebell eyes, "because we're all just archetypes and individuality is for the birds."

"You get it!" I exclaimed and gave her an exaggerated grin to emphasize my utter sarcasm.

"You're subtle," she giggled. That sound...good God, that sound. I wanted to bottle it.

"Preston has made it clear that subtlety is not one of my strengths, yes."

"You're close, then?" She asked, a small smile on her lips.

"Yeah." I nodded. "As has been established, we're not freaky twin close. But we've been each other's constant since we were tiny. We were inseparable as kids, and everyone always said we'd eventually start fighting. It's like they couldn't believe for a second that siblings could just be cool with one another."

"I know what you mean. My parents always said they expected my older sister and me to fight, but we never did. Thick as thieves from the moment I could steal her Barbies."

I wanted to take a picture of her expression as she spoke of her sister and maybe immortalize it. It was like she was looking back through time at a memory that brought her pure joy. Not the overpowering kind that makes you jump or yell, but the one that fills you slowly from the inside out like warm syrup, enveloping you in a feeling of contentment, warmth, and belonging.

I realized I was staring at her again. If I kept doing that, I was going to kiss her, and she deserved better than a mauling mid-flight. *Gotta break the tension, Brooks.*

"Don't get me wrong," I continued, "Preston can be annoying as fuck. But she's my annoying little tyrant, and I love her to pieces."

LB giggled and nodded eagerly. "I feel the same way about Sara Jean. She's the absolute best, but she's also the only person in the world who knows every single one of my buttons and how to press them just right, so I lose my ever-loving mind."

I sighed wistfully. "Sisters. Gotta love 'em."

"May as well, I suppose," she mused.

She glanced out the window. Every instinct in my being was telling me not to let this girl go—not to let this be our only conversation.

"You know, you got me thinking earlier." I may have agreed to her terms, but that didn't mean I was above attempting a renegotiation. Not after the banter we had. Not after I lost myself in her eyes so frequently, I felt like I may have had a secret lobotomy mid-flight.

She peeked back at me and that damn talented eyebrow— just the one—spiked again. "Oh yeah? That unusual for you?"

I snorted. Couldn't help it. She was quick as hell. "You know, for a Southern belle, you sure have a sharp tongue."

The smirk on her lips shot lightning straight to my groin, and I tried not to shift obviously. *Not now, man. Come on.*

"My momma taught me to be a lady," she retorted, a wicked glint in her eye. "And my daddy taught me to shoot first and ask questions later. I'll let you guess which lessons I took to like a duck to water."

"Vicious little thing," I murmured. I didn't even realize I was going to say it out loud until the words passed my lips. In the process, my voice had gone gruff. Husky.

She hitched a breath in response, and the motion drew my eyes down to the glimpse of cleavage revealed by her shirt. *I wonder if she's that responsive in every situation. Fuck. I want to find out.*

I realized we had both leaned into one another like we were telling secrets, and her lips were inches away from mine. Too far and too close at the same time, given our surroundings. Her lips parted and her tongue started to make an appearance.

"Nuh-uh," I chastised, that gruffness still thick in my tone. I reached up, eyes locked on hers, and gently pushed her lower lip closed with my thumb. "Put that thing away, please. A guy can only take so much."

Chapter 5

LB

My body was a live wire. Parker's thumb rested on my lip and his face was so close to mine I could smell his aftershave and a hint of minty toothpaste on his breath. My heart felt like it was going to beat straight out of my chest and my panties were a lost cause.

He swiped his thumb slowly from the center of my lip to the corner, pressing lightly there before he drew his hand away and straightened a bit, putting a sliver of distance between us. I felt the absence of his touch like a physical ache. *For fuck's sake, Laura Beth. You are a strong, independent woman!* My vagina severely disagreed. She was no longer a feminist because she was unashamed and simping for this man without regret.

His lips quirked into a little smile, and I ignored the pressure in my core. Okay, fine, I tried to ignore it. And, yes, goddamnit, I failed.

"As I was saying," he went on, his voice doing the raspy thing that made me think of luxe sheets and candles and orgasms, "your little stunt earlier—putting me in my place—well, it set off my spidey senses."

I was curious about where he was going with this, but I was

also highly distracted by my body's reaction to his infuriating proximity. *He's talking about a comic book superhero and I'm practically gushing. What is in his cologne?!*

"Is it fair to assume you've been on a few dates in the Bay?"

It was my turn to snort. "You could say that."

"Any winners?"

I gave him a "what do you think?" look, which, being the unlikely specimen he was, he interpreted with ease.

"Alright, so, no winners. Tell me something, spitfire. What would've been a winning date?"

I blinked at him. *First of all, spitfire? Where did that come from and why does it sound like foreplay?* I didn't know that I had ever had so many positive, slow-blink reactions to anyone in my life. He was uniquely gifted.

Second of all, what kind of jerks have you been spending time with, Laura Beth!? This should not be impressive.

"How are you the first guy who has asked me that?" I muttered.

The smile he gave me warmed me through to my toes. "Well, I'm kind of glad. Such a low bar gives me a great chance."

I rolled my eyes to hide the effect he had on me. "We're leaving this shit up to your friend Fate, mister."

"Sure," he agreed, too quickly. "Humor me."

I thought for a moment and glanced down at my hands to give myself a breath. Not about my ideal date—every girl knows that answer at the drop of a hat, am I right?—but about how much of myself I wanted to give to this handsome near stranger. Everyone's heart has thousands of keys. Giving any of them away should be considered with care.

I cleared my throat gently. "Dinner out," I offered, and he leaned in because there was a softness to my tone I couldn't quite erase. I felt his body heat like a drug. "Somewhere high-end but not pretentious, with real portions. A place that can make a perfect French 75."

I still wasn't looking at him, but I felt his attention on me like a physical touch. "Dancing after, maybe at a Latin bar. They're always so...alive." I made the mistake of looking back up into his eyes. The hunger in his gaze nearly bowled me over. Like I was a snack—a meaty one.

"Nothing wrong with working up a sweat to a great beat," he rasped, and my pussy clenched.

"But we'd have to end the night at a dive," I continued. Our eyes were locked now. It felt dangerous and exciting all at once. "Somewhere with Pabst tall boys and a floor so sticky we make sure to leave before close so we don't have to see the place when the lights come up."

"I like that you said 'we,'" he whispered.

I. Was. Aflame. His velvety voice, that feral look, and the fingers that were lightly brushing my thigh over the armrest— almost accidentally—were lighting up my being. I was vaguely aware that we were on a plane surrounded by people, but in that moment there were just the two of us. The tension between us was thick enough I don't think a knife would have done it. Maybe a chainsaw.

My lips parted, though I wasn't sure what I was going to say. He leaned forward ever so much more, and—

BING! "We're beginning our final descent into Boise. Please take a moment to put your tray tables up and your seat backs in their full, upright position. We'll be coming through the cabin to collect any service items. Thank you."

We didn't need a chainsaw, after all. Just a reminder of where we were and that our conversation had an expiration date.

I leaned away from Parker and gave him a wry smile. "Well,

that was the quickest this flight has ever gone. Thanks for keeping me entertained."

He looked reluctant to let go of our moment, but he followed my lead. I don't think he realized how many points that won him. "Is it corny to say the feeling is mutual?"

I shrugged, feigning nonchalance. "Unoriginal, yes. Not particularly corny."

I gave him a smirk and wanted to melt into a puddle when he sent one right back.

"Can I convince you to throw my 'friend' Fate out the window and catch a drink with me after we touch down?" He asked with a note of defiance in his voice.

"Afraid not, Pee-ter Parker," I quipped. I couldn't help myself with the pun, but I also knew I needed to hold my boundaries. *Nothing good can come of a distraction right now.*

He groaned at my emphasis on his unfortunate nickname and flung his head back against the headrest.

"I promise I'm not actually friends with fate, spitfire. C'mon, give me a chance."

I smiled softly at him. "I did. This was the best conversation I've had in a while, and I mean that. I got on this plane fully intending to work my tail off, per usual, and maybe make eyes at you through some seats. This was an unexpected treat and will be a lovely memory. Let's not tarnish it."

He watched my face intently while I spoke. I could tell he disagreed—there was a tension in his body that wasn't there for most of our conversation—but he didn't press. After a few beats, he gave me a slow nod.

"Alright, then," he relented. "We'll do it your way. But if Fate, who is my best friend now, by the way, brings us back together?"

I shrugged while a butterfly colony took residence in my belly. "Who am I to argue with fate?"

Chapter 6

Parker

I wanted to hack into her phone and figure out where she was
staying. We were both on a later flight than usual, one that
didn't leave any time to do business and get home. She was
staying in Boise, and so was I. It was too much to hope that we'd
be at the same hotel, so I wanted the details that gave me a surefire way to find her.

But I was not a grade-A creep. Maybe grade F. That's
better, right? Less of a creep? Whatever, terrible analogy.
However you want to phrase it, there are obsessed stalkers and
then there are well-intentioned guys who don't want to miss out
on what could be the most perfect girl they've ever met. *Those
two things don't sound that distinct right now, Brooks.*

I pressed my eyes closed and leaned my head back against
the seat of the car. I was so not interested in logic from my
conscience right then. She was perfect for me. I was perfect for
her. We were perfect. *You don't let perfect walk the fuck away.*

Okay, okay. I needed to take a beat. It was not status quo for
me to get tied up like this over a girl. I didn't have a revolving
door of partners, but I was making the most of my twenties. It
was normal for me to pickup a girl or two a month, usually when

I was out with the boys on the weekends. We would hook up, have our fun, and I would let things peter out. Chasing girls was not something I did, because putting that kind of effort into someone meant you wanted something more. And I was not at a place in my life or emotional maturity, if I was honest with myself, where I wanted anything more than the occasional good fuck. But if I continued with the theme of honesty, I had to admit that I didn't just want to fuck LB (though I wanted that, too). I wanted more of the banter from earlier, more glimpses into the person she was behind the makeup and corporate clothes. I wanted to peel back her layers and find her soul, the heart of who she was. And I think I wanted to devour it.

I looked out the window without seeing a damn thing. All I could see was her face. The way her forehead would crinkle, or her hands would wave as she talked, so animated it felt like a reliving, not a retelling. I felt like, if I had a single artistic bone in my body, I could fill a gallery with her different expressions.

A buzz in my pocket brought me back to the present.

Van the Man: Get it done, Parker.

Ah, the good ol' boss. Such an encouraging fellow. I wrote him back quickly.

Me: You know I will.

He wouldn't let me get the last word. He never would. Van Costa, Venture Partner at Athena Ventures, was anything but generous. At least when it came to his junior staff, that is. He had a reputation in the Bay for being commanding, exacting, relentless, and successful as fuck. *I still want to be him when I grow up.*

Van the Man: Leave the cocky shit at the hotel.
Call if you need to escalate.

His encouragement was overwhelming. I reacted to the text with a thumbs up so he wouldn't ask me for confirmation I received it in twenty minutes (yes, he would do that and, yes, I knew from experience). When I looked back out the window, we were pulling up to the hotel.

I hopped out of the car and thanked my driver before heading into the lobby. I happened to know the owner of this particular chain of hotels, and he had sent through a mobile key for my usual suite. No reason to linger when what I needed was a cold shower, possibly followed by a pep talk from my twin. My head and my gut may have been a mess after the best non-sexual encounter I had ever had with the opposite sex, but my cock was not. He had missed all the signs to slow down and was still chubbin' over my Southern spitfire. *Ah, fuck, Brooks, she's not yours.*

Yeah, yeah, my buzzkill of a conscience needed to shut the fuck up. *She's not mine...yet.*

I let myself into my room, tossed my leather overnight bag— a gift from my grandfather when I graduated high school—on the couch, and headed straight for the bathroom. I had every intention of taking that cold shower, but I couldn't get the image of LB's little pink tongue nearly poking out of her mouth out of my head. By the time I got my clothes off, my cock was as hard as steel.

Okay, fine. Change of plan.

I flipped the shower on and leaned against the door to wait for it to heat. Gripping my shaft, I gave it a slow stroke, my touch light, and let my mind's eye wander all over LB. I felt like a creep for two seconds until the pleasure swept all the guilt away and I lost myself in sensation. I continued the slow, lazy tugs until the steam built, then stepped gratefully under the spray. I faced the shower head and closed my eyes, tilting my head up and into the spray as I ran my hands through my hair.

The water hit my cock directly, and it twitched; the sensation sending a light tingle through me. I let my mind conjure up a scene, LB on her knees in front of me, those big blue eyes looking up at me over painted red lips.

"Fucking hell," I muttered. Just thinking about her in that position had me painfully hard. I leaned forward and braced one hand against the tiled wall, head bowed under the spray, and wrapped my other hand around my dick.

There was no gentle touch this time—I gripped it firmly and pulled, twisting my hand over the head as I imagined LB's hot, wet mouth in place of my fist. I could only imagine how well she'd take me. How pretty she'd look with tears making her mascara—so perfectly applied, like everything else about the corporate armor she wore—run in messy streaks. I wanted to make a mess of her entirely, from head to toe. I wanted her wet with sweat and rumpled in my sheets, her perfect pink lips parted as she recovered from the first orgasm.

"God...damn...LB," I gasped as I quickened my pace. My hips thrust into my fist as I continued the rhythmic strokes—squeezing at the base, tight up my shaft, then a twist as I turned over the head and glided right back down.

I could feel my orgasm building at the base of my spine, a heaviness settling into my balls as I pictured her bobbing on my cock, cheeks hollowed and face slick with spit and precum. She was giving it her all, one small hand wrapped around me while she swallowed my head, the other digging her nails into my thigh while she steadied herself against my thrusts. I saw stars in real life.

"Shit," I hissed. "So goddamn good."

And she was. She was fucking gorgeous in my mind's eye as

I rutted into my hand in real life like a teenager. She was taking me completely, her throat opening for me, her eyes locked on mine, those tear tracks a thing of fucking beauty. I groaned as my orgasm rushed through me. I pictured her desperately swallowing around my cock as I spurted, imagining my cum dribbling down her chin when she couldn't quite keep it all in. That pink tongue flicked out of her mouth and trailed along her lip, catching a drop or two, and she moaned at the taste. *Holy fuck, that's the hottest thing I've ever seen.*

I sagged against the wall, the cool tile a harsh contrast to the heat that was still vibrating through me as I caught my breath. My cock twitched, barely half-mast, as I let myself stare at my mental image of my perfect Southern spitfire. I wiped a hand over my face roughly, frustration simmering under my skin. I wanted to make that daydream real. I wanted that more than I'd ever wanted any sexual encounter in my goddamn life. My dick twitched again, as if he was just as ready to go again as I was, despite how hard I came. *So, we agree. That girl is mine.*

Chapter 7

LB

"What'll it be?" the bartender asked as he slid a coaster across the bar I was leaning against. I gave my head a shake in an attempt to orient myself and looked up to meet a pair of smiling green eyes.

"Gin martini please," I replied as I turned to survey the buzzing hotel bar. The room was dimly lit, creating a sense of intimacy and privacy within the shadows. Groups of two and three were huddled on sexy, low sofas and tucked into taller, velveted booths. Despite the low lighting, my eyes caught a well-dressed, dark-haired businessman's hand as it traced up the calf of the beautiful brunette he was seated with.

My pulse quickened, and I hurriedly turned back in my seat, not wanting to get caught gawking. It was obvious my traitorous body hadn't settled after its run-in with sex-personified, Mr. Parker.....shit, what was his last name? Did I even get a last name? How was I supposed to find him online with only a first name to go on? I meant what I had said about not wanting to give out my number–I may not have the time to balance dating and going after this promotion at work, but that didn't mean I couldn't admire from afar.

If I was being honest with myself, I was regretting not taking him up on his offer to get a drink. At the time, I had felt in control and assured, but now I was feeling more than a little horny and lonely sitting in this bar by myself.

As I sipped the martini that had just arrived in front of me, I wondered who those two guests I spotted earlier were to one another—a couple trying to rekindle a flame? Coworkers who wanted to be more? Strangers meeting for one night of fun? Hotels always seemed to hold a promise of unexpected meetings and chance encounters, the ideal place to assume a new identity, if only temporarily, and my imagination got the better of me.

I grabbed my phone to shoot off a quick text.

> Me: Just got to my hotel and grabbing a drink before I head up to my room for the night. You won't believe who I sat next to on my flight...

> Sis: WHO???

> Me: Mr. Snack Pack

My phone immediately started buzzing, and I let out a snort. After taking a long sip of my drink, I answered. "Hey, sis."

"I'm gonna need details, Laura Beth."

I chuckled, trying to decide how much I wanted to say. "There's not much to tell. He practically forced his way into the seat next to me, and we spent the rest of the flight chatting."

I bit my bottom lip to hold on to the inexplicable feelings and irrational thoughts that floated through my mind while remembering my interaction with Parker. Like how the entire cabin had disappeared when he turned that brilliant smile in my direction, or how my body responded with the faintest of his touches.

"Tell me you at least gave him your number."

36

I sighed. "You know I didn't. I deleted the dating apps months ago, and I'm serious about not seeing anyone right now. I don't need the distraction."

"It sounds like you need someone to look after your snack pack and help you relax," she fired back. Sara Jean sounded exasperated, and I knew where this was going. She wanted to tell me how I would never find someone to end up with if I didn't give them a shot and open up.

I interjected before she could start the lecture, "As much as I appreciate your concern for me and my snack pack, we're just fine. I should finish this drink and head up to my room. I've got an early start tomorrow."

"Whatever you say, sis. Be safe and text me in the morning, alright?"

"Sure thing. Love you."

"Love you more," Sara Jean sing-songed before hanging up. At that moment, the bartender appeared, swiftly removing my empty martini glass and replacing it with a full, fizzing champagne flute.

"Oh, I'm so sorry, but I didn't order this," I said.

The bartender chuckled. "No. You didn't, but he did." My eyes followed his finger as he pointed towards the navy, high-back booth in the far corner. Within the shadows, Parker sat with his elbows propped on the small table, his chin rested on his clasped hands, and his eyes fixed on mine. My jaw dropped as a small gasp escaped my lips.

"Thank you," I managed to mutter to the bartender, my eyes never wavering. Parker smirked and tilted his head to the side, as if in question. In answer, I grabbed my bag and drink and slid off my seat. Moving on autopilot, I strode through the crowd toward him.

Parker's smile as I came to a stop in front of the booth was devilish. "LB. Don't you look lovely tonight?"

How was he so relaxed? My palms were slick with sweat and condensation from the glass I was clutching.

"Nice to see you again," I murmured. I was trying to wrap my head around the fact that he was suddenly right there, in the same bar. I needed to calm down and see this as an opportunity gifted to me by the universe or fate or whoever the fuck else. Maybe Sara Jean was right. What would be the harm in indulging in this gorgeous man's company for a little while longer? *Come tomorrow, I'll have him out of my system and be able to refocus.*

His hands dropped, and he gestured to his side, and I slid into the booth beside him. The space was small, and my exposed knee was immediately pressed against his muscled thigh. God, it felt like much higher stakes than when we were at 30,000 feet. The thought crossed my mind that I left my bravado on the plane.

"It looks like fate is on my side after all." He smiled, and I swear those hazel eyes darkened.

My fingers found the stem of my champagne flute and began to fidget. "I suppose so. A French 75, huh?" I nodded to the drink he sent.

"Something you'll come to learn about me, LB, is that I'm very attentive when it comes to things I'm interested in."

"Is that so? What else did you learn about me then?" My flippant tone didn't belie the wild flurry of emotions I was feeling.

"Hm, where should I begin?" Parker asked as he reached across the table and stopped my fidgeting with a gentle press of his warm, large hand. He stroked his thumb across the tops of my fingers and said, "You bite your bottom lip when you're focused. You also absentmindedly chew your thumbnail, but you're trying to stop."

I blinked, surprised by his words. Tucking a loose lock

behind my ear, he continued, "You can't stand when your hair is in your face and you hate being cold."

My pulse was deafening in my ears. "Wow, I didn't realize I had a stalker," I joked to try and cut the tension.

"Just observant." He shrugged and leaned back, wrapping his arm around the back of the booth.

"And I assume you're staying here at the hotel? Do you typically send drinks to women you find in hotel bars?"

His lips twitched. "Yes. And no."

"So what changed?" I held my breath, unsure of what I wanted in response.

"A little blonde spitfire tried to get away from me, but Fate and I had other plans."

Chapter 8

Parker

Kissing LB wasn't what I thought it would be when I pictured all those salacious moments before. It was so much better. Her lips were soft on mine, her tongue was teasing and firm, and she molded her body to mine as though we were made to fit together. I refused to break the wild kiss we started in the elevator and managed to get my mobile key up and to my door without taking my mouth from hers. I pushed her gently against the door, my arm around her waist, and opened it. She stumbled slightly, but I held her to me with ease and walked us through, unwilling to let logic or common sense get a spare word in between us.

I leaned her back up against the closet just inside the door, being careful to avoid the handles, and pressed my forehead to hers. Her hands were on my biceps, grip firm, and her chest was heaving between us in an entirely distracting way. I closed my eyes briefly. "You are fucking stunning, Laura Beth Calhoun," I breathed. Her breath hitched, and I opened my eyes, meeting her wide, sex-drunk bluebell blues. "And if you're up for it," I said, raising a hand to cup her cheek as I swiped a line across her lower lip with my thumb, "I'd like to ravish you now."

Her chest rose in another of those big, desperate gasps and I groaned, pressing my body weight against her even more. I kept eye contact with her, watching as the internal conversation flickered across her face before she gave me a small, firm nod, followed by a breathy, "Yes, please."

I growled and captured her lips with mine again, my hand on her neck and jaw to tilt her head just the way I wanted it. I leaned into her, reveling in the feel of her softness against my harder frame. I could feel her nipples through my shirt and I could not wait to get them in my mouth. My tongue touched her lip, asking for entrance, and I surged into her mouth when she opened for me again, tangling my tongue with hers as I groaned lightly at her taste. *So sweet.*

When we came up for air, I didn't give her an inch. I kept her pinned, kissing down her jaw and appreciating every little gasp and moan as she tilted her head to the side, giving me access to that perfect spot below her ear. I placed an open-mouthed kiss there, and she shivered. *Fuck, yes, more of that.* I wetted my lips, then licked from the base of her neck up to her earlobe as she trembled against me, a whimper escaping her lips. I couldn't help my smirk as I sucked her earlobe into my mouth, lightly running my teeth over it as I pulled back.

"I'm going to make you come now, spitfire," I whispered, my lips against her ear. She sagged against me, her knees wobbly, and I grinned.

I wrapped my arms around her and swung her up into my hold. She squeaked and grabbed for my neck and shoulders, flailing a bit.

"Parker! What the hell!" Her accent was so thick right then, and it made my cock twitch.

"Hush, spitfire. I've got you."

Whether it was the confidence in my tone or the heat in my gaze, she stilled and stared at me with a slow swallow as I

41

covered the short distance to the bed. I leaned over most of the way, then let her fall lightly into the pillows. I enjoyed her little gasp and look of surprise far too much.

I stood by the bed and made quick work of unbuttoning my shirt, and I couldn't miss how her eyes tracked every movement. That tongue of hers—the one I was fast realizing I'd become addicted to—darted out again as my shirt fell open. She could look at me like that forever, and it would be too short. I quickly shucked off everything but my slacks, then crawled up the bed toward her.

She was looking up at me with those bluebell eyes, breaths still heavy in her chest. She opened her legs for me as I approached and I hummed my approval. I kneeled on the bed and trailed my fingers up her legs, starting at the ankle. She whimpered a little when I got to mid-thigh, and I took her wide-eyed look of lust and parted thighs as the invitation they were. As I reached up for her panties, I pushed her skirt up to reveal my prize.

"Fucking hell, look at you," I muttered. The sheerest little tease of pastel pink lace covered her pussy. I thought I was hard when we got up to my room, but it was nothing on the raging erection in my pants then. I could feel the wet spot from my precum blooming. "Perfection."

She watched me intently as I hooked my fingers in her panties, drew them down her legs, and leaned out of the way to take them all the way off. Looking her in the eye, I brought them to my nose, pressing them against my face as I inhaled. I couldn't miss her little gasp and whimper of surprise, but my eyes rolled back into my head and I groaned as her scent filled my nose. I shoved her panties in my pocket and quickly moved forward to place my lips on her inner knee, then trailed kisses up her leg.

"You are exquisite, Laura Beth," I murmured between soft

presses of my lips, nipping and sucking at her skin as I worked my way toward her pretty pink pussy. I looked up at her as I went, and she was biting her lip and whimpering, her legs twitching in my grasp. "Do you taste as good as you smell, spitfire? Is your honey as sweet as I imagined?"

"Dear god, the mouth on you," she muttered, her eyes wide and pupils blown.

I smiled at her from between her thighs. "Oh, sweet thing, you have no idea."

I licked a broad, firm line from the bottom of her slit to the top.

"Oh. My. GOD."

I smirked and did it again. "Parker's fine. Now be a good girl and stay still." I locked eyes with her again, enjoying the flush in her cheeks. "I'm hungry."

I feasted on her pussy. I nipped and nibbled her tender lips, then licked my way slowly between her folds before plunging my tongue into her. She writhed, and I wrapped my arms around her thighs and settled my hands on her hips to keep her still. Her thighs were quaking around my ears as I focused on her clit, swirling my tongue slowly around that little bundle of nerves in lazy, gentle circles. I could tell it was driving her insane because she was whimpering again and I was fucking living for those sounds.

I turned my attention back to her labia, and she moaned a protest, bucking against my hold. I held firm and speared my tongue into her, making her arch her back and thrust up against my face. *God, yes, more of that.* I pulled back to focus on her clit again, this time with more pressure, and pulled one hand around to tease at her folds. She was thrusting into my face with abandon, and I hummed in pure male satisfaction as she gasped at the firm touch of my fingers. I slowly pushed one into her channel and crooked it up, feeling for that rough patch.

I knew I'd found it when her whole body locked up.

"Fuck, fuck, fuck, fuck," she said. She arched her spine and threw her head back. "Don't stop, fuck, please, don't stop."

Her wish was my command. I kept the pressure of my tongue steady on her clit, working it in smooth circles, and I pushed against her G-spot in rhythmic strokes. She was trembling, bracing against the bed with her heels and pushing up to meet my mouth and touch. I could feel the tension in her muscles as she stilled for a moment. Then she shattered.

There was a rush of her honey on my tongue as she gasped, "Oh, oh, OH. Fuck!" Her body practically vibrated as she began to writhe with the wave of her orgasm, arching both toward and away from me as I continued to stroke her through it. She pulled away from my tongue and I let her, my finger still inside her as her soft inner walls squeezed the ever-loving shit out of my finger. *She's fucking magnificent.*

"Oh my God," she breathed, her legs tightening around my hand. "Fuck, honey, that..." She flopped back against the pillows, her fisted hands loosening on the bed sheets as she slowly released her grip on me. I could still feel the aftershocks fluttering along my finger as I slowly withdrew it and placed a single kiss on her clit. She flinched. "Fuck."

"Hmmm," I hummed, pushing her dress up further so I could kiss her hip bone. "You're a work of art, spitfire."

She huffed a little laugh as I kept working my way up, my lips and tongue carving a wet path over her stomach and to her bra. I kneeled up again to pull the dress over her head, which she sat up a bit to help me achieve. She flopped bonelessly back against the bed with a little smile, spread before me in nothing but her pink bra. *Of course it fucking matches. Perfect creature.*

I gave her a little smirk of warning, then leaned down and sucked the nipple of her right breast into my mouth through her bra. The lace was rough on my tongue as I swirled it around the peaked bud thoroughly, sucking and nipping through the material. She arched into me and I growled my approval, taking more of her into my mouth before drawing back to admire the dark, glistening spot on her heaving chest.

She was watching me watch her, with goosebumps and a fine sheen of sweat on her skin. "You look at me like I'm a meal," she murmured, licking her lips like she didn't know it was my undoing.

"You are," I confirmed, bending to give her left breast the same attention.

As I did, I trailed my fingers back down to that magical place between her thighs. She gasped as I teased her clit slowly with two fingers, rolling them in lazy circles. Her breathing was quickening already, and I knew her second orgasm wouldn't take much. *I want another before I'm inside her.*

I ghosted my fingers down and slowly pushed them both inside of her, the wetness from my saliva and her prior orgasm providing plenty of lube. I was still feasting on her breast and nipple as I did, and the long, low moan she gave as I filled her with my hand was the best sound I'd ever heard. Pushing my fingers into her, I curved them up, and gave my favorite little G-spot a stroke. She threw her head back and gasped, her hands grasping my head to her tit fiercely. I sucked harder, nipped again, and slowly thrust my fingers in and out. She rocked her hips up to meet me as she mumbled incoherent things, so close to falling over that ledge again. I reached up with my thumb and lazily circled her clit, and she slowly locked up as I released her nipple.

"Give me another, spitfire," I demanded as I peered into her eyes. "Show me again how fucking stunning you are when you come."

I swirled my thumb steadily and stroked with my curled fingers, and she was gone. Her eyes rolled back, and she bowed against me, her whole body trembling again while I kept up the pressure. She was writhing against me, clutching me where she could, completely lost to her pleasure. *A work of fucking art, Brooks. This girl is perfect.*

I gradually stopped my torture of her sopping cunt as she relaxed once more, little aftershocks making her twitch against me. I covered her lips with mine and she surged into me, wrapping herself around me without hesitation. It was impossible to miss how well we fit together, like two pieces of a puzzle.

"Fucking hell, Parker," she mumbled against my lips. She pulled back a bit to look at me, her legs around my hips and her hand settling on my cheek. "That was...that was better than Ms. Wilson's first peach pie of the season."

I laughed and grinned at her. "I have no idea what that's like, spitfire, but I'll take it you enjoyed yourself."

She gave me a lazy nod, biting her lip as she stared at me. "Mmmhm. I can hardly wait for the main event."

My cock twitched painfully in my slacks at the feral lust in her eyes. I kissed her again, taking my time, savoring her. "Is that so?" I whispered against her lips when we broke apart.

"It is," she answered, her hand dropping to work the button open on my slacks. "Gimme."

I chuckled and rolled to my back to finish what she started, shoving my pants and boxer briefs off in one quick motion. I intended to turn back to her, but she surprised me, shoving my shoulder as I started to move.

"Nope, you had your fun." She crawled over to me. Eying my cock appreciatively—I hoped—she licked her goddamn lips again. *Fucking temptress.*

I arched a brow at her. "Seems like you had yours, too."

She flushed at that, shooting me a glare. I grinned back at her, unabashed.

"Beside the point," she replied primly, pulling her hair to one side. "Moral of the story is, I'm in charge now."

My eyebrows crept up, "Okay, whatever you s—"

She stole the words from my mouth and breath from my lungs as she leaned down and wrapped her mouth around my cock, taking me halfway down her throat without hesitation.

"Jesus fucking Christ," I barked, as I threw my head back and clenched my fists. Whatever I imagined earlier in the shower was a poor imitation of reality, because her mouth was fucking magic. Hot, wet, tight magic that was going to cast a spell on me I feared I could never break. *Keep it together, Brooks!*

She was bobbing away, her hand around my base as she hollowed her cheeks. I breathed harshly, trying to get myself under control before it ended way too soon.

"Spitfire, you are fucking talented, but I really need you to stop before I blow in your mouth," I said through clenched teeth.

She made a lewd noise as she popped off of my dick that would be imprinted on my memory for all time, right alongside the image of her kneeling beside me in just a bra, flushed all over with saliva everywhere. *Utter perfection.*

"Somewhere else you'd rather come, sugar?" She teased.

Oh god, Brooks, where is your dignity? You can't blow your load because she says something sexy! Get. It. Together!

I swallowed and tried to think of anything to pause the impending eruption. "What's on offer?"

She smirked at me, and the look was pure evil lust. *God, I'm here for that.*

"You have condoms?"

I reached over to the nightstand and grabbed a foil packet I had tossed there earlier in hopes I'd find her. She laughed at me, not unkindly.

She shrugged a bit, waving the condom at me. "You can come in this, inside." She pointed down to the nirvana between her thighs, and I clenched *everything* to keep my shit together. "Or you can get yourself right to the edge," she said, as she reached back to unclasp her bra and push it off her shoulders, "and come on these."

Her breasts were heavy on her chest, perky pink nipples tight and rigid. It was the absolute best set of tits I'd ever seen in person, hands down. I wanted to suffocate between them.

She reached out and rubbed a gentle thumb over the corner of my mouth. "You're drooling."

I blinked up at her. At that moment, there was no longer time for talk—just action. I reached out, snagged the condom, ripped it open, and slid it quickly on my cock while she gaped at me and my lightning speed.

"I choose option B." I playfully tackled her and pushed her onto her back.

She squealed and giggled, opening her thighs for me without hesitation. I fitted myself between them and snagged a pillow before tapping her hip.

"Lift," I instructed. She listened, raising her hips so I could slot the pillow under her. "Good girl." She bit her lower lip and her eyes darkened at my praise, and I felt myself losing all sense of caution. "God, you're perfect."

Her whole body flushed at my words, and I decided to make my move before I had to think too long about the fact that I had said that shit out loud. I rubbed my cock against her pussy lips— still gorgeously wet from our fun—a few times, teasing and coating it with her cum, then notched it against her entrance. I watched, rapt, as I pushed inside with one slow, firm stroke. "Fucking hell, look at how well you take me, Laura Beth."

Her sharp inhale brought my eyes to hers as I pulled one of her knees up to my hip and leaned forward, bracing on one arm.

I leaned down and kissed her, then slowly dragged myself out just to plunge right back in. I couldn't help the groan that fell from my lips. "God, the way you squeeze me. So good."

She moaned and started thrusting her hips up to meet mine, creating a frantic rhythm between us. Her pussy was gripping my cock, squeezing every time she thrust up, sucking me in deeper. I could feel my orgasm building and I hissed, needing to change things up.

I sat back on my heels and grasped her hips, lifting her lower body as I pounded into her. She gave me a moan that could be a scream, and I grunted in satisfaction. "Such a good girl," I rasped, and her answering flush and pussy squeeze gave me way too much pride. "You were made for this cock, Laura Beth."

Her body started to tense again, and I hummed my approval. "That's it, gorgeous. Come for me. Give me another. I want to feel you come all over this cock."

"Fuck, Parker," she cried. "Ri—fuck—right there, don't stop!"

Like I could fucking stop right then. She was a goddamn masterpiece before me, skin flushed and sweat glistening, one hand gripping the sheets while the other scrabbled for purchase on my thigh. Getting her over that cliff was not optional.

I reached down and circled my thumb on her clit, and she detonated. Her pussy clamped down on my cock and I almost shouted at the sensation, losing all hope of coming all over those perfect tits as she dragged my orgasm straight out of me. My hips stuttered and my thrusts faltered, but I pushed through, keeping the motion up through the last wave of her pleasure as best I could. As she relaxed back into the mattress, breathing hard but looking so blissed out I could've fucking pounded my chest like a Neanderthal, I gently lowered myself against her.

I worried for a moment that I'd be too heavy, but she wrapped both her arms and legs around me and held me tight, so I stayed put. I could've remained there like that forever, and I could've certainly passed out in her warm embrace in no time at all, so I slowly peeled myself off to the side when she loosened her grip. I flopped onto my back and recognized that my breaths were heaving out of me just as hard as hers were. I closed my eyes and chuckled softly.

"I think Fate and I really are best friends," I mused.

She laughed breathlessly and smacked my chest so softly it was basically just her hand flopping onto my body.

"You broke me," she whispered, eyes still closed.

I propped myself up on my elbow and turned toward her, worried. "What do you mean? Are you okay?" I glanced down her body and onto the bed, looking for any sign of injury. I didn't think I had been that rough, but I had also been pretty lost to the fog of pleasure and desire for the most part.

She blinked her eyes open in surprise and looked up at me. Her gaze softened immediately. "You are the biggest softie ever, Parker. All that dirty talk and look at you. A big ol' teddy bear."

While she was definitely full of shit, thank you very much, I was still looking at her with concern. She laughed and rolled over to snuggle into me, pushing gently on my opposite shoulder. I took her direction and relaxed on my back as I tucked my arm around her.

"I just meant you broke my brain, silly boy," she mumbled, her head on my shoulder and the smile evident in her voice. "Three orgasms will do that to a girl."

I grinned. I couldn't help it. "It *was* three, wasn't it? Bet I can get four out of you next time."

She snickered and smacked me again, with a little more oomph to it the second time around. "Make it five, sugar. Dream big."

I barked a laugh. *Absolutely. Fucking. Perfect.*

Chapter 9

LB

I woke up slowly. My body was heavy with sleep, but my bladder was insistent that I pay attention and get a move on. I wanted to groan, but something stopped me. *Why am I so warm?*

My eyes flashed open, my whole body stilling. I was in a hotel room. *Parker's* hotel room. He was snuggled up against my back, his arm draped around my waist and leg tucked between mine. It amazed me I was so fucking comfortable because usually, I'm a kicker. It was also pathetically perfect how well we fit together. I glanced at the clock and grimaced. It was four in the morning. I had no reason to be up that early, but the rude awakening gave me the perfect opportunity to slip away.

Parker sniffed in his sleep and shifted slightly, taking the weight of his body off mine. I seized the opportunity and slowly rolled away from him, ignoring the throb in my core when I glanced back at him, prone on the bed. He was fucking gorgeous. When he had stripped down last night, eyes hot on mine and movements decisive, I swore my body liquefied. I'd never had sex like that before, never been *worshiped* like I was something worthy of devotion. He laid me on an altar and methodically tore down my walls one by one, then destroyed me for any other man. *Okay, drama llama, back it up. It was great sex. Now you have a job to do.*

I sighed. Sometimes, y'all, my conscience was a real party pooper. I grabbed my clothes from the floor by the bed and scooped up my purse from where I had dropped it by the door. Then I let myself into his bathroom. There was a nightlight on near the mirror, so I skipped the overhead in hopes that Parker would sleep through my sneak out. My very dignified sneak out.

I relieved my bladder with a sigh of relief before washing my hands and hastily throwing my dress on. I abandoned the bra and panties and wadded them into my purse–they were superfluous for a walk of shame. I hesitated for a moment, because there was nothing shameful about last night, and caught my gaze in the mirror. *Best sex of your life, Laura Beth, and you're walking away without a word?*

My eyelids fell, and I took a steadying breath. I had a plan, see. One I'd carefully outlined since I was a tween in a podunk football town in Alabama. I never felt like I fit in Pike Road with its small downtown, where the greatest ambition was a national championship for the Pike Road High Patriots. My parents were simple folk. They had married right out of high school and became parents to my older sister before either of them hit twenty. But as I grew up watching their love, watching my sister fall in love in high school and settle right into the same pattern, my skin felt too tight and my palms itched for something more. There was nothing for me in Pike Road. Nothing for me in Alabama. My path was clear–graduate high school, get a scholarship to a top university on the West or East Coast (any coast but the Gulf), and make my own way. Because, the alternative–staying in Pike Road like most of my classmates and my entire family–felt like giving up on a future that was unwritten. I didn't want to give up on everything I could be.

I opened my eyes and nodded at myself. Parker was fun, and sexy, and seemingly sweet—which was seriously rude because unicorns like that didn't come along often—but he was also a distraction. I'd been successful in achieving each step of my plan thus far. I was the only one of my graduating class who got into Berkeley. The first person in my family tree to secure an undergraduate degree. One of the few to pursue a white-collar job successfully. One of only a handful to 'make it' enough to not end up right back in Pike Road after college. I was not about to toss my future out the window for a decent dicking. *Even if it was a really, **really** good dicking.* I sighed. *God, such a nice dick.*

I shook my head at myself and tiptoed from the bathroom. I spared one last glance back at Parker, sprawled out in the muted light of the city through the window. The blanket was low on his naked hips, one leg sticking out. I flashed back to all that lean, corded muscle pressing me against the entryway closet and felt myself get wet. *Hang on to those memories, Laura Beth. They're all you're gonna get.* The temptation of Parker was far too strong—it was better to leave it here, at this perfect night, than to let him rip through my life. Because I knew he would. I could already feel the tension he had put on the tissue paper of my existence—one sharp tug and I'd be in pieces and adrift, and that just wouldn't do. It was best to walk away.

So I did.

The halls were deserted as I paced quickly to the elevator and navigated my way back to my room. I had taken the time to unpack the night before, worried my dress would be a wrinkled mess if I didn't. It was still well before 5 am, so I decided on a quick shower and a run to get my head in the game for the meeting with my potential client today.

Dr. Gaspar was a genius, and that was putting it lightly. He had developed and patented gene-editing technology that could vastly improve the nutrients in many common crops. With this most recent round of funding, he'd get closer to making a material difference in the state of malnutrition in our country and, ultimately, beyond. The man was as brilliant as he was eccentric, though, and he'd been putting me through my paces. And, given this was the first investment opportunity that Mr. Livingston had trusted to me and me alone, that had proven to be a unique and frustrating challenge. It wasn't like Dr. Gaspar was sexist—it would honestly have been easier if he was; I had been blowing misogynistic ideas to smithereens since I was knee high to a grasshopper. He was just particular, exacting, and fully aware that he held the power in our dynamic. We were acting early and, from what I'd gathered, we were not alone in our pursuit of his partnership. I knew at least one other firm was in the mix, based on what the doctor and his team had shared or let slip. Which only amped up the pressure.

As I stepped into the shower, I felt a twinge of remorse about losing Parker's scent. I had noticed the smell of him clinging to me on my way back to my room, and there was an uncomfortable clench in my chest at the thought of just washing him away. But washing him away, and walking away, was the right call. *Of course, it's the right call, Laura Beth. Get your head in the game.*

I knew a run would help me find my center. It always did. While Sara Jean, my dear big sister, opted for cheerleading in high school (and, yes, she married the captain of the football team because my family is one giant small-town cliche), I was drawn to track. An 'interesting choice for a little thing' like me, Coach loved to say, but a fitting one nonetheless. Few things had the calming effect on me that the rhythm and familiarity of running did. I always packed my running things, even on single overnights like this trip, because starting my day any other way was a surefire invitation for disaster.

I remembered spotting a gym on the elevator bank buttons, and the desk clerk had mentioned one when I checked in (not that I fully processed his words—I'd been highly distracted wondering how badly I'd fucked up by letting Parker walk away after the flight). I pushed him from my mind again and wound my way through the hotel to the fitness center. It was blessedly quiet, with only one other person using a treadmill on the far side of the room. I kept my eyes on my chosen machine on the opposite wall, popped in my earbuds, and selected a rigorous cardio program.

As I started my run, I ran through my goals for the day's meeting. So far, Dr. Gaspar had been reluctant to commit. He knew an investment partner like P&L would help him achieve the scale he needed to drive true impact in the agriculture industry, but that hadn't stopped him from being incredibly particular. Not only had he been exacting about the terms of a deal, but he'd also grilled me on the reputation of my firm. It was clear that who he partnered with was just as important to him as the specifics of the partnership agreement. I knew that the key to getting him to sign with P&L would be showing an understanding of and empathy for the things he cared about—once I figured out exactly what those things were. The last three meetings had been an extended introduction for both of us. He was still vetting me and P&L, while I was vetting him, his business plan, and doing my best to get a better understanding of the details of his patent—and the possible revenue and profit it could drive. All the bones were there for a winning opportunity: he had a stellar idea, there was tremendous demand and broad applications for his tech, and there was true potential for longevity if we could grow his business to become a market leader in AgTech.

I could feel the sweat beading, and the tension I was feeling over saying goodbye to Parker this morning faded from my limbs. As much as it would've been fairytale perfect to stay in his arms, in his bed, and let him continue to sweep me off my feet, I lived in the real world. And, at least in my experience, that meant there were no easy paths. There was only the work you were willing to put in to move yourself to the next step, against all obstacles.

And right then, I had plenty to focus on for work. Dr. Gaspar had asked that we spend our time that day talking about my firm, P&L Ventures. We were the venture capital arm of Price & Livingston Financial, one of the largest and most prestigious investment firms on the East Coast. P&L opened their offices in the Bay just five years ago, under the lead of Nathaniel Livingston, my boss, and heir to both his father's company and the family fortune. Dr. Gaspar had mentioned the importance of "doing business with like-minded people" multiple times. He'd also been insistent on face-to-face meetings with few exceptions. That day, I planned to walk him through our mission, vision, and the fledgling Foundation started by Mr. Livingston, which was focusing on food and housing insecurity among its five-year objectives.

The treadmill signaled that my cool down was imminent, and I switched mental gears to planning my next steps for the morning. By the time I got back to my room, showered again, and got ready, I would have an hour to catch up on emails and grab a quick bite. *You've got this. You can do hard things.*

I could. I had. I would.

———

A few hours later that morning, at 8:55am, I walked purposefully into the lobby at Gaspar Technologies. It was a small office and lab in an unassuming, low-slung strip of similar industrial spaces. The first time I had come here, I wondered if I'd gotten the address wrong. But the second you walked into the lobby, the space was bright, white, and inviting in its minimalism. My eyes were down as I entered, flicking over an email I got from Mr. Livingston this morning with his requests for outcomes for the day. I heard Courtney, the office manager, laugh and smiled to myself as I closed out of my email app. She was good people.

I looked up, and my step faltered. There was an all-too-familiar frame in front of Courtney's desk, clad in a dark suit that screamed money and fit like it had been made for his body. With the polish of it, it likely had. I just barely held in the "what the fuck?!" that went screaming through my mind at the sight of him. Just.

Courtney caught my surely stunned gaze and grinned. "Hey there, LB! Parker here finished up a smidge early, so Dr. Gaspar should be just about ready for you. Let me buzz him."

"Sure thing, Courtney!" I called, giving her a wide smile. I was pointedly not looking at Parker, but I noticed how he turned sharply toward the door when Courtney said my name. Not many "LBs" running around out there, I suppose.

I glanced at him in what I intended to be a brief meeting of eyes, but the intensity in his gaze snagged my attention. He slowly arched one eyebrow at me, his expression unreadable, and tilted his head to the side. There was a clear question in that look, and it mirrored my own from moments ago.

I gave him a quick and pointed shake of the head, clearly saying *not here, not now*. He smirked and his gaze darkened before he turned back to Courtney as though he couldn't be bothered by my presence. I tried desperately not to notice how she glanced appreciatively at him out of the corner of her eye

57

and gave a soft smile while she asked Dr. Gaspar if he was ready for his 9 o'clock.

"Understood, sir," she said, hanging up the phone and turning to me. "He needs five, LB. I can grab you some water while you wait?"

"Oh sure, Courtney, that'd be lovely. Thank you!"

She nodded and slipped from behind the desk, headed back to the kitchen. I turned toward Parker and found him smiling at me, his expression predatory.

"Who the fuck do you work for?" I snapped. He could look gorgeous and intimidating all he wanted, but I was not to be deterred.

He barked a laugh. "Ahhh, regretting the ol' work embargo from yesterday, eh?"

"Don't be cute, mister," I hissed. I could hear my accent getting thick and wrangled it back. "Just answer the question, please."

His eyes fucking sparkled, as they were wont to do, and he grinned. "You really are Southern, aren't you? Even polite when you're spitting mad."

"Oh, you haven't seen mad yet, I promise you that," I quipped back, sarcasm thick in my tone. "I asked you a question: who do you work for?"

He leaned casually against the desk and smirked at me. "Guess."

"No. I will not play your little game. You will tell me, and then you'll fuck right off so I can focus and get my job done."

There was a heat in his eyes that should not have been turning me on, but the fact that this man liked it when I got sassy really did things for my lady bits. Annoying-as-fuck things, but *things*.

"Athena," he said simply, and I cursed internally.

I could hear Courtney returning to the lobby, so I kept it short. "Thank you, Parker. Take care."

Giving him my back and putting on my best professional smile, I thanked Courtney for the water bottle as she offered it to me. I had exactly two minutes to freak the fuck out over this news, then I need to get my game face back on. Nodding to Courtney, I took a seat on one of the couches in front of her desk, pulling out my phone as I did. I was vaguely aware that Parker had wandered over to the other couch, where a sleek black backpack waited. I did my best to ignore him as I pulled up my messages app. He didn't make it easy, with his smolder resolutely aimed my way.

> Me: Good morning! Just letting you know Athena is the other firm in the running. Still confident it's just the two of us, but thought you'd like to know.

His reply was instant, but that wasn't a surprise, given the history. While my boss was the heir apparent to Price & Livingston and the Livingston family fortune, his 10-month-older sister, Alexandra, was the founder and general partner of Athena Ventures. To say there was tension between our firms would be the understatement of the century. Parker may as well be Romeo to my Juliet. *Now there's a depressing thought, Laura Beth, for fuck's sake.* My phone buzzing brought my attention back to reality.

> Mr. Livingston: Is it a partner?

> Me: No, sir. I just have a first name: Parker.

I could see him typing a response thanks to the little bouncing dots, but his reply took a minute. I assumed he was looking Parker up.

Mr. Livingston: Sr. Associate reporting to Van.
Good intel, LB. Now forget about him. Focus
on the goal and call me from the airport.

Me: Yes, sir. Will do.

I sighed and closed my eyes briefly, seeking the calm confidence I'd had walking in.

"You're all set, LB, head on back," Courtney called from the desk, giving me a grin.

"Thanks so much," I replied with a smile. I stood and turned to head down the hall without a single glance back. I didn't have time for Parker and his stupid, pretty face. *Game time, Laura Beth. Let's do this.*

I strode down the hallway to the single conference room in the modest space. Per usual, Dr. Gaspar was waiting inside. He was looking at something on his laptop, but he looked up and shut it without preamble as I walked in. He gave me his typical flat look in greeting.

"Hi there, Dr. Gaspar," I greeted warmly, offering him my hand.

As he always did, he reached over the table and took my hand, then gave it one firm pump before settling back in his seat. He was an intense man with heavy, dark eyebrows and thick salt and pepper hair, light on the salt.

"Morning, Miss Calhoun," he responded. "I'm interested to hear more about P&L. I had an enlightening conversation with your competition this morning."

My smile didn't falter, and I was damn proud of that. "I'm sure you did, Doctor. Athena has a great reputation in the Bay, for good reason." That earned me an eyebrow raise, but there was no point in mincing words—Parker and his firm were stiff competition, as they should be. "But I'm excited to share a little more about P&L and how we prioritize our own investments–in our clients and our community. Shall we begin?"

He gave me a nod, and I pulled up my presentation, connecting seamlessly to the TV on the wall. *Time to get it done.*

Chapter 10

Parker

I heard heels coming down the hall and had to fight back a smirk. I could tell LB was not exactly pleased to see me here earlier, but I was delighted at another opportunity to...talk. After her little disappearing act last night, I wasn't sure I'd see her again. Though I was ready to shoot my shot if we wound up on a few more flights together, I was also concerned my new best friend, Fate, had set me up to crash and burn. Either way, I wasn't ready for her to see just how happy I was that we were sharing the same space again.

She burst into view around the corner in a flurry of professional energy, eyes on her phone as she entered the lobby. She looked up at the receptionist and gave her a smile.

"Thanks so much, Courtney," she gushed, and I noticed her accent was nowhere to be found, just like when she had arrived. Interesting. "Dr. Gaspar mentioned his availability is a bit tight next week—can we schedule that follow up for Wednesday?"

"Afraid the good doctor is busy Wednesday," I called across the lobby.

LB whirled on me and leveled me with a death glare. If I

didn't know what her face looked like when she came, I might have been affected by it.

"Is that so, Mr....?" She snarked back at me.

It was a struggle to keep a straight face, but I managed it. "Brooks. Parker Brooks. And you are?"

Her nostrils flared in what I could only assume was indignation. "LB Calhoun, not that it's any of your business, Mr. Brooks." Her accent was showing itself a bit now, like a little flash of leg.

"Lovely to meet you, Ms. Calhoun. Dr. Gaspar will be with me Wednesday afternoon, and he made it clear I was taking the last available slot on his calendar that day." I wasn't even lying, either, despite how I desperately wanted to fuck with her.

"I see," she replied stiffly. She turned back to Courtney and flashed her a megawatt smile. "While I appreciate how willing Mr. Brooks was to offer up this information, Courtney, I'd like to confirm with you directly. Can we find a time on Wednesday?"

"Afraid Parker here has it right. Dr. Gaspar's only availability next week is Thursday afternoon. Shall I reserve the conference room for you at 2pm, per usual?" Courtney asked, a broad smile on her face. She was a nice gal, that one. Very reliable.

LB was practically vibrating with displeasure. I wanted to help her relax. I bet I knew just the buttons to push, too.

"I see. Yes, let's book it then," she gritted out, jaw tight. I could see the Southern politeness warring with her sheer frustration, and it was honestly one of the more entertaining things I've witnessed.

"Conference room, huh?" I taunted as I leaned against the front desk. "Awfully predictable."

LB dropped all pretenses, and straight up ignored me. Courtney glanced between us, her eyebrows slowly rising as she caught onto the fact that she was missing quite a bit of context.

"She's cranky," I mouthed silently behind my hand. Courtney almost stopped the snort that escaped her. Almost.

"Well, LB, you're on the calendar! Anything else I can do for you today?" She asked brightly.

LB gave her a genuine smile. The girl had a heart of gold under that honey badger routine, I supposed. "Thanks a million, Courtney. You're the best. See you next week?"

"You bet, LB," she confirmed, giving me a quick glance before turning back to LB with a wry eyebrow twitch. "Safe travels."

"Thanks, hun." LB winked—straight up winked—and turned away, moving to stalk right out of the lobby without another word.

I don't think so, spitfire. I tossed Courtney a wink of my own and followed LB out, stopping at the couch I'd been waiting on to grab my things on the way. When I emerged from the building, LB was staring intently at her phone. I walked up right next to her, close enough to brush her elbow with mine, and shifted my hand in front of her.

"Ever heard of personal space?" She snapped, not looking up.

That's good. Means she felt me, knew who I was.

"Ever heard of saying goodbye?" I tossed back. She flinched and I couldn't hold back the satisfied smile. *You should flinch, spitfire. I've got so much more in store for you.* I wiggled my hand a bit, making the coffee in the cup I was holding jump out of the little hole in the lid. "This is for you. Soy latte, triple shot. Thought you might want the extra caffeine."

Her gaze flew to mine, expression confused. "Excuse me?"

I wiggled the cup again, drawing her eyes to it. "Coffee. For you."

She reached out hesitantly and took the cup. With my hand

free, I reached back and pulled the little paper bag from my backpack and offered it to her.

"And what's this?" She asked, giving me a look of bewilderment and wariness.

"Croissant. Thought you might like a snack. Also thought you might've missed breakfast," I said, then tossed her a dark look. "Late night and all."

She flushed crimson, and I wanted to shout and fist pump like a buffoon. I didn't, but fuck did I want to. Knowing I was getting to her was my new favorite drug.

"Well," she snapped, recovering quickly, "I'm glad we got that out of our systems, anyway. Now we can focus on the task at hand."

I ignored the first half of her comment, for now. "And what's the task at hand, Ms. Calhoun?"

She looked me square in the eye and my cock took notice. He liked it when she was fiery. Liked it a little too much, if I was honest.

"Competition, Mr. Brooks," she answered, giving me one of her famous cocked eyebrows. "You're now the enemy."

I laughed because, *what—are we twelve?* And, also, she was adorable. Hard not to laugh.

"I see. You with a VC from the Bay, too?" Her unimpressed look made me chuckle. "Okay, fine, that one could've been an internal thought. Let's see..." I thought for a moment, running through a list of our competitors in my brain. Dr. Gaspar wasn't on many people's radar, yet, and he was serving a niche enough industry that Van and Lex—Van's partner and owner of the firm—were relatively confident we'd be one of maybe two players courting him this early. *Ah, fuck. Of course.* "You're not with P&L, are you?"

Her eyebrows both flew up. "How the hell did you figure that out so fast?"

I groaned a little, but my smile didn't falter. "Oh, hell, you are. That certainly makes all this interesting. That's okay, though, we can work with this."

"What do you mean? Work with what?"

"The family drama. No need to bring it into this," I gestured between us. "We're professionals. We can leave work at the door. Focus on the fun stuff."

She gave an incredulous laugh. I didn't like that sound. "And what, pray tell, would you define as the 'fun' stuff?"

I let my grin turn wolfish as I met her eyes. "Well, I do believe there was talk of me owing you five next time. I'd like to get started on that fun. Preferably as soon as possible."

She choked out a garbled laugh and took an immediate step away from me. *Huh. Not the reaction I had in mind.*

"I don't think so, *Mr. Brooks*," she bit out, shaking her head. "You are persona non grata to me, now. I have a job to do, and you will not distract me from it." She raised her coffee cup at me. "Thanks for the coffee, but I have shit to do. Good luck. See you never."

She went to turn away, but I was so not done with her yet.

"Spitfire," I called, my voice a soft warning. It had the desired effect—she stopped dead. "You don't want to walk away from this."

She looked at me full on; her face a hard mask. There was a twinge of concern and hurt deep in my chest, but I pushed it away.

"There is nothing to walk away from, Mr. Brooks. We scratched an itch. Now we're enemies. It's just business."

I stepped up into her personal space, savoring the way her breath hitched as my proximity forced her to look up to meet my eyes. I pitched my tone low, just for her, "Was it just business when you came on my tongue, fingers, *and* cock last night, spit-fire? Or was that just...scratching an itch?"

She licked her lip and restraining my groan was physically painful, but I did it. I could feel the tension in her body, could see a flash of want in her eyes that called to mine. But she resisted, and it seemed easier to do than I wanted it to be.

"An itch," she muttered, but her voice lacked all conviction.

"I see," I replied, softly. I looked up, away from her eyes, and straightened, putting a bit of distance between us. "I see."

I stepped back and looked back at her face, finding her watching me. There was a look I couldn't decipher in her eyes, but whatever I said next felt important. Like it could set the stage for whatever happened between us then and in the future. *And I still want this girl more than I've ever wanted anything.* Fucking up wasn't an option. But if all she would give me was enemies, I'd take it.

"Well, then, Ms. Calhoun," I said, my tone falsely light, "game on."

She blinked. "Excuse me?"

"You heard me. You want a battle royale, you'll get one. But can we call a truce for now? My ride has been waiting a while." I jerked my chin at the black car on the curb and she whipped her head toward it.

"Your ride?"

"Yeah. Hop in."

She narrowed her eyes at me and I widened mine back. "I went back to the hotel, grabbed my bag. I assume you're flying out on the 12:20?"

"Yeah, but I have to get—"

"It's in the car."

"Excuse me?"

"Your bag." I opened the rear passenger door. "It's in the trunk."

"I left it with the concierge."

"I know. I left mine with the concierge, too."

67

"Okay, but—"

"I told him we were colleagues."

"You what?!"

"I told the concierge we worked together. He believed me. And the tip I gave him."

"Are you fucking *kidding* me right now?"

She was close enough to touch, having walked closer as we went back and forth. I took advantage of her proximity and leaned toward her.

"I'd be fucking *you* right now if it was up to me, but it's not," I gave her a pointed look. "So, no. I'm not kidding you—fucking or otherwise. Get in the damn car, spitfire."

I ignored her sputtering and stepped away, walking around the car to the rear driver's side door. I opened it and slid into my seat. I had fastened my seatbelt and pulled out my phone by the time LB huffed her way in and slammed the door.

"I can't believe you stole my bag."

I tsked, still looking at my phone. "Buckle up," I reminded her. "I didn't steal it. I picked it up for you. Before I bought you breakfast." I gave her another pointed look.

"Why would you do that? Why would they let you!?"

I growled a bit, frustrated by her stubbornness. "Who ghosted who, again?" I asked, my tone firm. I leaned toward her to keep our conversation private.

"I meant it when I promised you five next time. I had every intention of waking you up with a *very* thorough kiss this morning, and not on your face." My eyes slipped down her body to her lap, then back up. "And of getting your number and setting up a date for when we're back in the Bay." I held her eyes for a beat, remembering her sprawled out beneath me post-orgasm, flushed and blissed-out. "After a night like that, why would I ever assume you would just walk away?"

My response seemed to catch her off guard. She was staring

at me with her jaw slightly dropped, mouth open. She closed it, then opened again. I desperately wanted to slide my cock between her lips, but, being the gentleman I was, I kept it in my pants. For now.

She looked down, swallowed, and sat back in her seat, gaze going toward the window. A few moments later, she cleared her throat and said, "Thank you."

I nodded, looking at my phone once more, though I desperately wanted to stare at her face and absorb every last expression. "You're welcome."

"But this doesn't mean we're not enemies," she continued, her voice earnest.

I blinked in surprise, then looked up at her. "Pardon me?"

"Seriously, Parker. I've worked hard to get where I am. This deal is important for me, for my future. I can't let you," she looked at me, her eyes flicking to my lap (which was not exactly a PG location just then) and back up, "or your *assets* get in the way of achieving what's next. Last night was fun, but now I have to work to make this deal happen." She sighed and turned her gaze back out the window. "Even more so now that we know Athena is at the table."

I stared at her, honestly a bit baffled. I was on board with a little friendly competition, but she was seriously shutting me down. Shutting *us* down. *There is no us, according to her.* That was a tough pill to swallow. So I didn't.

"Got it." I looked back down at my phone with a nod. "May the best VC win."

She wants to be enemies? I'll play.

She could fight for this deal, but I had something far more enticing on the line.

She's mine.

Chapter 11

LB

The ride to the airport was awkward. At least, it was for me. Parker didn't seem bothered. I didn't understand how the man could be so unperturbed all the time. It was honestly unnatural. But my words in the car clearly had an effect, because he was silent the rest of the way.

When we pulled up to the departures area, he grabbed my bag out of the trunk and handed it over with a perfunctory nod.

"We'll see each other again soon, I'm sure," he said, giving me a hot look.

"I'm sure. I doubt your boss is going to take it lightly that P&L is here to play."

He snorted, "My boss couldn't care less about you and your firm, to be honest. The rivalry there is largely one-sided."

After the flash of offense at his brash dismissal cleared, I found his stance a bit confusing. The rivalry between Nathaniel and Alexandra Livingston, and therefore P&L and Athena, was widely known in the Bay, according to anyone at P&L.

"Regardless," he continued, "we both have a lot of work to do. I'm going to head to the lounge since I'm here at such an unreasonably early hour. I'm sure I'll see you on the flight."

Even though I was the one putting up the boundaries, I was taken aback that he was just going to walk away now. I mean, it was a fair call and likely the best approach, but I didn't think he'd give in that easily. I glanced down at my suitcase and realized, to my complete and utter shame, that I was both pouting and fidgeting.

"Oh, spitfire," he crooned, and my core clenched at the dark promise in his tone. "Don't look so disappointed. I'd very much like to come over there and drag my thumb across your lip...and other places...and kiss you senseless, but you've set the boundaries. Enemies, right?"

I blinked owlishly up at him. My pussy was telling me to fuck boundaries. *Shut up, horny bitch.* "Right. Boundaries."

He nodded. "Boundaries, LB. But if we're going to do this little battle, I want to be able to reach you. For business purposes. Something tells me, given the conversation today and the good doctor setting us up to bump into one another, we may have to join forces here soon. For the greater good, of course."

He held out a hand, but I just stared at him.

"Your phone, LB. Give it to me. I'm going to give you my number. Use it if you need to, for business, or not."

"You don't want mine?"

His eyes flashed, and he made this grumbling sound that was not appropriate for public or my panties. "I want yours, LB. I want it badly. But I'm following your rules and trying to be at least a little bit of a gentleman here, so...you know, work with me. Give me your phone."

I handed it over wordlessly because, honestly, what was I going to say to that? The man growled at me and he couldn't have made it any clearer that he wanted me. And not as a business rival. *Fate, you're a cold bastard.*

"Hey, that's my new best friend you're talking about,"

71

Parker teased, and I nearly died when it registered that I had let that little statement slip out loud.

"Ah, ignore me." I accepted my phone back with a nod. I glanced down and snorted at the name he'd given his contact. "Bold choice, My Competition."

He gave me this nonchalant shrug that shouldn't have been attractive but still had heat coiling low in my belly. "Gotta make myself memorable."

I threw him an exasperated look that told him exactly how subtle he was being—*the man knew he was memorable as fuck, let's not play*—and his smirk turned into an all-out grin that stole the breath from my lungs and somehow turned it into moisture between my thighs. *I don't think that's how that works, but apparently my reactions to this man defy nature.*

"Catch you later, LB," he murmured as he gave me a jaunty salute.

Then he walked away. And I just watched him go.

I gave myself five seconds—I counted them, silently, Mississippis and all—to stare at his perfectly slack-clad ass, then I turned on my heel and headed to the other security checkpoint. If there was anything I'd learned in the last 24 hours, it was that Parker's hold on me was only increased by proximity. The more distance I could put between him and my pussy...I mean, body... the better. For both of our sanities.

My mind wandered as I went through the motions with the airport's security screening. The process was like second nature for me, between the work trips and my admittedly infrequent flights back home. Well, back to Montgomery by way of LA or Salt Lake or Atlanta because there were no direct routes, and it was at least a 10-hour travel day, then the 30 minutes to my parents' or sister's house in a car that would've felt at home in either a junkyard or a museum. I much preferred the easy breezy nonstop adventure with business class options and the comfort of anonymity. There was none of either in Pike Road.

I relegated thoughts of home to the little lockbox in the back of my brain. I'd let it all out again soon enough–I planned to call Sara Jean once I got to my gate and after I caught Mr. Livingston up on the events of the day. The airport was on the smaller side, and I made decent time through the line. So decent that I hadn't quite figured out the best way to cover off on the happenings with Mr. Livingston when my phone buzzed.

"Hi, boss," I said, answering quickly as I grabbed a seat by the gate and near an outlet.

"LB," he answered, in his clipped, I-don't-have-time-for-this voice. That didn't exactly bode well for me. "What's the outcome?"

That's something I had learned in this business–no one ever asked me how something went, or how I was feeling about it, or what the prospect or client said. They only wanted to know the answer to "what's next?" It still took me a minute to rewire my brain for the inevitable interrogation, because that's just not how my brain worked. I stripped back the things I noticed about what Gaspar was interested in, the questions that he asked, and the way he lit up when I mentioned certain details about our operating model or the foundation. Experience told me they would all be immaterial to Mr. Livingston, anyway.

"Another meeting next week, this time to discuss market size and projected revenue for the first three years."

He was silent, but I'd worked with him enough to know he was likely pursing his lips. "Will that be a virtual meeting this time?"

"No, sir. Planning for Thursday afternoon."

"I see. How many more conversations is it going to take, LB?"

I had known this question was coming, but I still didn't have a good answer for it. "As many as he needs, boss. Dr. Gaspar isn't motivated by the dollar signs or the resources we can bring. He's got a deep network of his own that he could mine independently. He cares more about finding the right partners to make the right connections—the ones that will make his bold growth plans a reality. And he's vetting us as thoroughly as we're vetting him, and it's not our annual report he's interested in. He cares about the—"

"It's still a business transaction, LB. I know you're a bleeding heart for some of this stuff, and I respect it because it's given you excellent instincts, but sometimes being a leader means recognizing when to shift the narrative. Was this next meeting your idea or his request?"

"His request, sir."

He made a small noise of affirmation, like he wasn't surprised. "I want you to change the plan. Think of something that will make him see you and P&L in a different light—one where you're asserting your expertise and leadership more effectively. It's a power play, but not an overt one. We need to get in the driver's seat to get this anywhere near to closing."

I stared off into the distance as I contemplated his words, nodding as I did. "Um. Okay, yeah. I can see how it would be helpful to direct things more firmly. I can do that. I think he wants to see how we collaborate, because he has ideas beyond just this initial patent. He seems interested in working with multiple investors—"

"If you're angling to suggest we get in bed with Athena Ventures on this, LB, you need to change tactics. That's not something our leadership will approve. My sister may have built a successful firm, but P&L doesn't need anyone else at the table to make this viable for the short or long term."

I had known he was going to shut me down on that, but I

also knew ending up with some level of collaboration was the better call. Dr. Gaspar wanted to see if we could do things differently. Athena, our competition, prided themselves on putting the needs of their clients first—it was central to their brand. As he held us up against that standard, Dr. Gaspar needed to see that P&L wasn't a typical VC that was full of big egos and bureaucracy. But it was going to take me no small amount of time and luck to get Mr. Livingston to come around to that.

"I understand there's a unique dynamic between our firms, sir. I'll send you some thoughts by tonight on how to turn the tables in our favor for next week."

"That's fine. Did you get anything out of Parker?"

"Excuse me?" I choked.

"Parker, the senior associate from Lex—I mean, Athena. Did you get any information out of him about their strategy? Anything that can give us an advantage as we head into the next round of conversations?"

"Uh, no, sir. We didn't discuss much business," I stumbled a bit over my words, cursing myself silently.

There was a pause, then a sigh. "LB, you're a good kid. Smart, reliable, and so detail-oriented it's honestly a bit scary. But this business also needs some level of ruthlessness and aggression. I need to see more of that in you. Think you can prove to me you deserve more responsibility? You've got senior associate on the line, here. Maybe more, in the future."

My heart was speeding up in my chest, because he was laying my path out before me on a silver platter. *Get in at the ground floor, work your way up. Get to VP by 30.*

"I know I can prove that to you, Mr. Livingston."

"Hm. I don't. I need to see it," he said, and the challenge lit a fire in my gut.

"I'm not one to back down, Nate," I said, using the nickname I'd heard his executive assistant and others at the office use, but had never uttered myself.

"Not from your challenge, not from the goals I've set for myself, and not from the plan I've mapped out for my career. That promotion is mine. If your recommendation is to get ruthless, then I'm ready to take the gloves off."

"Atta girl," he said, and I could hear his smile.

I wanted to ignore the feeling of pride that filled me at his praise, condescending as it may have been, but I couldn't. I wanted to impress Nate. I wanted him to be rooting for me, like he had always claimed to do.

"Get what you can out of Parker the next time you cross paths. Alexandra will not back down from this, especially now that we both know we're toe-to-toe. She's got too much to prove," he said, absently, as if he was talking to himself for a moment. He snapped back to the present quickly and continued, "Send me your proposal for next week, and let's switch the narrative. Get behind the wheel, LB. This is your race to lose or win."

"You got it, bo-...Nate."

He chuckled as he hung up. The moment we disconnected, the energy that had filled me rushed away, and I sagged into my seat. When I started this job, I took it because it seemed like the right thing to do. I was a top student in my undergraduate program, studying Business Administration. I took every internship opportunity I could get my hands on, and when the opportunity to interview for P&L came up, it seemed ludicrous not to take it.

I never envisioned myself in a job like this. Even though I had studied business, I still had these ideas in my head that somehow I'd end up doing something that helped people. Venture capital seemed like an interesting option because it was all about helping make people's dreams come true. They even called individuals in my line of work, those not backed by a firm like mine, angel investors. I had assumed I'd be working with people who had big, bright ideas for how to change the world for the better, and that we'd find a way through money and connections to help them do it. But I had been naive.

In reality, most of the projects I had supported in my two and a half years at P&L had been more about lining the pockets of the people involved than making any real difference in society. That's part of why Dr. Gaspar's file was so interesting to me when Nate brought it up. He was a man who was actually trying to change the world, make a difference, materially impact agriculture as an industry, and ultimately help end malnutrition. I didn't just want to succeed because the next item on my list was that damn promotion. I wanted to be part of what Dr. Gaspar was building toward.

I leaned my head back and took a deep breath. I used to get energy from this job because I was constantly learning new things about business, negotiation, and communication. Learning had always been a surefire way to keep me engaged. With this being my first solo project and Nate encouraging me to "be aggressive," I felt more disconnected from this career path than ever. I didn't want to be aggressive, or ruthless, or any other adjective that suggested a lack of care for the humans involved. The goals here weren't just about business to me. It was Dr. Gaspar's livelihood, his passion, his dream for a better future for so many. But to Nate, none of that mattered as much as the bottom line. It was about the revenue. The growth potential. The competition. The win.

I rubbed my hands over my face and sighed. If I didn't snap myself out of this morose mood, I'd be stuck in it for days. I fished my phone out of my pocket and opened my favorites. There was one person who I knew would distract me.

"For fuck's sake, Laura Beth, I expected to hear from you this morning!" she screeched. *Screeched.*

"Hello, Sara Jean. I'm just lovely, thanks for asking. How are you today?"

"Shut your piehole and tell me you saw Mr. Snack Pack last night."

I snorted a laugh. "Which is it, sis? Shut my piehole or tell you about my night?"

She squealed. "I knew it! You did see him! You hussy! You were supposed to text me!"

"Ah, fuck. I was." I winced. "Sorry, sis." Missing an "I'm alive" text was a cardinal sin in the Calhoun family.

"Don't give me your 'sorry sis', Laura Beth. Give me one good reason why I shouldn't tell Momma how worried you made me all day."

"You wouldn't dare," I gasped. My momma would skin me alive if she thought I'd put Sara Jean out at all. I'd never hear the end of it, and I'd be facing down a week of twice daily calls with texts every few hours to make sure I was a) okay and b) communicating frequently with all members of the family. "Sara Jean, she's still calling me every other day over the last bullshit you fed her about me giving up on love. Don't you dare make my life any more difficult than it already is!"

"I won't have to if you spill! I know you have a good reason for missing the check-in text–you're as fanatical about those as Momma is."

I sighed. She wasn't wrong. As much as I had desperately needed to flee Pike Road, I had never really wanted to flee my family. They were all pretty great. Clingy as fuck and almost toxic in their codependence, but great nonetheless. "Okay, okay. Fair. I did see him last night."

"And? Did he *buy* you a snack or make *you* one?" she asked, and I could hear the salacious eyebrow wiggle in her voice.

I groaned, "Stop with the puns, woman! You're incorrigible."

"You and your big ass college-educated vocabulary. Bring it down to grade school level for us poor folk."

I rolled my eyes but couldn't help my chuckle. As I had known she would, Sara Jean was turning my mood right around. "He sent me a drink at the bar right after we hung up. Turns out he was staying in the same hotel."

"OH. MY. GOD," she yelled. "I knew it! I darn well knew you were going to see him again! All your talk of fate and all that nonsense. Laura Beth Calhoun, I'm saying it now: you're going to marry that boy."

My brain legitimately derailed. I heard the word "marry" and it just completely went offline. I stared straight ahead, mouth gaping like a fish, and searched for a reasonable reaction to that absolutely absurd suggestion.

"SARA JEAN!" I whisper-shouted. Okay, not my best work in the comeback department, fair. But holy hell, this girl wanted to talk about marriage?!

"LAURA BETH!" she shouted back.

I blinked and realized that quite a few folks were giving me the wide "excuse you" eyes. I winced and mouthed "sorry", turning in my seat to give them my back as I snuggled up to the wall.

"It was a good time, Sara Jean. Not a marriage proposal."

She squealed again. The girl had lungs on her, and I pulled the phone away from my ear with another wince. "You slut! I knew you were gonna get some last night!"

"Shhh! I'm at the airport, woman, and you are way too loud."

"TELL ME THE DETAILS OR I WON'T STOP SCREAMING!"

"Gaaaah! Stop! Hush! Take a pill or something! I just told you I'm in public, I'm not telling you shit."

"Laura Beth Calhoun, that's bullshit. I have only ever been with one man, and it is your sisterly duty to let me live vicariously through you. Now. Tell me everything!"

"You kiss our momma with that mouth?"

"You know I do, and I'll kiss you, too. LAURA BETH! Stop stalling!"

I laughed, and she did, too. It felt good, almost erasing the miles and months between us.

"Fine, big sis. I'll give you something."

"Some*things*. Make it plural, please. My vagina is growing cobwebs these days thanks to the rugrats."

"Ugh, thank you for that dose of birth control. Okay, I'll give you some*things*. First, three."

"Three? What the fuck does that mean?"

"I'm in public, Sara Jean. Use your imagination."

"Hours?"

"No."

"Men?"

I cackled. "No!"

She gasped. "Oh my god, ORGASMS!?"

I collapsed into giggles. "For fuck's sake, Sara Jean, my attempts at subterfuge and privacy mean nothing if you're just going to scream the salacious things!"

"Okay, okay, sorry! Three!? What the hell, woman, you're making that up. I'm lucky if Dex gets one out of me, let alone three."

"Ew, TMI, sis," I grimaced. Dex was a great guy, husband, father. I'd known him nearly my whole life and loved him to death. "I have no desire to hear any intimate details about my brother-in-law."

"Ugh, prude. The city has turned you uppity, but I'll forgive you because you're giving me details. Continue."

"You get two more details and not a word more, Sara Jean."

"Fine! Go on then!"

"Okay. Calm down. Second, um...tongue."

"You bitch! Dex hasn't eaten me out in months. It used to be all the time, but for some reason you have kids and 'oh!' it's suddenly too much trouble."

I gave a strangled laugh and tried to think of what I could read on the plane that would serve as effective enough brain bleach to delete all memory of this conversation. "The last detail is contingent on you not saying anything about Dex, Sara Jean. I mean it!"

"Fine," she grumbled. "Lay it on me. Make it juicy."

I thought for a moment. The things I wanted to say, like how it was the best sex of my life and he made me feel things I didn't know I could feel, would set off her sisterly radar in a big way. I had no desire to weather a Sara Jean inquisition any time soon.

"Um." I was racking my brain, searching for something spicy that wouldn't put my heart on my sleeve.

"Spit it out, sister."

Her words triggered something, and I said it without even thinking. "He calls me spitfire."

She was quiet for a moment, and I knew I'd done it.

"I'm sorry, he calls you what now?" I could hear the mile-wide grin in her voice and I groaned, knocking my forehead gently against the wall.

"Forget it. I'll come up with a different detail!"

"Nope, I don't want any more. Those three are perfect. Three! Ha! It's perfect. He makes you come three times, at least once with his magic tongue, and he calls you *spitfire*. Which means you've let him see you. The real you, not that corporate robot you call LB."

"Hey, I'm fond of my LB persona."

"Bullshit. You hate that bitch."

"Sara Jean! Play nice or I'm hanging up."

"I said *you* hate her. I love you in all your forms, but I especially love you when you're happy and free and true to *you*, which you haven't been any time I've seen you in LB mode. So if this guy brings out your Southern enough to call you *spitfire* after one plane ride, then I like him. A lot. And I stand by my prediction: you're going to marry this boy."

I was gaping at her words again, searching for something to say.

"Now, I know I just broke your brain again, so I'm going to leave it at that and tell you I love you. You're perfect just the way you are. Fly safe and text me when you get home, okay?"

"Uh, yeah. Yeah, okay."

"Don't forget, Laura Beth! I'll tell Momma in a heartbeat."

"No! I won't forget, don't tell Momma. Love you."

"Love you, pretty girl."

And just like that, she was gone. Even though I was in a state of mild emotional shock, I recovered quickly. There was just something about the healing effect of a sister.

Chapter 12

LB

The office was quiet when I arrived at 7am. I was an early bird by force of habit, something I taught myself as a kid. It wouldn't do to waste a moment of the day, especially not as a small-town girl with big dreams of escape. I was never quite able to leave that determined little girl behind in Pike Road, though I often wished I could see the world with her clarity. She wanted few things in life, and she'd look at where I was these days and cheer for my success.

I sighed and settled into my office chair. I'd stopped and gotten a soy latte and croissant from the coffee shop downstairs, and they were sitting on my desk serving as a reminder of how yesterday had started. After what was arguably one of the most eventful mornings of my life, the plane ride back to the Bay and my rideshare home had felt mundane.

Parker was indeed on my flight, but we were seated far enough apart that I was successful in ignoring him after glimpsing him walking down the aisle. Mostly. I managed to keep my eyes on my laptop, despite how my skin burned with what I assumed was his gaze, but when I snuck a glance after takeoff, he was just as focused as I was. I took that for the sign it surely was and didn't look for him again. And once we landed, I let folks fill the distance between us and took an honestly cowardly extended bathroom break to ensure we didn't stumble into one another on the way out.

Last night was quiet. I caught sight of my roommate, Maya, for a brief smile and hello as she headed out for her night shift at the teaching hospital. The alumni network at Berkeley introduced us, two transplants to California with few connections in the Bay. Our schedules were opposite, so we were mostly like two ships passing in the night, but there were little things about our small shared apartment that reminded me I wasn't alone in life. She would buy my favorite oat-based creamer when she did the shopping and I would always add extra fruit to the bowl on the counter—typically things with peels I knew she could easily toss in her bag as she dashed out the door. Our friendship was largely nonexistent, but our cohabitation worked. Until I could afford my own place in the neighborhood I wanted, it was just fine.

After I had unpacked and started laundry, I sat down to work through how I could take Nate's words to heart and embrace my inner cheer captain. It was time to: Be! Aggressive! (Yes, I could literally see my cheer captain sister in her uniform in my mind's eye as I thought those words, leading the squad in a riotous rendition of "Be! Aggressive! B! E! Aggressive!") I owed Nate a plan, and I cobbled one together and crossed my fingers before sending it off. I remained vague on the details, but the gist was clear. I was going to push to get time with Dr. Gaspar earlier in the week, and I'd double up with Parker's time slot if I had to. Though I suspected Parker was right about collaboration being the path forward, I wasn't going to credit him for that insight just yet.

Refocusing, I popped in an earbud and opened my laptop, plugging it into the monitor at my desk. My first order of business for the day was to firm up the plan for how to get Dr. Gaspar on board. As I shared with Nate, our next conversation was supposed to get into the brass tacks of his growth plan for Gaspar Technologies and what projected revenue could look like in three years. But the doctor's questions about P&L and how we worked had me wondering if our skill set overlapped with Athena's, or if perhaps it was complementary, instead.

I had the Athena Ventures website pulled up when Ana, a fellow associate and the closest thing I had to a friend in California, bounced in. She was a ball of frenetic energy, per usual, and was impossible to miss in her bold red pantsuit. The girl wore power suits like armor and I had always admired that about her.

"Whoa, there, chica. You jumping ship? Bold move for a Thursday."

I looked up at her in confusion and she raised her thick, well-defined eyebrows and gestured at my laptop screen.

"Oh! No, god, of course not. Girl, there's so much to catch you up on. I found out that the other firm going after Gaspar Technologies is Athena."

Her eyes widened as she folded her tall frame into the seat next to me. "Whoa. Did you meet her? The other Livingston?"

"What?" I blinked at her, temporarily lost, before her meaning clicked. "Gosh, no. She's pawned it off on a lackey, just like Nate has."

"Oh, so he's Nate now? Since when?" she cast me a smirk as she asked.

I rolled my eyes with a sigh. "So I might've finally gotten up the courage to call him Nate. Starting yesterday."

"Took you long enough," she laughed. "Pretty sure you and the intern are the only holdouts at this stage."

"Whatever," I muttered. I may have lived on the West Coast, but my Southern roots were deep. Respecting those older and in positions of authority was basically written on my soul, right next to honorifics like "sir" and "ma'am".

I looked up, and Ana was studying me. She did that a lot. She wasn't as gifted at reading me as Sara Jean was, but she only had so much to work with–I was in my full "LB persona" around her. Always.

"What changed, LB?"

I sighed. "Nate challenged me. Suggested I didn't have the aggression or leadership skills to actually do what I need to do to prove myself for the Senior Associate position."

She gave a low whistle. "That would do it. That's like waving a red flag at a bull."

I snorted. "Close enough. That's not all, either." I pulled up the "Our team" page of the Athena Ventures website and scrolled to the "Sr. Associates" section to hover over Parker's stupidly handsome face. "That's my competition."

Ana choked on the sip of coffee she was taking. "Excuse me? What do you mean?"

"He's the other guy. The Athena Ventures lead for Gaspar."

She whistled suggestively before her lips, red to match her suit, curled devilishly. "Hot damn, just look at him. Have you met this gorgeous specimen?"

I nodded slowly. "You could say that."

Ana looked up at me with wide eyes. "Say more, please. Right now."

"We made eyes at each other a couple times on the flight, and we ended up in the same hotel. Which wasn't a stretch because Boise is, well, Boise. Pickings are slim." I was deflecting, and she knew it.

"Stop talking about pickings and start talking about why you're blushing, LB Calhoun."

I felt myself flush harder. "I am not blushing!"

"Oh, so 'lobster' is the standard shade of your blush?"

I huffed. "Fine. But I wasn't until you suggested otherwise. Ugh. Yes, he's hot, but can we please focus on something else? I have to figure out how to 'get in the driver's seat' on this one sooner rather than later."

"Nate's words?"

I nodded again, and she gave me a resolute nod. "Fine, I'll let you off the hook. For now! We're coming back to...this." She twirled her index finger in a circle around Parker's face on my screen.

I quickly closed the tab and turned to her. I took a moment to catch her up on the details, explaining my thoughts on collaboration and how scheduling had gone down for the next week.

"So you want to propose something that will get all of you in the same room for the first time? Sure that's the right approach?" she asked when I was done.

"No. But I'm confident it will get us closer to a deal than we are at the moment. I don't think Gaspar is even going to entertain exclusive terms, though I know that's what Nate wants. I think he'll be more likely to invite us to the table in an official capacity for the long term if we show we can play ball."

She thought for a moment, then nodded. "Okay, that makes sense. How are you going to swing this with the living god at Athena?"

I fought my eye roll and motioned to my phone. "He gave me his number for this express purpose."

Her eyebrows climbed her face, and she gave me a look. A very pointed one.

"He was very explicit that he was giving me his number and not asking for mine," I explained. I conveniently left off the part where the only reason he didn't ask for mine was because I had laid boundaries earlier. *Stupid, stupid boundaries.*

"Riiiiight. Yeah, you're not telling me everything, but that's okay. I can deal with a cryptic bitch as well as the next girl. Okay. So, you have to get close to the enemy."

"And Nate wants me to see what I can get out of him. Like, intel. So we can...win."

Ana cracked a laugh. "Girl, you sound sooooo excited about this. And yes, that was sarcasm."

"I know," I groaned, dropping my head into my hands.

And, at that very moment, our colleagues Cristoph and Brandon walked in. Together, of course, because they played into finance bro culture like nobody's business. Pretty sure they were both robots and possibly carbon copies of one another.

"What is up, ladies!" Brandon called as they walked up.

"Did you get this party started without us?" Cristoph echoed.

Internally, I sighed and grumbled at their particularly annoying flavor of toxic masculinity. Externally, I kept my LB persona firmly in place. "Oh, hey guys! Morning. I was just catching Ana here up on the latest with Gaspar."

"Dope. Anything you need help with?" Cristoph asked.

I didn't intend to take him up on the offer, but Ana jumped in. "Actually, yes. She's going toe-to-toe with someone from Athena and needs to plan how to get intel out of him. And win, of course."

The internal cringing I was doing could have been considered cardio. "I mean, it's really not a big–"

"Oh, HO! Toe-to-toe with the enemy, LB, niiiiice!" Brandon said with an unhealthy amount of enthusiasm. "Yes, let's talk about this. You have to get intel out of him and you absolutely have to mess with him, too."

"Yes," Cristoph piled on, a grin on his face. "Sabotage is the name of the game. Nothing wrong with a little friendly prank war to try to tank his chances."

I gave them a blank look, a bit stunned at the suggestion. This wasn't high school. "You can't possibly be serious."

"Of course we are!" Cristoph crowed. "It'll be epic! You could run him right out of the competition and win the deal. Isn't this your first solo? Means that a promotion is coming up if you want it, right? It's a no-brainer, LB!"

I glanced at Ana, and, to my complete dismay, she looked far too interested in this plan. "Oh no, not you, too!?"

"It's perfect, LB!" she cried, and I started to think I had entered the twilight zone, or my Southern sensibilities were creeping up on me. If it was the latter, I needed to smack them right back down like a game of whack-a-mole and pony up to what needed doing.

"Think about it," she continued, "Nate wants this thing to be anything but a collab and you think that's out of the question, but if you trip Athena's guy up enough, then the only logical choice will be exclusivity. And then your promo is basically in the bag."

My instincts were telling me this was a terrible idea. But my instincts were hardly reliable in the VC industry–I'd had to train them hard in the last few years. I nodded slowly at them. Perhaps I needed to shut down the little voice in my head telling me this was a terrible idea and instead get on board. *The promotion is the next milestone on your plan, Laura Beth. It's worth it.*

"Okay. I can see it. Tell me more, what kind of sabotage do you have in mind?"

Brandon and Cristoph high fived and turned dual grins on me. And then they lobbed ideas back and forth, one after the other.

"Plant something on him before he goes through TSA."

"Change his flight."

"Put something nasty in his bag."

"Cancel his ride."

"Give him bad info, so he misses a meeting."

"Send him nudes mid-meeting."

"Bro!" Brandon laughed so hard he doubled over.

"Uhhhh, no," Ana interjected, a look of concerned amusement on her face. "Not that one."

I choked on a laugh. "Duh. Seriously," I scoffed. After a moment of consideration, during which time the boys continued to throw increasingly inane ideas back and forth, I continued my musing aloud. "I think there are some ideas I can work with in there."

After all, I knew Parker hated airports. And if I kept to pranks that were largely harmless...could it really hurt? And if I could do what Ana said and manipulate my way to exclusivity and then that promotion...well, then my plan would stay on track and I would be moving forward. *Can't stop moving forward, Laura Beth.*

Ana was watching me process, and she smiled when she knew I'd accepted their ludicrous idea. "This is gonna be fun, LB. You're going to go all boss bitch on this project and Nate's going to promote you. And, if you're lucky, you'll get to have some fun of your own with that hottie from Athena."

Brandon and Cristoph were suddenly both staring at me.

"Ooooooh," Cristoph taunted, his brows wagging obnoxiously. "He's a hottie, is he? Get it, LB!"

I flushed and shook my head. "This conversation is over, boys. Entertain yourselves at someone else's expense."

"Aw, c'mon, LB!" Brandon whined. "No fun."

He gave me an exaggerated pouty lip, and I just shook my head again and turned back to my laptop. I couldn't stop the small smile on my lips, though, because they were both so over the top. Ana and I referred to them as Brandoph when they weren't around, though Tweedle Dee and Tweedle Dum might have been more accurate.

I knew the boys had moved on when Ana turned to me again. "Don't back down, LB. You deserve this promotion, and you said it yourself–Nate expects exclusivity."

"He does. I'll figure it out, Ana." *I have to.*

"I know you will, girl. And I'm here for you." She squeezed my shoulder and headed toward the kitchen.

I refocused on the email draft I had pulled up, intended for Dr. Gaspar. In it, I mentioned his Wednesday afternoon meeting with Athena, and how I thought we'd all benefit from a joint conversation about his market and revenue projections. I highlighted themes of collaboration and impact and offered to join him and Parker for what I was sure would be a productive conversation on Wednesday afternoon.

That done, I turned my mind toward a little bit of sabotage. Parker was a textbook finance bro of his own, after all–just like Brandoph–and if his stories on the plane were any indication, he was no stranger to some good old-fashioned pranking. He could take it. And there was a small slice of the poor little girl from Alabama that relished the opportunity to stick it to someone from the other side of the tracks. *Better buckle up and make it fun, Laura Beth.*

Chapter 13

Parker

I hit the office right after the airport, because home was anything but conducive to wrapping up the last part of my workday. I had a few irons in the fire in addition to Gaspar Technologies, and lately I'd felt like I was neglecting the other companies in my portfolio.

My position at Athena was a unique one. I was one of the younger team members, but I held a decent amount of seniority and responsibility. I hadn't actually applied for a role here, though it had been my father who had introduced me to Lex. They weren't friends, but they ran in overlapping circles, so LB's assessment from the plane was largely accurate. But I didn't credit my father's tenuous connection to Lex for my position at Athena. Quite the opposite–upon meeting me as "billionaire Jonathan Brooks's son", Lex had been ready to write me off as another trust fund kid with a silver spoon in my mouth and a complete lack of ambition.

But then we got to talking. I shared, with enthusiasm, some of my thoughts on startup trends in Silicon Valley and mentioned the companies I'd supported based on my own connections and research. Several of them made it big, fast, so

I'd been able to keep building a portfolio with even greater investments each time. And, while I didn't share it with Lex in our first conversation, I'd been able to do it all with my own money–funds I'd earned and grown through my investments–without touching my sizable trust fund. In fact, I'd gotten access to it legally at 25 and hadn't spent a dime. It was important to me to prove to myself, and to no one else, that I could stand on my own two feet. After growing up the way Preston and I did, all I wanted was to create the life and family I wanted for myself without IOUs or obligations to anyone.

When Lex learned about my motivations, she and Van dove deep into my portfolio before offering me a job. She knew I didn't need it–my dad was an official member of the three comma club and, through my trust fund, so was I–but she empathized with my need to make it on my own. And Van appreciated my keen eye for potential, much like his own. So, because I knew I could learn from them both while accessing even greater resources for the businesses I was supporting and courting, I took the gig. And I'd been steadily growing my wealth and reputation ever since.

As I wrapped up for the evening, feeling settled after a productive few hours, Van stopped by my desk. He was a big, burly motherfucker, but he still wore a suit like he was born in one. He had that tall, dark, handsome Italian thing going on and while I was as straight as they came, even I could admire that look on a guy.

"Parker," he greeted as he approached. That was all, like my name was a full sentence. Total power move, that.

"Hey, boss." I closed my laptop and rose to my feet. "What can I do for you?"

"Anything of note from today?"

"The doctor wants to learn more about our charitable giving and any plans we may have to open a foundation. I mentioned we didn't have a formal philanthropy arm established yet, but that it's on the firm's five-year roadmap."

Van nodded. "Good. What's the next step?"

The thing about Van was that he expected a lot from his team and he was unabashed about setting high expectations and providing blunt feedback. He would give you the rope to hang yourself with (professionally speaking) without hesitation, because he had no time or patience for people who needed their hands held. Lucky for me, I'd always been independent.

"He won't sign an exclusivity deal willingly. P&L is at the table and they've assigned an associate to the account. If I were a betting man, I'd put money on their angle being all about maximizing revenue. But ours will be about maximizing human impact, namely malnutrition in the US to start, and willingness to collaborate. I gave my number to the P&L associate as a first step toward collaboration and I'm headed back to Boise on Wednesday."

As I spoke, Van nodded and stared off at the far wall, processing. When I mentioned my number, he flicked his eyes to me. Nothing could get past the man. After a moment, he gave me another nod.

"Keep me posted." He tapped my desk once, then turned to go.

"No notes, boss?" I asked, because I couldn't help myself.

"Don't go fishing, Parker. Get it done."

That was as close to an all out compliment as I'd gotten from Van, so I took it. He'd been more than a boss to me in my handful of years at the firm—he'd been a dedicated, grueling, and exhausting mentor. I knew VC life would not be forever (I had far too much ambition to work for someone else for too long), but my years with Athena were no doubt going to be some of my best. And that was entirely thanks to Van and Lex.

I packed up my laptop and grabbed my overnight bag, then

headed out for the quick walk home. It was a beautiful evening, and I took a moment to appreciate where I was. I was a lucky bastard—grew up right here in Palo Alto, went to the best private schools money could pay for and then to Stanford. My parents both came from money, so even though they split when Preston and I were twelve, we never wanted for anything material. We were short on family bonding and parental chats, though. Dad had his new family, and Mom didn't keep her new husbands— already on her fourth—for very long. It was mostly just Preston and me against the world, with all the *things* we could possibly want. Maybe that's why it sometimes felt lonely in my apartment, and why I often found myself at Preston's place. There was something comforting about the idea of being surrounded by the warmth and energy of others.

I looked up at my building and smiled. I bought the luxury condo in downtown Palo Alto while still in undergrad, renting out the additional bedrooms. Preston had moved in just a few blocks over with her best friend and business partner, Cami. After graduation, the roommates moved out to a tech incubator nearby, and I was solo for the first time in my life. Preston and I kept each other close and filled our days with work and found family, at least for the most part.

As I let myself in, the quiet of the space surrounded me. It was always loud when the guys lived there—an atmosphere resembling a college frat house—with blaring video games or the aggressive playlists the guys loved to work to. I didn't mind the silence, exactly, but our regular happy hours were welcome.

I moved into the kitchen and grabbed a beer, walking to the wall of floor-to-ceiling windows to appreciate the view. My phone buzzed in my pocket, and I chuckled as I opened the group chat my former roommates and I used as our primary channel for communication. Apparently, all I had to do was think about them, and they appeared.

Raj: Yo Parker! You back in the Bay? We on for happy hour?

Me: I'm back. I'll be there tomorrow

Raj: You see the little blonde thing from the plane again?

Sipping my beer, I pondered over the interesting 24 hours I'd just had. The mere thought of LB had her appearing in my mind's eye, stretched out on the bed before me. *Magnificent.*

Me: Sure did

Raj: What happened?

Me: Stole the seat next to her

Me: talked the entire flight. I've honestly never gotten along with a girl so well

Me: extremely smart, funny, gorgeous

Me: she refused to give me her number though

Me: said we should leave it to fate

Trey: fuck that

I smirked. Of course Trey had to pipe in. The guy wasn't known for his patience, and when he wanted something, he would doggedly pursue it. It made him successful professionally, and a pain in the ass as a friend at times.

Me: I would've agreed with you yesterday morning

Me: now? Me and fate, we're tight

Noah: DETAILS?!

Me: I'll keep those to myself

Noah: Dude

Trey: What does she do?

Me: Turns out she's my competition. An associate at P&L Capital

Trey: The new VC from that massive private equity firm back east?

Trey: I read an article about them. The general partner sounds like a total douche

I barked a laugh. Trey's assessment wasn't wrong from what I knew of LB's boss.

Noah: Next steps?!

Me: I think I'll ask her to marry me

I was kidding, I thought. But I did know I wanted to pursue this woman, which was unlike me. In fact, I was far more likely to pick someone up in a bar and send her on her way the next morning, never to be seen again, than to talk about my intent to get close to someone. And my former roommates knew me.

Raj: Woah

Noah: P!!!

The old nickname made me huff a laugh, but it also conjured images of LB on the plane, her face filled with mirth at my expense. I didn't mind her laughing at me, if it meant I got to see her embody joy like that, like she took energy from the emotion and could cast it out to those around her.

Raj: So it's serious then? You in love?

He was giving me shit, I knew it, but *was I in love? Was that something I'd even be willing to entertain?* Everything in my past told me no. I'd watched my parents' marriage go up in flames. Oh, what a fiery death that had been. And not even a year later, Dad had been remarried with a new kid on the way, and we were second fiddle. Then I'd watched Mother flit from meal ticket to meal ticket. I loved the woman out of obligation, but I could also objectively recognize that she hadn't married a single one of her many husbands for any reason other than greed and a desperate need for security.

But the things in my present? LB's laugh, her accent. The way she lit up when she talked about her family, or how she flushed with pleasure when I said something suggestive. All of those little moments had been carefully cataloged and filed away in my brain. I'd been viewing them on repeat at will, experiencing each of our moments together over and over while life went on. I wanted to crawl into those memories and get cozy. I wanted to hunt her down and demand to know why she hadn't used the number I'd given her mere hours ago. I wanted to strip her down and toss her in my bed and see what it took to get her to five. Those things...they told me that perhaps my view of love had been warped. And while I was nowhere near ready for a paradigm shift, maybe I should be willing to see where it all could go.

For years, I had been sure I didn't actually believe in love. At least, not the kind of love Raj meant when he asked that question. The kind that led to marriage and a white picket fence. That kind of love might have existed for other people, but I would've put money on it not being in my future. But there was a growing part of me that acknowledged that I felt something different for LB–something new. Something that was ever-present, and at times, all-consuming. Something that felt like both ownership and devotion. Something I felt loathe to give up, even just 24 hours in.

> Me: I don't know about that, but I'd like to think there is some runway with her

> Me: and I'm willing to put in the work to find out

———

"Thanks, have a good one," I said to my driver as I ducked out of my car on Wednesday morning. I'd received an email from Dr. Gaspar on Friday that informed me there had been a slight change of plan for the week. He hadn't elaborated, but he had asked me to come in a few hours earlier for our meeting.

I was looking down at my phone as I walked into the airport, so I didn't see her right away. But when I glanced up to find my way to the security line, there she was.

"LB," I called, "fancy meeting you here."

The thought crossed my mind that I'd always seen her either in the boarding queue or on the plane—she didn't leave things to the last minute like I did. She gave me a smirk and stepped toward me.

"Morning, Parker," she said, lightly squeezing my bicep in greeting. "Good to see you."

I cocked my head to the side and gave her a long look. *What are you playing at, spitfire?*

"Good to see you, too. I thought you were headed out tomorrow?"

Her smirk deepened, and my cock took notice. "Change of plans. He's keeping us on our toes, isn't he?"

"I suppose so," I murmured. "Are we still enemies?"

"Hmm, good question," she said nonchalantly. "I'd call us more rivals, wouldn't you? Enemies seems so...harsh."

"I'd just call us professionals. No need for drama to enter the mix."

She grinned. "Bless your heart. Isn't that good of you?"

I nodded toward security and started that direction with a wry smile as she turned to follow. "I know enough about Southern culture to know that wasn't a compliment."

She snorted a laugh, and it was pathetic how much my heart lifted to hear that sound. "All in good fun, Mr. Brooks. All in good fun."

"I'm sure," I said, trying to figure out her angle. "Why were you waiting for me, spitfire?"

She smiled and stepped into the security line behind me. "Who said I was waiting for you?"

"I wasn't born yesterday, Ms. Calhoun. You're a habitual early bird. Being on this side of security has you twitchy. Don't think I can't see it."

She flinched like I'd hit a physical nerve and I couldn't restrain my chuckle. Whatever game she was playing, she was certainly making it hard on herself. She just shrugged in reply, though, focusing on her phone as she pulled up her boarding pass in preparation for the security agent. She bumped me slightly as she moved forward, eyes still locked on the screen.

"Sorry," she mumbled, moving back out of my immediate orbit.

"I don't know whether I'm more offended by the bump or the fact you're clearly giving me the cold shoulder," I teased, raising an eyebrow at her.

She flushed, and I cheered internally at the effect I had on her. "I'm doing no such thing. Not everything is about you, Mr. Brooks."

ARRIVED

"Touché." I stepped up to the agent just as she was called to the security booth one over.

I kept my eyes fixed on her as we moved through our respective lines, watching the quick and efficient way she approached the mundane task. The dance we were both performing was clearly familiar, not a single wasted movement. Her line moved a smidge faster than mine, and she disappeared through the metal detector before me. I peered after her for a moment, then had my attention called back by the security agent clearing his throat and motioning rather aggressively for me to step through. I did, then proceeded to the conveyor belt to pick up my bag.

"Sir, is this yours?" A TSA agent held up my bag, a stern look on his face.

"Yes. Problem?" I answered.

"Come with me," he said, leading me over to a testing station.

I racked my brain for what could have set things off. Like it clearly was for LB, this was a practiced and familiar exercise for me. I cleared my bag before I left the house to ensure I didn't have any contraband, my toiletries were all under the size limit, and I knew exactly which shoes to wear that looked professional and wouldn't set off the metal detector. There was nothing I could think of that would necessitate testing.

"Do you have any weapons in your bag, sir?"

"No," I said, firmly. I kept calm, because I knew nothing good would come of anger or hysteria.

"Did you leave your bag unattended at any point?"

"No. I got out of my car five minutes ago–there was no time to leave anything unattended."

The stoic agent said nothing. He just systematically began opening every exterior pocket of my bag and emptying the contents thoroughly.

"Sorry, but I have a flight to catch–"

"I have to inspect your bag."

"Yes, I understand that, but how long will that take?"

He gave me the look. The one that said that I was resembling a Karen and had no business asking something so asinine. I glanced at my watch and groaned internally. I had maybe 15 minutes before my gate closed. I looked up to see if I could catch sight of a flight monitor for a status update (for once hoping for a delay), and my eyes caught on LB.

She stood just beyond the security checkpoint, a smug little smile on her pink lips. She gave me a little wave of her fingers, making damn sure I saw her, then turned and sashayed away, unhurried. I stared after her in mild shock and no small amount of desire, knowing without question that she was behind whatever had gotten my bag flagged by TSA. I felt a flash of frustration, followed by undeniable heat. If there was anything I was always ready to do, it was rise to a challenge. And one leveled by LB, of all people? Oh, I knew how I wanted that to end, and it would be satisfying for both of us. *What did you do, spitfire? More importantly, are you ready for what happens next?*

Whatever she had done, she was going to pay for it. I'd make sure of that.

Chapter 14

LB

"Ladies and gentlemen, welcome aboard Flight 1485 with nonstop service from San Francisco to Boise. We are currently third in line for take-off and are expected to be in the air in approximately seven minutes. We ask that you please fasten your seatbelts at this time and secure all large electronics and baggage underneath your seat."

I stared at the empty business class seat I knew Parker should be in, and my nerves kicked into overdrive. *Fuck, I really did it. He missed the flight.*

Putting my plan into action had been surprisingly easy. Between our back-and-forth banter in the line leading up to security and the deliberate physical contact, Parker was entirely focused on me. I could tell he was suspicious, but he never would have suspected I slid anything into his open briefcase. But the moment the TSA agent found my pink hair cutting shears I used for split ends in the briefcase's interior pocket, Parker would know exactly what had happened and who was responsible. *I wonder how angry he'll be with me? And why does the idea of making him angry excite me?*

Pulling me back to reality, my phone buzzed.

> **My Competition:** So it's going to be like that, LB? Petty pranks? Isn't that a bit beneath you?

I swallowed and stared down at the phone. *You expected this, Laura Beth. No retreating now.*

> **Me:** You know what they say Parker, all is fair in love and war. It was nothing personal.

> **My Competition:** I don't think you know what you're getting yourself into. Are you sure you want to do this?

No, of course not! I'm absolutely not sure about any of this! What I am sure of is the need to put as much distance between me and Parker Brooks as humanly possible.

> **Me:** It's a little bit late for that, don't you think?

> **My Competition:** It's never too late for you to surrender to me, LB. In fact, I'm quite looking forward to it.

> **My Competition:** Have a safe flight, spitfire. See you in Boise ;)

Gaping at my phone, I struggled to make sense of Parker's reaction and obvious dismissal. *He wasn't angry? He was looking forward to me surrendering? Why did that sound so suggestive?* I crossed my legs and clenched my thighs together while taking several steadying breaths.

"And we're cleared for takeoff. Cabin crew please take your seats."

I glanced at the texts one last time and switched my phone

into airplane mode. I had intended for my stunt to throw Parker off his game, and yet here I was feeling anything but on top.

———

My foot tapped anxiously while I sat waiting in the golf course's clubhouse. Despite Courtney from Gaspar Technologies calling me earlier to confirm the new later tee time worked for Dr. Gaspar, I still arrived 20 minutes early.

The devil works fast, but Parker Brooks works faster. He must've found another direct flight to Boise, called the golf course to change plans, and then contacted Courtney to let Dr. Gaspar know not to come at our original tee time. All while I was inflight.

LB: 0. Parker Brooks: 1.

A bell chimed as the Pro Shop's door opened and Dr. Gaspar and Parker entered.

Holy shit, he looks good.

The white fitted polo accentuated his chest and biceps, all the while bringing out his tan. And those shorts showed off just the right amount of thigh. Making my way back up his body, Parker's eyes caught mine, and he winked. *Busted, Laura Beth.*

"Ah, Miss Calhoun. It's wonderful you could join us!" Dr. Gaspar exclaimed as he and Parker stopped in front of the sofa I was perched on. I smiled and met his outstretched hand while standing.

"Yes, I'm glad you suggested we meet Miss Calhoun. I, for one, am excited to get to know you and P&L Capital better," Parker said while extending his hand. "And who knows? This may be the start to a productive collaboration," he added, while giving my hand an extra squeeze before letting it go. I looked up at him and desire flared in his eyes.

"You can call me LB," I replied as I fidgeted, patting the skirt of my halter dress.

"Should we head out?"

"Of course, after you," Parker replied cooly and nodded for me to go ahead. Striding forward, I couldn't help the small flinch at the feel of his hot palm pressed into the small of my back, leading me towards the door. *This is going to be the longest golf game of my life.*

I couldn't remember the small talk we made while making our way to the first hole. I was present, but somewhere else entirely. My eyes kept drifting to the way Parker's legs filled out his shorts and the corded veins tracing his forearms as he gripped the steering wheel.

If it weren't for Dr. Gaspar in the back of this golf cart, I'd be begging Parker to pull off into the woods. For a moment, I let myself imagine it...Parker stopping the golf cart and picking me up, settling me on his lap. Those strong hands sliding up my exposed thighs and under the thin skirt of my dress. He would grip my hips, letting me feel his hard erection.

"LB, what strategic partnerships has P&L established in the space?" Parker's voice cut through the picture I was painting in my head.

I coughed, clearing my throat. "That's a great question, Parker. I'm so glad you asked," I stalled, trying to come up with an acceptable answer.

"Didn't I just read an announcement about a partnership with The Rural Aid and Access Fund? That will be huge in bringing help to rural communities," he added, his lips quirked in a private smug smile meant only for me.

Did Parker just cover for me? Here I was ignoring Dr. Gaspar, fantasizing about riding Parker in public, while he's trying to stop me from making a complete fool of myself.

"Yes, that's right. Dr. Gaspar, I'd be happy to walk you

through the details of the partnership and how we could bring your technology to more farms through the Access Fund."

"Yes, yes, I'd love to learn more. But no more talk of business until at least mid round and, please, call me August. I want to get to know the people I'm considering working with better first."

Chapter 15

Parker

After our 9 holes, I was pretty sure August was nearly as enamored with LB as I was. He gave her a warm smile, the friendliest I'd ever seen on the man, as we said our farewells, grasping her hand in both of his as he thanked her for the brilliant idea. I couldn't help but feel a flare of pride at that—it had been a great call to open the door for collaboration, and I was glad she'd been the one to recommend it. But, I couldn't let her little stunt at the airport keep me from maintaining the upper hand, of course.

While I wasn't one to flaunt my wealth (much), I also wasn't about to let her upstage me in front of my client. I flew commercial most of the time because it was the reasonable and environmentally conscious thing to do, but there was no reason to be late to our meeting when my jet was at the ready. After I cleared things up with TSA and thoroughly missed my flight, I switched plans and called my pilot. He had the jet fueled up and ready in 30 minutes, and we'd been off.

The look of rueful resignation on LB's face when she saw I had still beaten her to the club, despite her tricks, had filled me with immense satisfaction. I hadn't been joking in my text—I couldn't wait to see her submit. And after the conversation we'd just had, I was just as excited to get to know more about who she was.

When the doc had asked her to share more about herself, she'd looked like a deer in the headlights for a few seconds before giving a strangled laugh.

"Well, August, there's not much to tell," she'd said. "Just a small-town girl trying to make something of herself, I suppose."

"Oh, go on, then," he pushed. "What small town?"

I could see the realization dawn on her he wasn't going to let her get out of this line of questioning. At nearly the same moment, I saw her resolve to rise to this challenge, too, no matter how uncomfortable it might make her.

"Pike Road," she said, and I found myself already searching for her accent with every syllable. It came and went so quickly. "Just outside of Montgomery. Alabama, that is." She chuckled and shook her head. "All the people in Pike Road care about is football."

August had leaned forward in interest. "Alabama is an interesting case study. So much poverty there. What was it like growing up in small town America?"

She blinked at him, processing his bluntness, then smiled softly. "In a lot of ways, it was simple. I didn't grow up with much, but we always had enough. My parents kept us fed, clothed, happy. We did family dinner every night and twice on Sundays." She chuckled, a far-off look in her eyes. "It's a tight-knit community, Pike Road. People know everyone's business, which makes things challenging in its own right, but they also care."

She gave him another smile, which he enthusiastically returned. "For all the bad rap small town America gets, there's a sense of safety in knowing that they'll be just as willing to support you as they are to gossip about your faults."

He laughed, "Yes, yes, I've seen that play out. Why did you leave?"

Her gaze turned longing for a moment, as she looked out across the course. "I never fit in Pike Road, August. I didn't want to believe the world could be that small, and I needed to see what else was out there, and not just for me. It felt important to experience something bigger than me, or my small town, or my state." She shrugged a bit, then met his eyes. "Ever since I was in elementary school, I knew I wanted to do something more, something that would take me out of my life and give me the ability to build one I wanted. My whole family was born into their lives, and there they stayed. I wanted to create my own."

The doctor was beaming at her by that point, and nodding as she spoke. I could barely keep the grin off my face, but I figured his enthusiasm was sufficient for now. The conversation didn't stop there, and as he pushed and she teased back another few layers, I realized there was far more to LB than I'd previously seen. She was ambitious, driven, and almost single-minded in her quest for what was next. But the more she shared, the more I wondered if she truly knew what she wanted "next" to be. I was coming to understand why she had put those boundaries up between us, though, and it only made me more determined to break them down piece-by-piece.

From what I gathered of her self-deprecating comments and stories of her childhood, and her fierce desire to "make something of herself", she envisioned anything that wasn't a stepping stone toward her next professional achievement as an obstacle. Now, I wasn't exactly a romantic, but even I could acknowledge that the human soul was capable of creating and achieving more than just one dream.

There was a moment, when August had asked a followup question about her internships in college, when she'd told a simple story of a mixup leading to an embarrassing moment during an interview. She'd made the most of it and spun it well enough that the person she'd gone to interview with had hired her on the spot. She threw her head back and laughed as the doctor chortled with her, and it struck me. At this moment, with her walls down, she seemed like a completely different person than the one who had stalked into his lab last week. Here, she was real–warm, playful, and boldly vulnerable in her transparency. Seeing her like this, it was clear that she didn't feel she could be herself in her job. I could only imagine how that might weigh on a person, especially one as determined as LB.

I shook myself mentally, focusing back on the present and the girl beside me.

"You headed back to the airport, spitfire?" I asked casually.

We were standing outside the club entrance, watching the doctor's car disappear down the drive. As we'd reached the end of our outing, he'd requested another collaborative meeting in follow up–this time, a dinner. He felt he'd learned a great deal today, he said, and he wanted to get into more of the business in a relaxed environment that would "encourage free conversation between us". We'd agreed, and I hadn't missed the flash of accomplishment in LB's eyes when she did.

LB turned to face me and smiled softly. It wasn't quite the beaming grin she'd sported for much of the last two hours, but I'd take it. I was realizing I'd take nearly anything, no matter how small, if she was the one offering.

"May as well. Wouldn't want to miss my flight," she teased, her eyes flashing with mirth.

"Oh, it's like that, is it?" I asked, stepping up to face her. She stilled, her face turned up and attention wholly on me. *I like that way too much.*

I reached out and swiped a thumb across her cheekbone before settling my hand on the side of her neck, my fingers wrapping around her nape and just grazing the other side. Her eyes widened, and she leaned into my touch immediately, the heat of her skin pressing into mine. I squeezed, just a bit, my thumb teasing the lobe of her ear as I did. She swallowed thickly, and I swore I heard the tiniest whimper break free.

"You're playing a dangerous game, spitfire," I breathed, looking deeply into her bluebell eyes. "I don't know if you're truly ready for the consequences."

She heaved a breath and let it out slowly, her eyes searching mine. I knew full well I was crossing all sorts of professional boundaries at that moment, but I didn't care one fucking bit. I needed to get my hands on her, needed to feel that rapid heart-beat against my flesh.

"And what consequences might those be?" she asked, her voice thready with a desire that nearly had me throwing all restraint out the window and tossing her over my shoulder. *She has no idea what she's doing to me.*

"That's for me to know," I said as my lips curved into what I knew was an evil smirk, "and you to find out. But you should know..." I leaned down and whispered directly into her ear, "I never lose."

I placed a kiss in the hollow of her throat, more pleased than I could articulate when she shuddered in my hold. I was going to have fun with this, with her. She'd been threatening war for the last week, and today she'd made her first move. But I had no doubt she'd severely underestimated her opponent.

I straightened and dropped my hand, ignoring the urge to bundle her up in my arms and stepping back.

"Since my plans were changed for me," I gave her a pointed look, satisfied when her cheeks pinkened, "I don't need my ride. You should take it."

I gestured toward the car moving up to the curb. She glanced back at it, then up at me. "Wait, what?"

"The car, LB. It's going to the airport. You should take it."

"But—"

"I scheduled it ahead of time. I'm a planner." I placed my hands on her shoulders and turned her toward the car, then urged her forward with a firm press of my palm to her lower back. "You wrecked my plans, but the driver doesn't have to suffer for those mistakes. Take the ride. Get home safe."

She looked up at me, clearly flustered. "Parker, there's no need for this. Take the car into the city or something, I—"

"I don't need to. I arranged for an office here at the club for the next few hours to chip away at my to-do list."

She opened her mouth, clearly about to protest again.

"You need me to give you something else to do with that mouth?" I growled, cocking my head at her. "Don't argue. Go."

She shook her head with a huff and turned toward the car.

"Good girl," I murmured, just loud enough for her to hear.

She stiffened, but I didn't miss the way her thighs clenched. Those words had an effect, and I was happy to file that tidbit away into my ever-growing file of Things to Know About LB. She gave me a little look over her shoulder, then tossed her bag into the car and slid into the seat. I leaned in after her, which was unexpected, judging by her gasp, and drew the seatbelt from her side, across her chest, and to her hip. I let my fingers touch far more than they needed to, feather-light, as I did, and was rewarded by a flush of goosebumps on her arms as I buckled her in. I leaned in close to whisper in her ear again, soaking up every tiny reaction.

"I hope you're ready to play, spitfire," I said, running my nose from the base of her neck to her cheek and inhaling her scent. "Game on."

I leaned back and smiled down at her. She was a master-piece—hair mussed, skin flushed, chest heaving, and thighs pressed together.

"Text me when you make it," I said with a smile.

She blinked up at me with those big doe eyes before nodding once, ever so slightly. I itched to dive right back into her. Now wasn't the time, though. *Soon. This one is going to take some patience. And a whole lot of fun.*

I winked and shut the door, then patted the roof. The car pulled away, and I tossed a little finger wave after it before turning, adjusting myself slightly, and heading back into the club. *Hope you don't mind a little walk down memory lane, spitfire. Rural Idaho is calling your name.*

Chapter 16

LB

Two salt-rimmed margaritas appeared in front of me.

"Alright, spill. How are things going with Gaspar Technologies and the Athena hottie?" Ana asked as she hopped onto the barstool across from me and flipped her long, sleek hair over her shoulder.

After arriving home from the airport late and not getting nearly enough sleep the night before, I spent all of Thursday playing catch-up at work. Ana had immediately pounced, demanding a full status update on Parker, and I had only managed to evade her questioning by agreeing to happy hour that evening. *Welp, no more excuses to avoid this conversation.*

I took a long drink before answering. "Terribly, and can we please not call him 'the hottie'?"

I wasn't going to explain all the reasons why I didn't need to be reminded of Parker's looks, the first of which being that it was something I couldn't forget. And believe me, I had tried.

Ana laughed and breezed right past my sour attitude. "Come on, it can't be that bad! I've seen you work. Clients love you, and I know you worked your ass off preparing for this. What changed since last week?"

Stuffing a tortilla chip into my mouth, I mulled her question over. What had changed since last week? A lot. I had learned I made a terrible saboteur for one. And Parker's reaction had thrown me for a loop.

"Well, my plan to make Parker late for our meeting with Dr. Gaspar was a complete failure. And if that wasn't enough, the asshole decided to get me back by dropping me off at Middle-of-Fucking-Nowhere Municipal Airport with no way of getting a ride. Have you tried ordering a rideshare in country Idaho, Ana? Let me warn you, it's not a thing." I paused briefly to swallow back my drink, and Ana wordlessly raised her hand to signal the bartender for another round. She could clearly read my mood.

Exhaling deeply, I went on. "I had to beg a sweet old woman to take pity on me and give me a ride 20 miles. I didn't even have cash to thank her because who even carries cash anymore? I gave her an old Starbucks gift card I had in the back of my wallet! It was mortifying."

Ana picked up her drink but set it back down, dumbstruck. "Hold on a second, you're telling me he stranded you at the wrong airport? That's incredible. What did you do to warrant that level of retaliation?"

I scowled at her. "It was not incredible. I was lucky I made my flight."

"You're not answering the question, and I know how early you leave to head to the airport. I bet you still had time to kill, even after the detour to bumfuck nowhere. Fess up. What did you do to him?"

Sighing, I peered over at her over the rim of my glass. *Here goes.* "I may have slid a pair of scissors into his briefcase before we went through security at SFO and it may have caused him to miss his flight to Boise."

"Geeze, LB. You think you maybe took the boys' sabotage

suggestions a little too seriously?" she asked with a laugh. "You planted a weapon on the guy and probably got him strip searched. All he did was give you the scenic tour of Boise in return?"

I scoffed, and distracted myself from that discomforting thought, gathering my hair up off my shoulders and into the claw clip I had stashed in my bag.

"Well a lot of good it did. He made it to the meeting on time and was as smooth as ever. How he managed to find another flight to Boise so quickly, I have no idea," I said.

Through a bite of guacamole, Ana continued her interrogation. "Okay so prank war aside, how was your meeting with Dr. Gaspar? Did you take him golfing like I suggested?"

Thinking over our time with Dr. Gaspar, I decided it ultimately had been a success. August seemed less dismissive than in previous meetings at his offices and had opened up a bit on the golf course. He shared more about his time as a pediatrician, and I had already begun incorporating some of what I learned into my business proposal.

"Yes, thank you for that, by the way. He seemed much more interested in the idea of a joint investment from the two firms and suggested we discuss more over dinner next week."

"That's my girl!" She smiled as she squeezed my arm. "You may not have knocked your competition out of the running just yet, but you're still in the game. I know you got this."

Slapping her hand on the table and leveling me with a look, Ana exclaimed, "Okay! After those two margaritas, I'm dying. I'm running to the ladies' room. When I get back, I need to fill you in on Hot Yoga."

Laughing, I watched her dash inside. Hot Yoga in this instance was not, in fact, the workout. Hot Yoga was Ana's latest boy toy she met in (you guessed it) hot yoga class. He was just the latest in the string of men she entertained herself with. They never stuck around long enough for me to try and remember names, and after two years, I was used to referring to them as their occupation (Mr. Masseuse), their physical attributes (Red Beard), or their personality traits (Turtle Man). Ana was the main character in her life, and the men she saw were nothing more than guest stars for an episode or two.

I sipped my margarita and looked out across downtown Palo Alto. We were seated at a small bar top that perfectly allowed for people watching, and Broadway was filling.

At that moment, I saw a head of dark hair and a tall, broad frame slide out of a blacked-out SUV parked on the curb behind three other, slightly-less built guys. They were laughing boisterously and had that apparent familiarity with one another that only came with years of friendship. It dawned on me that I knew that dress-shirt clad back and tight ass. *That* was Parker.

I snatched my phone from the table and opened my messages. I didn't know how he made it back from Boise, but seeing him there in the city reminded me I hadn't followed his instructions.

> Me: You made it back, I see.

Out on the sidewalk, Parker slid his phone from his pocket and smirked. I ignored the way that look made my core clench and watched as he looked up and glanced around.

> My Competition: Well, no one put a bomb in my suitcase, so.

A surprised laugh bubbled up as another message came in right away.

> My Competition: Is this your way of letting me know you made it back safely? Stalking seems excessive, spitfire. Should I be flattered?

I bit back a laugh and shook my head. He was still looking around, trying to spot me, but our table was tucked away. I had a clear view of him, but he would be hard pressed to find me.

> Me: Figured you weren't really that interested in my safety, considering where that car left me.

He still had his phone in his hand as his friends talked and milled about outside. I got the impression they were waiting for someone or undecided on where they were going. As he read my message, his eyebrow raised (just the one), and those luscious lips pursed.

> My Competition: Don't play, LB. You should know your safety is very important to me.

I watched as that little smirk returned, the three dots flashing in my app to tell me he wasn't done.

> My Competition: Anyway, I've been to the Nampa Municipal Airport a few times. It's lovely.

Oh, no you don't, sir.

> Me: Lovely?! You and I have different definitions of that word, clearly. It was NOT lovely.

He laughed, and I swear I could feel the effects of it in my soul. He was mouthwatering on a bad day, but like that? Head tossed back, throat exposed, and endless mirth on his face? Just bury me already. I was dead.

At that inopportune moment, Ana slid back into her seat.

"Okay, so, Hot Yoga. The man can fold himself like a pretzel, and let me tell you–," she stopped mid-sentence and gave me a narrow-eyed look. "You're not paying attention. LB, I'm about to give you a Kama Sutra masterclass and you're tuning me out."

She snapped in front of my face a few times, and I jerked my eyes off my phone. She gave me a pointed look, then glanced at my phone and back at me. I bit my lip and considered how much to say.

"Bitch, spill. You wear your entire heart on your damn sleeve. I know I've lost you to whatever the Athena hottie is saying to you right now."

"What!" I spluttered, "Why would you think–"

"Nope, uh uh. Stop." She held up a hand. "I'm not stupid and, contrary to what our esteemed colleagues Brandoph might say, my worth is not only in my tits." She gave said rack a little squeeze with her upper arms, boosting her cleavage. "Doesn't take a private investigator to notice how you light up whenever you mention him, even when you're pretending to hate that he cared enough about you and this little prank war you instigated to play along."

I blinked rapidly at her. "What does that even mean, play along? We're rivals!"

She rolled her eyes and gave me another look. "LB, honey. The man's a senior associate at probably the top firm in the country. His portfolio is impressive as fuck; I should know, I looked it up. He could close Gaspar Technologies tomorrow on his track record alone, but he's collaborating with you, his junior. And he fucking pranked you back, harmlessly, in a way that did not interfere with your chances at a deal whatsoever. The man is *playing along*."

I gaped at her. I probably looked like a dying fish, but I honestly didn't care. Nothing she said was untrue–I'd looked into a bit of Parker's resume, too. He was a force, clearly. But the way Ana spun it, it was like she thought Parker was only in it–whatever the "it" was between us–for...me. *That can't possibly be true.*

Ana snagged my attention back by tapping one perfectly manicured finger on my phone screen. "What did he say, LB?"

"Oh," I looked down. "I realized I hadn't texted him I made it back safe, which he asked me to do."

She laughed like she was privy to an inside joke, then nodded at me with a flourish of her drink, indicating I should continue. I'm not sure why I left out the little tidbit about seeing Parker with his friends, but I didn't want her to know he was in reach. I had a feeling she'd heavily abuse that knowledge, likely to my complete and utter mortification.

"And, uh, I was complaining about the runaround." I said as I shrugged.

"Uh huh, okay. Sure," she nodded at me again. "Okay, you're holding back, but I think it's because you need more time to process. I'm going to go to the bar and flirt with the hot bartender, get us another round, and let you piece through what you want to share with the class. M'kay?"

She was up and gone before I could fully respond. I immediately looked outside to see if Parker was still in view and nearly fell off of my seat when I found him alone and looking right at me. He was sitting on a bench across the sidewalk, phone in hand. He gave me a slow smile and waved his phone a bit in the air. I glanced down at mine and saw several texts had piled up during my conversation with Ana.

My Competition: My definition of lovely is anywhere a certain 5' nothing blonde with bluebell blue eyes happens to be. What's yours?

My Competition: Cat got your tongue, little stalker?

My Competition: Ah, there you are. I see you.

My phone buzzed as another message popped up.

My Competition: This place any good? I've been meaning to try it.

I scoffed and looked up at him, shaking my head.

Me: I'm not letting you off the hook that easy, sugar. You dumped me in the middle of nowhere.

My Competition: You appear to have survived to tell the tale.

Me: Physically, sure! But I may never recover from the emotional trauma.

I met his eyes and gave a little smile so he'd know I wasn't serious. He grinned back at me.

My Competition: Oh no, not emotional trauma. I've got a great therapist if you need one. I'll even cover the first session.

Me: Thank god! Chivalry isn't dead.

My Competition: At least not today. You ready to give in, spitfire? Did the emotional trauma push you over the edge?

Ha! This guy. This fucking guy.

> Me: While I've never been a quitter, humor me.
> What would giving in entail, exactly?

The way his gaze darkened as he typed furiously on his phone had goosebumps pebbling on my arms.

> My Competition: I want your honey on my tongue again, spitfire. And then I want you on your knees.

Oh. My. God.

Heat flashed through me and I pressed my thighs together, desperate for friction.

> My Competition: Do you want to taste me, spitfire? Be a good girl for me?

I gasped a bit, then slowly forced the breath out through my nose. *He's trying to kill me.*

> My Competition: I think you do. I think you want me to fill all of your senses until everything else falls away and there's nothing but me, you, and your pleasure. I promised you five orgasms next time.

I glanced up to find his eyes on me again. He tapped his phone without looking down, and mine buzzed.

> My Competition: And I always keep my promises.

Good lord, give me the strength to survive this man. I licked my lips and looked back at my phone, desperately trying to come up with a reply to that statement. As I did, Ana waltzed back up with our next round. My phone buzzed.

> My Competition: Have fun with your friend, spitfire. When you want to surrender, you know how to find me.

When I glanced back, he was walking down the sidewalk, hands in the pockets of his designer jeans like he had not a care in the world.

"You ready to talk yet?" Ana asked.

I turned to her and took a deep breath, then nodded. I wanted everything Parker promised in his text messages, wanted it so badly I could taste it. Taste *him*. I could perfectly picture myself on my knees for him willingly. And that's why I needed to push more professional distance between us. I'd never been one to fall head over heels for a guy. I didn't have the time, patience, or—honestly—motivation to invest in a relationship of any kind. My sister used to tease me for not having any crushes when I was in high school, wholly convinced something was wrong with me because I hadn't picked out my future spouse from the football team roster like she and our mom had. But with Parker?

It would be easy to give myself to him. Easy to walk away from my career, simple to just put it all on a shelf and lose myself completely in this gorgeous, intriguing, mildly domineering man who looked at me like I was the most interesting and beautiful thing he'd ever seen.

And Parker didn't just see my physical attributes, though he'd listed them well enough earlier. He saw straight through to the heart of me, and that meant he had power. Power over me, over my future.

Power I didn't want him to have.

"I need to drink, then I need to figure out what I'm going to do about the Athena hottie," I finally said.

Ana whooped and clinked her glass against mine. "Damn straight! Let's do this!"

I downed far too much of my margarita in one go after that, desperate to put some distance between me and my own damn feelings. Ana was all too happy to join me in my escapism, and we grinned and laughed at one another as we set down our glasses. *You've got this, LB. Eyes on the prize. The promotion prize, not Parker.*

Chapter 17

Parker

I was up with the sun on Saturday, eager to get to my sister's house for our biweekly hike. Thoughts of LB on Thursday night still crowded my mind—the dark red lipstick she'd been wearing, the way she'd smiled and laughed with her friend, how she'd flushed and bit her lip when she'd read my text messages. I'd had nothing but filthy dreams of her since, and I and my perpetually-ready cock desperately needed a distraction. If anyone could provide one effective enough to derail my thoughts, it would be Preston.

As kids, our lives had been anything but consistent. When our parents were together, they were almost constantly at odds. Dad was at work, Mother was attempting to one-up her "friends" with reputation-building events thinly disguised as charity work. Then, when they split, Dad disconnected from us entirely and Mother immediately started the hunt for her next husband. I'd always wondered why Dad hadn't taken us in the divorce. His staff raised us as it was, and there was no maternal bond for us to mourn had he fought for custody. But I think he knew we were part of our mother's carefully constructed image. And he was well aware how much she'd make his life hell if he tried to tear even a small part of that image down.

So, she got primary custody, and we spent the odd week or weekend with our dad when it was convenient for him. One of the few bright spots was the evenings and weekends with our grandfather. Though his relationship with our mother wasn't close, he had cared for us deeply and took every opportunity to spend time with us. Anything of value I learned outside of school was learned on his knee or at his side. We lost him early, when we were barely twelve, and I've often wondered how we would've turned out if he'd been there through high school.

As Mother hunted and landed different new husbands, our schedules, schools, and traditions changed on a whim. Whatever my mother thought would make her husband of the hour happy, she did, consequences be damned. More often than not, that meant that the only constants in our young lives were the traditions we built together, rituals we could have just for us despite our parental insecurity. As adults, those traditions had only matured and become more deeply ingrained for us both.

Every other Saturday, Preston and I got together for a hike. Every Sunday, without fail, we brunched. Tuesdays we had lunch together, either physically or through a video chat, to catch up one-on-one. Sometimes those lunches were 15 minutes long, other times they dragged for hours. The important part was that we were there for one another. And we always would be.

I hustled down to the street and glanced at my smartwatch. Preston was going to kill me for being five minutes late, but it would be an entertaining death, at least. Vicious and cunning, my sister.

I jogged the few blocks over to her building, buzzing myself in. We had a set of each other's keys for emergencies, though sometimes we stretched the definition of "emergency" a bit.

What else were two siblings going to do if not rib one another when the opportunity presented itself?

I was halfway up to her condo when my phone buzzed.

> **Twinkie:** You're late. You'll be expected to make up every minute and then some at brunch tomorrow.

> **Me:** Literally in the elevator. You know this. I know you stalk the notifications, creep.

> **Twinkie:** I'm sorry, would you rather I didn't ensure my own safety through using the features of my security system to their full advantage?

I let myself into her condo with a loud laugh. "You're full of shit, Preston!"

"Dude!" she said, walking around the corner from her bedroom, dark hair swaying in a high pony. "The key is for *emergencies*. Knock, for fuck's sake."

"I consider threats to your safety an emergency, you know this."

"Then don't be late and I won't suggest otherwise," she sniped, tossing her nose in the air in an exaggerated expression of haughtiness.

I swooped her into my arms for a quick hug, which she returned without hesitation. "Hey, twinkie," I greeted teasingly as I released her.

"Hey, big," she said, with an eye roll to accent her genuine smile.

"Parker!"

A warm voice called from just behind us, and I turned to find my sister's roommate and business partner, Cami. She was dressed in yoga pants and a sporty tank, and I grinned.

"Cami! You joining us again today?" I asked, reaching out for a quick hug from her, too.

She nodded brightly, "Sure am! Couldn't skip a chance to hike The Dish with the twinkie twins."

"Awesome. Let's do this?" I rubbed my hands together and smiled at them both.

"Did you send Ralph over?" Preston asked. She grabbed a small backpack from the hook by the front door and slung it over her shoulder.

"Saw him downstairs when I walked up," I confirmed.

"So, it's just you who's late, then?" she goaded, giving me a pointed look.

"I really think we need to revisit your definition of late, Pres," I said. "It was five minutes."

"I could figure out the cost of those five minutes based on my trust fund, but that sounds like way too much work. It's easier to say my time is valuable. So is yours and Cami's. Our time matters." She gave me a pointed look. "Do I really have to remind you of that?"

"Sure, time matters. But so does flexibility and understanding," I offered, giving her my most amicable smile. I was winding her up, because of course I was. Twins, remember?

The piercing look she shot me was well worth it. I held in a chuckle at Cami's amused expression. That girl had been around since college, and she was well used to our antics by now.

"I am very flexible and understanding, thank you very much," Preston quipped. "But you can't monetize that shit and you know it."

"Since when are we getting paid to hike together again? I must have missed that memo at the last estate planning session."

Cami laughed while Preston slugged me in the arm, both

perfectly true to their personalities. Pretty sure if you looked "sunshine" up in the dictionary, Cami's picture would be featured as an example. Preston, on the other hand, could be found under "lioness" or maybe "tigress" or possibly "Amazonian". She was constantly ready for battle and would win nine times out of ten, regardless of her opponent, either through skill or sheer force of will.

We reached the sidewalk and found Ralph waiting for us with the back passenger door of the black SUV wide open. He smiled and nodded at us all as we hopped in, then closed our door and headed for the driver's seat. The second he was in place, Cami piped up.

"Ralph! How are you? How was Allie's soccer game last week?"

Ralph beamed at her in the rearview mirror. She never failed to ask about him and his family, the pride of which was his teenage daughter. "I'm well, Miss Cami, thank you. And Allie's team won the match. She was very excited; she scored a goal."

"Of course she did! How exciting. Congrats to her!"

"Thank you, Miss Cami."

Preston gave me a look over Cami's head that clearly said "this girl, I fucking love her, isn't she the best?" and I returned the look wholeheartedly because, quite honestly, I agreed. Cami was a gem of a human being.

"Where the fuck have you been this week, big?" Preston asked.

"Ha! Easing right into it, I see. I was in Boise again, then out with the boys Thursday night. Work's been busy."

"Boise has been a thing a lot lately."

"Sure has."

I could feel Preston's laser focus on my face and sighed. "Have a question, there, twinkie?"

"Who is she?"

I leaned my head back against the headrest. "Say what now?"

"Raj said there's a girl."

That motherfucker, I should've known. Raj had been crushing on Preston ever since he'd first met her years ago, but he knew it was and would always be unrequited. A true gentleman, he'd pivoted to being her mole, which had won him plenty of free lunch from the healthy catering service she and Cami ran. It had also won him endless ribbing from me and the guys, but he took it on the chin, the asshole.

"There's not a girl. Yet."

Preston's eyebrows disappeared into her hair. Cami gave me a warm smile and patted my knee. She knew full well Preston wouldn't drop this topic, but she wouldn't pile on. I appreciated that about her.

"Pres, I love you. Let's talk about literally anything else, other than LB."

"So her name's LB."

I groaned. "Preston, I need a distraction today. You're supposed to keep my mind from wandering. Can you do that, please?"

She studied me for a minute, then nodded. "Fine. I'm putting a pin in this conversation, though, Parker. We're not done."

"Of course we aren't," I murmured, looking straight ahead.

I caught Ralph's gaze in the rearview, and he gave me an encouraging smile. I returned it half-heartedly. Preston and I told each other everything, within reason, but I wasn't ready for her personal brand of interrogation. We were closer than most siblings had any right to be, but the twin connection was next-level.

"If we're changing the subject, then you should know I heard from Mother this week," Preston said, her voice tight.

I groaned and dragged a hand over my face. That wasn't news I typically wanted, but a small part of me was glad we'd moved off the topic of LB.

Preston and I had each reacted to our parents' questionable involvement in vastly different ways—I'd focused on my education and career goals, and Preston had focused on control in just about every aspect of her life. That girl had the whole world on a string, and she knew it. Ever since we were kids, she'd been an expert at understanding people—their motivations, their desires. She could sell anything to anyone, and they'd still come looking for more. Once she'd figured that out, she'd had us all in the palm of her hand. Raj was just one example of the many connections she orchestrated throughout her life to get the information and outcomes she wanted.

While I might be quietly succeeding on my own as a fuck you to my father's legacy, Preston was flaunting every single move in their faces. She dove into her trust fund the second she could access it, funding not only her business with Cami, but also taking my direction and investing in a few startups to grow her wealth. And then she turned around and poured it into youth charities throughout the Bay. She was a media and society darling, which immediately raised her value in our mother's eyes. For Dad, she became something to manage. Nothing was more important than the sanctity of the family name. Naturally, she heard from both of them with far more frequency than I did.

"And what did Mommy Dearest have to say this time?" I asked, turning to look at my twin.

She grimaced. "There's an event next week. She wanted me to come and 'bring a date'."

I raised an eyebrow at her. I knew for a fact she had no more desire to spend time with our parents than I did.

"Yes, exactly, that," she said, pointing at my face and drawing a circle around it in the air. "My exact reaction. Why the fuck she thinks I'm going to perform for her when I haven't done so since kindergarten is beyond me."

"You did make an adorable Virgin Mary," I said with a smirk. Preston had gotten the lead role in the kindergarten rendition of the Christmas play through sheer intimidation. Our elementary theater instructor was terrified of her.

"Shut up, Wise Man Number Two," she snapped. "Anyway, while I was informing her I would not be attending with her, she told me some news."

I glanced at her as her tone dropped into more serious territory. "News?"

She nodded. "Her husband got a terminal diagnosis last week."

"Oh, hell. That's awful," I muttered. I didn't know much more than the man's name, but I wasn't heartless. I didn't wish that kind of suffering on anyone.

"Mmhm, sure is. She asked if I could please bring a date, preferably one with a single father."

I choked on air as Cami gasped between us.

"What the actual fuck?" I said, stunned.

Preston gave me a look. She gave me *the* look, really. The one we'd developed together as kids that meant "stop acting surprised, this is our normal now". I scrubbed my face with both hands and felt something crack in my chest. There was no love between me and my mother—no affection. She tolerated us as her children and celebrated us as her accomplishments when our achievements could bolster her. I shouldn't be surprised, but there was some part of me hoping that she'd redeem herself. Somehow attempt to repair the chasm between us.

"So, I'm not going," Preston continued, matter of fact. Her coping mechanism with our parents was to bottle up every emotion and put it on a shelf. I imagined she'd push us hard on this hike, taking her anger and grief out on her body. "But I thought you should know."

"Yeah, thanks for telling me," I said softly. I looked out the window as Ralph pulled up to drop us off at The Dish. "You okay?"

Preston gave me a long look, her green eyes both dark and fiery. I could tell she was raging under the surface, eager to take a chunk out of our mother in some way. I wasn't prone to violence or retribution, but Preston fed on the stuff. I had no doubt she'd find a way to put our mother in her place at some point, and I'd happily be her partner in crime.

"No," she said, emotion cracking through her facade for a moment. She swallowed, looked off, and pushed it back. She sighed and grabbed the door handle. "I'm not, Parker. But I will be. We will be."

I nodded at her and reached out to squeeze her shoulder. "We will."

Preston nodded briefly after a moment, opening the door and stepping out into the sunshine. Cami climbed out after her with a concerned look on her face. Based on her reaction in the car, I assumed my sister had saved that story for when I was around.

"It's okay, Cami," I said, slinging an arm over her shoulders. "I promise you'll never have to meet the folks."

"Oh! Thank goodness for that, Parker," she said in a rush. "I don't think I could keep it together in front of your parents, especially not your mom. I have a few choice words I'd like to say to that woman."

"Mother is a cruel bitch, that's for sure," Preston agreed. "Not worth your time, Cami."

"Not worth ours, either." I bumped shoulders with my twin. She was tall, just a handful of inches shorter than I was, and

I only had to bend a little to do it. She smirked up at me as I moved past her to take the lead on the trail.

"Agreed! That was my only topic for today, big. Whatever will we cover now?" she asked, giving me a pointed look.

I barked out a laugh and shook my head. "Nice try, brat. Cami, tell me–what's new in the allergy-friendly catering world? Any suggestions for my next farmer's market trip?"

I glanced back over my shoulder at them both and grinned. Preston was giving me a narrow-eyed glare while Cami beamed at me, clearly pleased with my question.

"I have so many recommendations, Parker! You should just come with us next time, and I can teach you everything I know," she gushed.

"I just might." I smiled, turning back to the front. "But in case I miss it, let's cover it now."

I could hear the shuffled kick before a spray of dirt and small rocks hit the backs of my calves. I laughed and skipped forward before turning to face the girls as I kept going down the trail, backwards.

"That all you got, twinkie?" I taunted, throwing my arms wide. "Bring it."

Preston got a feral look in her eye and launched toward me. I barked a laugh and spun around, taking off up the trail. Even when she caught me, I knew I'd be in the clear–she despised losing enough to not engage in a battle she knew she couldn't win. I'd come to her about LB when I was good and ready, and not a moment before.

Chapter 18

LB

Monday brought clouds and a sense of restlessness I felt deep in my bones, even after my morning run. As a kid, I'd spent hours outside. Our home was small, cramped, and always too warm. My mom was one of those petite little things who was almost constantly cold and considered 80 degrees Fahrenheit to be an ideal temperature. I'd frequently escaped the oven of my room to seek shade and fresh air.

Whiling away hours under–and in–trees around town, I would bring books to pile next to me or tuck into the branches. I had read to escape and to learn, fierce in my determination to succeed. Knowledge had felt like a critical and achievable first step.

Working in an office for hours on end had always put me on edge. Confined yet again by four walls, I itched to spend more time in the sun. I filled my weekends with runs around my neighborhood and spent hours in the park, stopping in at my apartment only for the necessities. Now that I was again surrounded by the gray walls and bright lights of P&L, I struggled to focus.

"Hey, girl, how you feelin'?" Ana walked up at that

moment, coffee cups in hand. She raised one with a smile and set it on my desk.

"Ugh, bless you." I snatched it and took a small sip, groaning in appreciation. "That's the stuff."

She chuckled as she slung her bag on her desk and took a seat. "Someone is a big fan of Mondays, if I remember correctly."

I rolled my eyes at her, and she just grinned back at me.

"You made it home okay Thursday, I take it," I said, giving her a look. She'd stayed at the bar when I'd gone home, intent on adding Hot Bartender to her stable of men.

"Sure did," she said primly, a wicked glint in her eye. "Wasn't my home, but I definitely made it."

I laughed and shook my head at her. I turned back to my laptop, coffee cup still in hand, and glanced at my hotel reservation info. As I'd booked the trip for our dinner with Dr. Gaspar on Thursday, the system had thrown an alert that only one room was left at my usual hotel. Ana peeked over at my screen, blatant and unabashed in her snooping.

"All set to see Parker on Thursday?" she asked.

I raised an eyebrow at her. "I'm all set to see Dr. Gaspar on Thursday, yes."

She scoffed. "Come on, LB. You're way more interested in seeing Parker."

I wish she was wrong. I wanted to kick myself, seriously. Here I was, finally on the precipice of what I'd been striving toward since I first cracked *The Seven Habits of Highly Effective People* while tucked away in the tree behind my childhood home. Every moment since then had been a carefully constructed journey of key milestones to achieve financial independence so I never had to feel stuck, so I'd never have to settle. And this promotion was a critical milestone in that journey.

With the raise I'd get, I could get my own place. I could

afford to fly my parents out to visit me, so they could see this city where I lived and maybe get a little closer to understanding their conundrum of a second born.

Honestly, I would also be one step closer to having the financial freedom to actually stop for a moment and maybe answer the question I'd been putting off in favor of moving forward. *What do you actually want to do with your life, Laura Beth?* I didn't have the time or energy to answer that question yet, but if my bank account could breathe a little easier, I just might be able to give it some thought.

"Only in the sense that I still think collaboration is the way to go to get the deal signed," I said, turning back to Ana.

"Right," she drawled. "Sure. Okay, so, what's the plan on that front, then?"

"I have a few deal terms I'm going to mention at dinner–ways we could do a collaboration that would still give both P&L and Athena equal stake, while ensuring we're also benefiting in the short and long term."

"Solid. Want to walk me through it?"

I smiled and nodded. "Yeah, let me just close this out."

As I went to close the browser window with our travel system pulled up, Ana asked me to stop.

"Does that say your hotel is sold out?"

"Yeah, but that's okay. I got the confirmation."

She gave me an evil little smile. "I'm not worried about your room, LB. I'm thinking about Parker. You still want to mess with him a little? Draw out this little prank war of yours?"

I gave her a long look, considering. Did I want to continue pranking Parker? That's what it was, now–pranks. I didn't truly believe I could sabotage his chances with Gaspar Technologies, and I didn't want to. But there was something delicious about our back-and-forth. I wasn't sure I was ready to give it up.

Another part of me, though, the part that had built a future bit by bit for a little girl from nowhere with not a prospect in sight...that part wanted me to focus on winning that signature. That part of me was telling me to let go of petty games and get down to business.

"Honestly, Ana, I'm not sure it's a good idea," I said, closing my laptop. I stood and smoothed my skirt. "I'm grabbing water–need anything?"

I should've been suspicious of the innocent look on her face as she shook her head, but my mind was on other topics as I wandered to the kitchen. Namely, how I could convince Nate to get on board with a collaborative deal. I had a feeling that might be the biggest challenge ahead of me, and the least enjoyable.

I was drafting a fictional email in my head as I walked back from the kitchen to my desk, thinking through how to give Nate an update without setting him off about working with Athena. He'd been pleased with my pivot to golf and the adjusted timetable last week, but he'd been skeptical about the merits of meeting over dinner this week. Fortunately, Dr. Gaspar (I still struggled to call the man August–that Southern politeness drilled in too deep) had taken that one out of my hands entirely– he'd made it clear that the dinner this week was mandatory.

As I sat back down at my desk, I noticed Ana shoot me a glance. She was sporting a smirk that spelled nothing but trouble.

"Girl, what did you do?" I asked, leaning away in concern.

"Well," she mused, tapping her chin with a single finger and looking up at the ceiling. Her brown eyes flashed as she looked back at me, a grin spreading across her lips. "I helped you out. I called and canceled his hotel room."

"You did what?! Ana!" I gasped, reaching out to grasp her arm.

"Oh, simmer down," she said dismissively, patting my hand.

"It was easy. I pretended to be his executive assistant and begged them to take care of it so I didn't get fired for my error. They didn't even ask for the confirmation number or anything!"

"I'm not worried about *how* you did it, you ridiculous human! I can't believe you did that!"

"It'll be fine. Who knows, maybe you'll end up having to make room in your bed." She gave me a very not-safe-for-work wink and eyebrow waggle.

I groaned and dropped my head onto my crossed arms on my desk. "I hate you," I mumbled.

Ana cackled beside me. "No, you don't." I could hear her perfectly manicured nails–a lovely deep red this week–clicking away on the keyboard. "Anyway, I have a feeling you'll thank me later."

———

Walking into the hotel on Thursday afternoon was a uniquely stressful experience. I was on high alert, worried Parker would pop out of the woodwork and I'd have to witness the inevitable fallout of Ana's rash actions. I hadn't seen him on the flight earlier, which was odd. There weren't many directs to Boise, and I couldn't imagine that he'd be arriving later. But if he got here earlier, what was his angle? *Your flight was probably sold out, you nut. Not everything is about sabotage.*

I really needed to listen to myself on that front. As Ana had pointed out last week, Parker had been careful to "play along" in a risk-free (or close to it) way. His absence distracted me as I checked in and made my way to my hotel room. I had enough time to shower, do my hair and makeup, and get dressed before we had to meet Dr. Gaspar at the hotel's restaurant.

Just as I was stepping out of the shower, I heard my phone

buzz on the bathroom counter. I hurried over to it quickly, wrapping my towel around me as I went.

> My Competition: It appears my room has been canceled and the hotel is sold out.

My heart raced, and I instantly felt overheated. The water from the shower was mixing with the sweat from the adrenaline and guilt.

> Me: Oh no! So sorry to hear that.

> My Competition: I'm sure. You wouldn't happen to know anyone named Mariana, would you?

For fuck's sake, Ana. Could you be any more obvious?!

> Me: I'm not sure I like what you're implying, Mr. Brooks.

> My Competition: And what might I be implying, Ms. Calhoun?

I shifted from foot to foot and stared at the foggy mirror. Was he mad? He didn't sound mad, but he didn't *not* sound mad. *God, I am so not cut out for this shit. I'm not doing this again.*

> Me: That I had something to do with your hotel situation.

> My Competition: Did you?

I worried at my lip as I opened the bathroom door to let the mugginess out, deciding how to play this.

> Me: I can neither confirm nor deny.

His reply was instant.

> My Competition: Hmmm. This is going to cost you, LB. I thought you were my good girl.

My knees nearly buckled as I opened the door. I just caught myself on the door frame as I pushed through, sagging against it as I stared down at my phone.

> Me: I'm not sure I realized I was "your" anything.

> My Competition: I'm patient.

> Me: And, anyway, it's not like I can't be naughty.

> My Competition: You can't see it, but I'm smirking.

I rolled my eyes at the phone.

> Me: What, don't believe me?

I walked over to the closet and looked at the two dresses I'd brought. It was impossible for me to pack only enough clothes for a trip. A girl needed options, y'all. One dress was simple, fitted, black, to the knee. Professional, sensible, while still being formal enough to be appropriate for cocktail attire. The other was a bright royal blue in a soft, flowy material. It was a wrap style with a modest v-neck and fitted top, with a skirt that hit a couple inches above the knee. As I looked over my options, I realized I'd brought one of these dresses with Parker in mind.

> My Competition: Honestly? Not one bit.

"Ugh," I scoffed at the phone. "Men. Go on and underestimate me there, big guy."

I nodded at my clothing choices and turned back to the bathroom to start on my hair and makeup, phone still in hand.

> Me: I'm full of surprises.

I set my phone down and got to work drying my hair.

> My Competition: Don't I know it, spitfire.

> My Competition: But I think you want to be good.

> My Competition: For me.

He had me by the short hairs. I don't know how he'd gotten hold of me so firmly, but the man knew exactly what buttons to push. I craved seeing those two words pop up again, and he would not give them to me. They did something to my insides, made me feel like the only woman in the world. Like the only woman he saw. *I do want to be your good girl, Parker. Goddamnit, I wish I didn't. But I do.*

> Me: We'll see.

I had nothing more clever in me. I turned my focus back to my hair and makeup, styling my blonde locks in loose waves and keeping the look natural.

> My Competition: Prove it, then. Show me how naughty you can be.

I eyed my phone, considering his challenge. With the sexual tension between us, good and naughty seemed so very close to one another. As I was about to step into my panties, I paused.

What would a naughty girl do? I looked at the black lace in my hand and smiled. *Let's see how well you can concentrate after this, Parker.*

I left my panties on the bed and quickly pulled on my bra, dress, earrings, and heels. Before I left the room, just a few minutes earlier than necessary, I gave myself a once over in the full-length mirror by the door. I turned and looked over my shoulder, double checking that nothing looked obvious beneath my dress. Satisfied that I was professional and modest enough, I stepped out into the hall, panties discreetly in my hand. Parker and I had arranged earlier in the week to meet at the elevator outside the restaurant on the top floor so we could try to greet Dr. Gaspar together.

I hit the elevator call button and waited patiently, mind whirring through the agenda for the evening. As the doors slid open, I barely glanced up, vaguely noticing just one other person inside. I stepped in quickly and checked that the right button was pressed.

"Fuck me, you're gorgeous."

I whipped my head around in surprise. My eyes widened at the sight of Parker standing just behind me, dressed head-to-toe in black. I had only a moment to soak in the sight of him, lean muscles clear through his fitted shirt, before he crowded me back against the elevator wall. He leaned in and I both felt and heard the long inhale as his nose grazed the side of my neck. Goosebumps prickled across my skin and I had to concentrate on staying upright.

"Parker," I breathed. I reached up with one hand to steady myself against his arm, and he chuckled.

"You look stunning in this color, LB," he said. He straightened and looked down into my eyes, a soft smile on his face. "Bluebells, just like your eyes."

He was right there. Like my filthiest fantasy made flesh, he was right in front of me, body pressed lightly against mine, arousal obvious between us. That strong jaw, light stubble–it made me swoon. Add in those warm, hazel eyes, and I wanted to melt. Drop right into a puddle at his feet.

Instead, I pushed up on my tiptoes and crashed my lips against his. He groaned in immediate approval, sliding a hand into my hair and tangling his fingers in the strands. He surged against me, pinning me more firmly against the wall and pressing his hard length against me. I'd like to say I held back the whimper that rose in my throat, but in his arms I was weak.

He had one arm around my waist and then slid the other from my hair to under my jaw. He pushed gently to angle my chin up as he deepened the kiss, his tongue sliding between my lips to caress mine. I clung to his shirt with one hand, pulling him to me, drawing in his taste, his smell, his heat. The man was aflame, and I was all too willing to burn in him.

The elevator slid to a stop and dinged, and we broke apart. I stared up at him for a moment, drinking in his kiss-swollen lips, and smiled softly. I loosened my hold on his shirt and slid my other hand to his pocket surreptitiously, depositing my black lace panties there as I patted his chest and turned to exit the elevator.

I felt like I'd just wrestled back a modicum of power. Yes, I melted at his touch, but he was just as susceptible to mine. I had no doubt he was equally distracted by our chemistry as I was and, if he thought this good little Southern girl couldn't play, he was in for a rude awakening. I couldn't wait for him to find my underwear in his pocket. He wanted naughty? *I'll be naughty for you, sugar.*

Chapter 19

LB

P arker gave me a quizzical look as he stepped out of the elevator. I smirked and ran a hand through my hair to settle it, then quickly looked around to see if Dr. Gaspar had arrived. When I looked back to Parker, not spotting the guest of honor, his posture had stiffened. He had one hand in his pocket, his eyes laser focused on me.

Heat pooled low in my belly as his gaze darkened, the motion of his fingers in his pocket barely visible. I boldly gazed right back at him, waiting for him to say something or step closer, anything to break the taught cord of tension between us. Just as I heard the rumble of a growl start in his chest and felt an answering tingle between my thighs, the next elevator over dinged and the doors whooshed open for the third and final member of our party.

"Ah, LB, Parker. You're here," Dr. Gaspar said with a small smile.

"August, good to see you," Parker said, turning toward him as he slipped his hand from his pocket. They shook hands firmly before turning to me.

"Thank you for inviting us, August," I said with a smile, offering my hand. "This place looks divine."

Dr. Gaspar gripped my hand with his customary single firm pump and nodded. "Yes, we don't have as many options here in Boise, but we do have a few gems. Shall we?"

He gestured toward the host and I nodded, moving aside so he could inform them of our reservation. Parker stepped up at my side, the heat of his body pressing into me as he stood just a hairsbreadth too close to be professional.

"You're playing with fire, LB," he breathed, just loud enough for me to hear.

I looked up at him and smiled into those fierce hazel eyes. "I like the way it burns," I whispered back, rewarded for my boldness by his sharp intake of breath and a flare of heat in his gaze.

The host asked Dr. Gaspar to follow them to our table, and I turned and hurried after them, leaving Parker to follow tight on my heels. The restaurant was dark with lush appointments, warm lighting, and gold accents on the fixtures, floor to ceiling. The space was divided into sections that ensured a measure of privacy for most of the tables, keeping traffic low and allowing for a relaxed ambience.

The host led us to a velvet-upholstered booth along the far side of the room, a low-lit gold sconce on the wall setting an intimate mood. Parker gestured for me to slide in, then followed me on one side, leaving Dr. Gaspar opposite us.

"I highly recommend the steak," Dr. Gaspar said, picking up his menu.

"Few things better than an excellently prepared cut of quality meat," Parker agreed, reaching for his menu. I froze momentarily thanks to the sheer suggestiveness of his tone.

He was sitting close enough on our shared side of the booth that his firm thigh was touching the full length of mine. How he was both so unyielding and so warm, I couldn't fathom. It took conscious effort for me to focus on the menu he passed over to me, and when I looked up to thank him for it, the open desire in his gaze lanced straight to my core.

"Th-thank you, Parker," I said, too softly. I dropped my eyes to my menu and internally screamed at myself. *Get a fucking grip, Laura Beth! You're on the clock, bitch.*

I could feel his answering smirk, but I refused to look up at him.

"So, August, tell us–how did the tests go this week?" Parker asked, eyes still on his menu.

I peeked at Dr. Gaspar to find him casually watching us both, his menu discarded. I flashed a quick smile and nodded my encouragement and interest in the topic.

"Better than expected," he said perfunctorily. "We still have some kinks to iron out, but I'm confident we can move our estimated timeline up by at least a month."

"That's excellent news!" I said, beaming at him. "Quicker to market means you'll be on that path to profitability–and making a true impact on underserved communities–in no time."

He nodded. "True. I'm thinking we will do a soft launch, though. Make sure everything is in order before we go broad. I'd like to know how your firms might support such an approach."

"Of course," Parker said, setting his menu aside as well. "We have deep connections in the agriculture community in Northern California. In fact, a close friend of mine comes from a family who has farmed the land in some capacity for three generations. Not only am I confident that they'd be willing to be early testers of your crops, I also know they have deep connections with some of the inner city charity organizations that focus on food insecurity. And that's just one of the introductions I'd like to make."

"Yes, that sounds promising Parker. I'm glad to hear it," Dr. Gaspar said, nodding.

At that moment, the server stepped up to the table. He gave us a professional smile and nod, then asked, "Good evening. My name is Will and I'll be taking care of you tonight. May I bring you any beverages or appetizers to start your meal?"

"Scotch, neat," Dr. Gaspar said.

"I'll have the same," Parker chimed in. "My colleague, though—she'll take a French 75."

I could feel the flush in my cheeks—partially from the sheer audacity of this man, partially from the unexpected hotness of him ordering for me—as Dr. Gaspar glanced over to see my reaction. The server met my eyes to confirm, and I gave him a smile and a nod.

"Please," I said. "Thank you."

"Very good. Are you ready to order your meal, as well?" he asked, gathering our discarded menus.

"The filet," Dr. Gaspar said. "Medium rare, please. Extra mushrooms."

"Of course, sir," the server turned to me, as I realized I hadn't so much as glanced at the menu since we sat down, "And for the lady?"

"Oh, I—"

"The filet, as well," Parker answered for me. "Medium rare. I'll have the same."

The server tossed me that same glance of confirmation and I felt my cheeks heat to dangerous levels. I gave another nod of agreement.

"Very good then. I'll be back shortly with some bread for the table," he said, before turning and walking briskly away.

I looked over at Parker and cocked an eyebrow at him. "Bold of you."

"It really was the best choice on the menu," Dr. Gaspar assured me. "You won't regret it." His eyes wandered over to the bar along the far wall, and he beamed. "Oh! Excuse me, please. I see an old colleague I've been meaning to connect with about next week's tests. I'll be back shortly."

Without a glance our way, he slipped from the booth and set course for the other side of the restaurant. He'd barely turned the corner when Parker shifted his body to both face me and effectively block me from the view of the other patrons.

"I'm not the only one feeling bold tonight," he said, his voice low and sultry.

I smirked up at him as I tried desperately to control my heaving breaths. "Oh? Whatever do you mean?"

He chuckled and shook his head, looking down at the table. He dropped the hand closest to me onto my thigh, resting the other casually on his water glass.

"You know exactly what I mean, spitfire," he rumbled, and I felt the wetness begin to gather between my thighs.

I squirmed, suddenly regretting my lack of undergarments when faced with the threat of soaking through my dress. His hand tightened on my thigh, stilling me.

"What are you going to do about it?" I goaded him, because all sense of self preservation had fled the building, along with my tact.

His fist tightened on his water glass as he took a sip, seemingly ignoring me. But his hand on my thigh slipped down, under the loose material of my skirt, then slowly back up. My lower lip dropped as my mouth fell open.

"Ah, ah, ah," he tsked, hand stalling in its progress. "There are prying eyes everywhere, LB. Close those naughty lips and act like nothing's happening. You can't make a sound."

He finally turned to meet my eyes again, the lust and dominance in his own nearly drowning me in a flurry of single-minded need. "Do you understand, Laura Beth?"

"Yes," I gasped softly, goosebumps rising on my arms as

tingles radiated out from where his skin made contact with mine.

He cocked his head at me, his hand immobile against my inner thigh. "Yes, what?"

I licked my lip, and his fingers dug into my flesh. I wanted so desperately to moan or whimper, but I held it in. Searching his gaze for a moment, I somehow knew without a doubt what he wanted to hear. "Yes, sir."

He closed his eyes briefly in appreciation, his grip on me tightening. "Good girl," he murmured, his hand resuming its upward trajectory.

It was incredible, the effect those two little words had on me. I felt a tremble start in my core and my goosebumps extended over my thighs, the most delicious tingle weighing heavily on my pussy. When his fingers brushed my bare skin, slick with my arousal, he growled softly and pressed his thigh harder to mine.

"I want to take my time with you, spitfire, but I don't know how long the good doctor is going to give us. And while I'm not one to leave you wanting, I really want to see just how naughty you'll be for me."

He met my gaze, and I fucking swooned inside. He searched my eyes for a moment and must've found what he wanted. Stroking my center with one firm finger, he slowly pushed past my pussy lips to find my clit. I bit my lip when he made contact, my eyes widening at my own boldness in allowing this to happen and at the electric current of pleasure that ran through me at the touch.

"That's it," he whispered, nodding. "Hold it together, spit-fire. I've got you."

He circled my tight, swollen bundle of nerves a few times as heat spread from my core into my belly, thin tendrils of it looping up my chest. A second finger joined the first, swooping around my clit in soft circles. I took a shuddering breath and tried desperately not to melt into the booth completely.

"Look at you," he murmured, eyes flashing as he drank in my sex-drunk features. "Such a good girl."

I almost moaned, and he took advantage of my scrambled attempt to silence myself and speared one strong finger into me. His fingertip found that rough, sensitive patch of skin along my channel with startling precision and began a rhythmic stroke back and forth. I could feel my body tightening on the sensation, the sheer pleasure of it only heightened by the fact that we were in public, surrounded by people, at risk of getting caught at any moment. Just the thought of our surroundings had me dancing precariously close to shattering.

Parker had lit me on fire and I had no desire to stop it, even though I knew I should. The pressure against my G-spot was just right, bringing me right up to the edge as he pushed his finger in, then dragged it out just an inch before pushing in again. His pace was both maddening and perfect, that slow build starting in my core and radiating out around me as my pleasure built. I was already so close, so desperate for the release. Looking up to meet his eyes again, I couldn't stop the tiny whimper that escaped. I needed something to cling to, my fingers seeking purchase on the seat of the booth between us.

Parker turned toward me a bit more and grasped my hand in his, holding me steady as he slowly tore me apart.

"Fucking hell, woman," he growled, pulling my hand into his lap. "Do you feel what you do to me?"

My knuckles brushed the hard length against his slacks and I gasped, feeling more wound up than I ever had in my life. He was still working along my inner walls, stroking that perfect spot, his pace slightly elevated as he pushed deeper inside me and ground the heel of his hand against my clit in a circular motion.

"Parker," I gasped, eyes falling closed as my orgasm broke, waves of pleasure rushing out from my core to my limbs, heat chasing it as my muscles spasmed. Parker pressed his shoulder and thigh more firmly against mine, masking the shudders that rocked through my body as he stroked me through the after-shocks, drawing them out with alternating attention to my G-spot and clit.

"Beautiful," he whispered, leaning away and releasing my hand. "Just stunning, spitfire."

I drew a ragged breath and nearly sobbed when he slipped from inside me and slowly pulled his hand away, his fingers trailing along my thigh. He rested his hand briefly on my knee and squeezed, and I looked down. It was oddly erotic, staring at his large hand as it engulfed so much of my flesh. His skin was tan against mine, a soft juxtaposition in the low light of the restaurant.

"Have a nice chat?" Parker asked.

I looked up, surprised, to find Dr. Gaspar nearly back at the table. I flinched and straightened before I could catch myself, but his eyes were on Parker, who casually pulled his hand from my knee and shifted ever so slightly away. Under the guise of placing my napkin on my lap, I pulled my skirt down a bit more.

"Indeed," Dr. Gaspar said, nodding eagerly. "Marcus is going to stop by next week to assist. It will be good to have his expertise in the lab."

"How fortuitous," Parker said with a smile, as though he hadn't had his fingers inside me mere moments ago.

Unable to stop myself now that I'd had the thought, I glanced at the fingers of his left hand and nearly died of mortifi-cation. Even in the low light, they were glistening. As though he could feel my panicked eyes on him, Parker pulled his napkin under the table and surreptitiously wiped his hands.

We were saved—or, honestly, I was, because I seemed to be

the only one of the two of us slowly spiraling in the wake of my very public orgasm–by the arrival of our server with our drinks and the promised bread.

"Your French 75, ma'am," he said, handing the drink over with a pointed eyebrow twitch and a judgmental gaze. *Holy fuck, did he see that? See me?!*

Before I could lose the plot completely, Parker spoke up. "Thanks so much, Will."

"Of course, sir," he said, giving him a pointed look of his own before turning to place Dr. Gaspar's scotch before him. "Would you prefer oil and pepper, or oil and balsamic?"

"Balsamic, certainly," Dr. Gaspar answered promptly.

"Right away," Will said, turning on his heel to fetch the oil and vinegar.

"So, we have much to discuss this evening," Dr. Gaspar began, turning to us both. "As I'm sure you've gathered, I'd like to consider a joint deal that would be beneficial for all parties."

"Of course," Parker said, nodding. "It only makes sense, from Athena's perspective. We bring a different set of resources and support to take Gaspar Technologies to the next level. P&L has strengths that are complementary to ours. There's truly no reason to compete."

"Exactly," Dr. Gaspar enthused, punctuating his statement with a nod. "I know P&L typically works alone, LB, but I'm confident you'll bring that boss of yours around, yes?"

I fought the tremble in my voice, both from the ongoing adrenaline rush from what had just transpired between me and Parker, and from my complete lack of confidence in my ability to convince Nate to support a joint deal. "I sure will, August."

"Good," he said. "That's good. Let's talk strategy."

As he and Parker began to discuss the finer details of how we could come together, I struggled to stay engaged. My drink disappeared quickly, and I nodded almost frantically when Will offered me another. Getting myself back in the game seemed a monumental task, but I internally slapped myself and worked to focus. I just needed to get through this dinner. Then I could make my way to the bar and drink away the feelings bubbling up to overwhelm me.

"Excuse me, Parker," I said gently when there was a break in conversation. "May I slip past you to the ladies' room?"

"Of course," he said, sliding out of the booth to let me pass.

"Thanks, sugar," I murmured, sliding after him and moving purposefully toward the restrooms.

Once there, I locked myself in a bathroom stall and took a long, steadying breath. *Get it together, Laura Beth! You can do this. You have to fucking do this.*

I shook out my hands then dug my cell phone out of my clutch, intent on getting a sisterly pep talk if I could reach her. Instead, I found a text message waiting for me.

> My Competition: I can still smell you on my skin, spitfire.

I whimpered out loud, unable to stop the noise after bottling everything in at the table. Another message followed quickly.

> My Competition: You may have started tonight naughty, LB. But you just proved you're my good girl.

And, just like that, my defenses fractured and crumbled into dust. I didn't know how to protect myself against a man who turned me inside out emotionally and physically. Who played my body like it was an instrument he'd been studying for years. Who looked at me as though I had hung the stars and moon. I could barely remember my own name, let alone the strategies and conversation points I'd been working on for the last several days in hopes of wowing both Parker and Dr. Gaspar tonight.

I felt things welling up in me that had no place at a business dinner, nor a place anywhere near my suddenly vulnerable and very eager heart. Things that were not factored into the plans I had carefully laid for my future. Things I'd seen my sister feel and give into, that had changed her future. Things that had locked my momma into the life she led, instead of the life she had once dreamed of.

I stumbled as I let myself back out of the stall and stepped up to the sink. Staring at myself, I took in the wild look in my eyes and slightly mussed look to my hair. I didn't recognize the girl staring back at me. She looked both unhinged and terrified, and I felt that tornado of emotions in my soul. I couldn't be Parker's good girl. I couldn't be his naughty little plaything, either. I needed to be his professional competition–the smart, capable, savvy associate who blew him and our client away.

But when I was around Parker, I didn't want to be the professional version of myself. I didn't want to don my LB armor, as Sara Jean called it. I wanted to strip all that away and flounce up to him in my floral print sundress and bare feet, heart on my sleeve, and not have to worry about softening my accent or thinking so critically about the words I chose. I wanted to do all of those things to make my heart happy, but none of them would win me that promotion. None of them would ensure I could support my parents when they were next struggling to make ends meet. None of them would help me realize the goals I'd been pushing toward since a childhood spent educating myself under the trees of Pike Road.

Get through this dinner, Laura Beth. Show them what you're made of. Hold it together. For now.

Taking a deep breath, I eyed myself in the mirror. I wasn't the naughty little vixen who let her gorgeous business rival finger her into oblivion *in public*. I was LB Calhoun, smart, strategic venture capitalist, with an eye for detail and killer instincts.

You can do hard things. You can do this.

I nodded at myself, smoothed my dress down one last time, and turned for the door. *Time to prove yourself, Laura Beth. As more than just a good girl.*

Chapter 20

Parker

"There you are, spitfire."

LB had her back towards me, her blonde locks spilling over her shoulders, as she perched on a high-backed stool. Coming to her side, I observed the two empty champagne flutes next to her.

What do we have here?

She briefly acknowledged me, nodding in agreement and twirling the remnants of her drink in the glass.

"You've been busy, I see." I plucked the glass out of her hand and grabbed her seat, twisting her to face me. I stared into her watery eyes, searching for answers.

As we had finished dinner and headed to leave the restaurant earlier, LB had said she needed to visit the ladies' room again. She urged August and me to go ahead without her, thanking August and saying her goodbyes. Once I had walked the good doctor out of the hotel, I was intent on finding LB and finishing what we started back at the dinner table. A call from Van interrupted my search, and I was delayed briefly. LB had obviously used that time to knock back a few.

"I think it's time we call it a night. Let's go," I said as I opened my wallet and dropped a stack of twenties on the bar. Signaling to the bartender, he nodded in reply.

LB's eyes widened as if in realization, and she gasped. "Oh no," she groaned. "Ana canceled your room, you have nowhere to stay."

As if a canceled room was the disaster LB made it out to be. It wasn't even a minor inconvenience. For fuck's sake, I golfed with the son of this hotel chain's founder. I could have an entire floor cleared with a phone call if I wanted. Her innocence about how money solved most of life's challenges was endearing.

"Ah. And the confession comes," I chuckled. I'd looked into her team at P&L and recognized the name.

Slipping my arm around her waist, I walked LB towards the elevator and was surprised when she didn't put up an argument. *Nice to see her armor is still missing. I like this version of her.*

Waiting for the elevator to arrive, I thought about the night and how we got here. LB's little pranks had done nothing to annoy me and everything to kindle that simmering flame of desire. I wouldn't admit it to her, but the teasing, the pranks, the bratty attitude–all any of it did was turn me on. She could play as much as she wanted, as long as it was with me. And only me.

After the most beautiful unraveling I had ever witnessed at my hands, LB had taken a moment to gather herself in the restroom and returned ready to perform. She was truly a marvel to witness. Every question August had pointed in her direction, she easily answered. Her projections and proposed deal terms were irrefutable. Her savvy business mind, combined with her innate poise and charm, had August reduced to putty in her hands. Honestly, so was I.

The elevator door chimed, and I guided LB into the lift, pressing the button for the floor she had joined me from on our way up. She leaned into my side more firmly and sighed. "How do you think the dinner went? Do you think Dr. Gaspar is ready to sign a deal?"

Was she really so unaware of her talent? How could she possibly have any doubts?

"That was the single most impressive performance I've ever witnessed at a business dinner," I said as I squeezed her hip. Looking down at her and catching her eyes, I winked.

LB slapped my chest but kept her tiny hand on my pec, spreading her fingers wider and clutching my shirt. "You know that's not what I meant, Parker."

"And you have to know you were brilliant with August. Gaspar Technologies would be lucky to have you as their investor and supporter."

"Thank you," she whispered.

Arriving at her floor, I let LB lead us out of the car and stroll us to her room. She was drunk, and I accepted things weren't going any further tonight, but that didn't mean I wanted to leave her. For the first time in as long as I could remember, I had a woman I didn't want to say goodbye to at the end of the night.

"Give me your clutch," I instructed when she stopped at a door. LB handed over the bag, and I located her key card. The door clicked, and I opened it for her, motioning my hand for her to walk in.

She stepped into the doorway and whipped quickly back to face me. She clung onto the door as she began asking me rapid-fire questions. "Wait, where are you going to stay? Where are your bags, anyway? Fuck, are you like sleeping in the lobby?" Her eyes widened comically, and she groaned, "I feel like such an asshole."

I smirked. "It's very kind of you to worry about me now, spitfire. That orgasm give you a change of heart?"

"Ugh, can we not mention that again? And get in here before I change my mind," she said as she walked backwards into her room.

As if I could turn down that invitation.

She stumbled on her heels, and I caught her forearm. Gripping her waist and holding her steady, I backed her up to the bed.

"Parker...about earlier...," she began, as she plopped onto the mattress.

"Shh, not right now. Let's just get you into bed and let you sleep off that champagne. We can talk tomorrow."

Kneeling, I slid my hands down her milky legs and smooth calves to the straps at her ankle.

"What are you doing?"

"I thought we just agreed, getting you ready for bed." Undoing the clasp, I slid the first stiletto off. Tracing my fingers over her ankles, I couldn't resist the opportunity to briefly knead her foot. LB groaned in response. *Yes, I most definitely like unguarded LB.*

"Parker, what the hell? That feels amazing," LB whimpered as she dropped her upper body back onto the mattress. "You have my permission to do that whenever you want."

"Watch out, spitfire. You give me permission to get on my knees in front of you, and I'll make this my home."

LB choked in reply, and I chuckled. Playing with her was my favorite thing in the world. *Fuck. When had it ever been like this with a woman?*

Focusing on my task, I moved on and quickly slipped the heel off her other foot. Standing, I saw LB was sprawled out on the bed, arm draped over her eyes. Her chest was rising and falling as she took deep, relaxed breaths. The thought struck me I wanted to see her this at peace more often. None of the stress or worry that often settled on her face when I watched her work over the past few weeks was there.

I moved, gathering a few necessities and spotting her pajamas laid out on the bedside chair.

"Alright, Laura Beth. Time to get out of that dress." I peeled her arm off her eyes and tugged her up to sit next to me. LB laid her head on my shoulder and sighed.

"I really stuck my foot in it this time, didn't I?" she asked. "I canceled your room and got so drunk you had to take care of me. And all you did was give me the most earth-shattering orgasm ever."

I smirked at that comment. "Arms up," I commanded. She complied, allowing me to slide the blue dress over her head and toss it aside.

I made eye contact with her, waiting for her to give me the go ahead. She nodded slowly, and I reached around to unclasp her bra and slide it down her arms. I stood and set her clothes back on the chair.

I turned back around, and she moved to cover her chest, pressing her forearm against her naked breasts. Looking up at me with nothing but want, she was a vision. Her long waves cascading over her tiny frame, chest rising and falling, completely bare to me. *I must sear this picture into my mind.*

There will be another opportunity for that, Parker. Focus on the task at hand. Shaking my head with a rueful smile, I grabbed her nightie and gathered the fabric into my hands. Gently, I tugged the pajamas over her head and helped her slip her arms through the straps. Propping her pillows up, I twisted her legs under the covers and tucked the sheets up around her waist.

"Drink up," I instructed as I removed the cap and passed LB a water bottle. She smiled softly and accepted, taking several gulps.

162

"Thank you, Parker. For everything. You really are sweeter than cherry pie."

She settled down into the bed, fluffing her pillows, pulling the covers up around her chin, and peering up at me.

"You don't need to thank me, spitfire." *It's me who should thank you. Allowing me to continue to exist in your presence should necessitate my thanks.*

"But I do. I've been nothin' but a thorn in your side. And you've been nothin' but a gentleman in return."

Her Southern is showing.

I clicked off the light beside her bed, and I felt her hand clasp mine. My heart squeezed in reply.

"You're staying, right? You have to stay, you have nowhere else to go."

"That's sweet of you, but you should really get your sleep, spitfire. You need your rest."

"I'll sleep better if I know you're not sleepin' on the streets because of me. Stay." LB exhaled as she closed her eyes.

"Alright Laura Beth, whatever you want," I conceded. *Whatever you want, spitfire.*

I slipped out of my jacket and tie, unbuttoning my shirt and sliding out of my shoes and pants. I settled into bed beside Laura Beth, and she rolled to form her curves perfectly against my side. Her head laid against my pec and her exposed thigh draped over mine. *How fucking perfect she fits.*

Stroking her shoulder softly, I stared up at the ceiling and pondered her earlier words, *"You've been nothing but a gentleman."* Had I? Had I really shown her a modicum of the respect a woman like her deserved?

I didn't need to ponder long, I knew the answer was no. Laura Beth Calhoun deserved so much more than I had given her. If I wanted her for more than just the fun we'd had–and I did, I really fucking did–I needed to do better. I needed to show her exactly who I was and why I deserved a spot in her bed and in her life. Not just on business trips and not just on drunken, sex-fueled nights. Permanently.

As I luxuriated surrounded by LB's warmth, a plan began to form.

Chapter 21

LB

Five more minutes.

I needed five more minutes under the hot water of the shower to, hopefully, wash away the embarrassment and regret I felt over last night.

I had woken to a dry mouth, a pounding headache, and an empty bed an hour before. Parker must've slipped out once I fell asleep, but not before leaving me with a water bottle, pain reliever tablets, and a cryptic note on my bedside table:

> *Spitfire—don't punish yourself. Take the tablets and drink all the water. I'll be seeing you very soon.*
>
> *xx Parker*

While I had wanted to be angry at his bossy tone, I knew I couldn't justifiably direct any of my frustrations at Parker. I was entirely responsible for both the pounding headache and the embarrassment I was experiencing. So, I grumbled before tossing back the water and medicine.

Shutting off the shower, I stepped out of the stall, wrapping a towel around my frame. Detangling my locks, I wondered about the rest of Parker's note. "I'll be seeing you very soon." What did that mean? Had we talked about meeting again? *Not that I could recall.*

Last night was, for the most part, accounted for. I remembered drowning my overwhelming feelings at the bar after my dinner with Dr. Gaspar and Parker. Then Parker found me and escorted me back to my room. I remember inviting him in, hoping we would continue what we had started in the elevator and escalated at the dinner table earlier that night. My drunken logic had said that if I had already indulged, I might as well have my fill. Instead, Parker treated me like an injured bird, all soft hands and precision, as he helped me out of my clothes and into bed. I had been the one to encourage him to stay, and even then, he only held me before I fell asleep.

I didn't know what to make of any of it, because it all felt a little too real and heartfelt. So, I decided to do the only thing I could at that moment: put those discomforting thoughts and feelings into that little box inside my mind and set it aside to consider later. Preferably when I didn't feel like I was on the verge of death.

I had a flight to catch and a deal to secure.

————

"Good morning, beautiful. Glad to see you made it out of bed."

Walking into the departures terminal an hour later, my head snapped to the voice calling from the curb beside me. There was Parker, looking far better than he had any right to look, leaning casually against a blacked out SUV. His dark locks were arranged in perfectly sculpted waves across his tanned forehead, with the beginnings of stubble accentuating his sharp jawline.

He looked like he stepped right out of a men's fashion magazine, and not at all like someone who crashed for a couple of hours in a woman's hotel room. *What the fuck.*

Spinning my luggage, I marched in his direction. "Parker, what are you doing out here? Were you waiting on me?"

Ignoring my questions, he leaned down and placed a chaste kiss on my cheek before taking the handle of my rolling luggage. "Here, let me get that for you." *Okay, cool...but also, what the actual fuck?*

Parker turned towards the vehicle, handing my suitcase over to the SUV's driver.

"Hold on a second, I'm heading inside. I'm on the 10:15 flight, I don't have time to go somewhere with you–"

"Calm down spitfire, I'll get you back to the Bay," he chuckled. Opening the car door, he motioned his hand for me to get in. "Hop in, and I promise I'll explain."

I rubbed my temples, not having the brain capacity to sort out what this game was about. I did trust he was being true to his word, and I'd make my flight, so I played along and climbed into the vehicle.

Sliding into the seat beside me, Parker unbuttoned his suit jacket and set those caramel eyes on me. *Seriously, how the fuck does he look so good? Didn't he crash in my room?*

"LB, did you hear me?"

Nope, not a word, sorry. My brain is incapable of multi-tasking right now, and I was lost in your eyes.

"Sorry, no. What was that?"

He grinned, turning more in his seat to face me. "I was just asking you how you're feeling. For someone pint-sized, you sure can hold your liquor. Are you doing okay?"

"Well, let's just say growing up in Pike Road, I was already well acquainted with Jack and Johnny by the time I reached legal drinking age. Champagne is tame by comparison." Laying my head against the seat, I said, "But to answer your question, my mouth feels like I just sucked a polished boot, my head is throbbing, and I feel drier than a corn husk."

Parker winced in reaction and reached his hand over my forehead, sweeping his fingers down and holding my face in his hand. Looking down at me with sympathy, he nodded.

"Right, that's about what I thought you'd say...albeit with less colorful metaphors. I did try to get you to hydrate last night but was worried you'd be in some pain today, regardless." Glancing out his window, he opened his door and continued, "Hopefully, this will help a little."

Looking out the open door, I noticed we were still at the airfield, just in a different area I'd never seen before from the main terminal. And we were literally on the tarmac–the SUV was parked just a stone's throw from the runway.

I opened my mouth to ask Parker what we were doing when he cut me off, wagging his fingers to direct me to follow him out of the SUV. "Come on spitfire, we've got a crew waiting on us."

"Good morning Mr. Brooks, Ms. Calhoun," a pilot nodded in greeting to us as I stepped out. *Huh?*

Before I could ask any questions, Parker took my hand and led me up the waiting jet's small stairs.

Entering the plane, a gray-haired flight attendant greeted me with a warm smile. "I can take that bag for you, Ms. Calhoun. There's still and sparkling water at your seat, but please let me know if I can get you champagne or anything else."

"We're all set, James, thank you. We won't be needing you for the flight, so feel free to have a seat and read your book," Parker said, patting the man's shoulder in acknowledgement.

Parker led me to two leather seats facing one another and motioned for me to sit down.

Dropping into the seat with a huff, I couldn't hold back the dam any longer. The questions burst out of me. "Parker, what in God's name is all of this? Is this how Athena treats all their Senior Associates? Why the hell have you been flying commercial for the past few months?!"

Laughing, he slid out of his suit jacket, laying it over the sofa to our left, before taking the seat opposite me. He draped his arm over the seat next to his and leaned back, taking a good look at me, before he shrugged slightly.

"No one should have to suffer commercial air travel hungover. That's just cruel," he replied nonchalantly.

I scoffed at the preposterous notion people had alternatives.

Crossing my arms, I threw another question his way. "So, what—you can just pick and choose when you use Athena's jet? That seems a bit excessive for someone so junior."

"LB, why are you so preoccupied with my transportation? Can't you just see this as one friend helping another friend in need?"

"Because it doesn't make any sense, Parker!" I winced, my headache pulsing. I did not have the energy or brain power for that conversation. "And anyway, since when did we become friends?"

His eyes flashed as he leaned toward me, and his voice dropped to a near-growl. "Well, spitfire, I'd say the moment you wrapped those perfect thighs around my head felt pretty friendly."

Fucking hell. I could feel the impact of his words in my core, as though my nerve endings had their own memory of just how talented Parker was. As I shifted in discomfort, his eyes darted to my thighs and his lips twitched up in a smirk.

"If that doesn't qualify as 'friendly' enough for you, though, I'd say tucking you into bed and ignoring my raging hard cock simply to hold you last night certainly should," he raised his gaze to mine slowly as he spoke, as though he was

ASHLEY JACOBS & S. S. RICH

trailing his touch up my body with nothing more than his eyes.

He raised one eyebrow at me and tilted his head in challenge. I gulped and ran my sweaty hands along my thighs as I tried to unscramble my brain.

"I stand corrected," I mumbled, my voice wavering.

The heat rushing through me was overwhelming. I had never met someone who could light me up with just his words and the intimate drag of his gaze. I felt like putty in Parker's hands, and it terrified me as much as it warmed me through.

"Thank you," I said finally, meeting Parker's intense hazel gaze. "For taking care of me, I mean. I...I needed that, last night."

His expression softened, and he nodded. "I could tell. Want to talk about it?"

I chuckled, shaking my head in awe. "You're something else, Parker Brooks."

"I may have heard that a time a two," he said with a boyish grin, "but tell me why *you* think so, LB. I want to know more about what goes on in that brilliant brain of yours."

This man. This beautiful, thoughtful man. He seemed just as interested in my mind as my body, just as resolute in supporting me as a person as he was in pursuing my pleasure.

"Last night, Parker...," my voice trailed off, and I glanced out the window briefly, gathering my scattered emotions into something coherent. I turned back to face him, my expression vulnerable. "Last night was a lot."

He nodded, slowly, "It was."

"I don't know if you've noticed," I gave him a wry little smile, "but I'm...I like to be in control."

He returned my smile in kind. "I've noticed."

I huffed a laugh. "My sister teases me for it endlessly; it's just who I am. I've always had a plan. But with you...," I held his gaze in mine, "with you, Parker, I feel like chaos personified. You turn me inside out and encourage and inspire me to do things I never would've imagined a few months ago."

His expression was kind, open. "And how do you feel about the things I've inspired you to do, spitfire?"

I breathed in slowly as I let myself drown in his attention. "Caught. Untethered," I said on a sigh. "I feel conflicted."

"There's a lot to unpack there," he said earnestly. "Look, beautiful, I know none of this is easy for you. I've seen how hard you work—how much of yourself you pour into what you do and the people you do it with. How many people pour that same effort into you?"

I'd never felt more like an open book than I did in that moment. "To be honest, Parker...I don't know. Before you, I didn't know what that felt like."

His expression suggested he was a little proud of us both for this conversation. "And now that you do know, what do you want?"

Heat flared through me as I considered his words. I knew what I wanted in that moment—I was staring right at him, soaking up every emotion written on his handsome face. But what would it cost me to give in? What would it cost to give myself to a man like Parker Brooks? I could almost see my carefully architected future crumbling under the weight of his attention, his intensity. It was so tempting to give in to that fantasy, to the real life man before me. But how long would I remain his focus?

As if he could read me, Parker gave me a warm smile to break the tension. "That's not something you need to answer in this moment, spitfire. But I do want to hear your answer someday."

I nodded, a grateful smile on my lips even as the tightness in my chest persisted. "Someday," I echoed.

"For now," he continued, "I'd like to propose a truce."

I blinked at him. "A truce."

"Indeed. You and I have been enjoying being one another's competition, but I'd like to put the pranks and teasing aside."

"Okay," I said, slowly, drawing the word out. "Is this a permanent truce, or...?"

He grinned. "I thought you might balk at that, honestly, so what if you gave me the weekend?"

"That sounds doable," I said. "It's not like I expect to see you much on the weekend, anyway." I gave him a teasing wink.

"Well, you might find this weekend different than most, spitfire."

What are you up to, Mr. Brooks? I arched my eyebrow at him, deciding I couldn't miss an opportunity to tease. "Are you going to explain that cryptic statement, sir?"

The effect that word had on him was palpable. He stiffened, his tongue darting out to swipe at his lower lip.

"Call me that again tomorrow," he rumbled, his voice deep and growly as he leaned towards me, "when I can do something about it."

Um, yes, please. I'd like to order a time machine.

His answering grin was downright feral. "I'll pick you up around eleven. That should give you enough time to recover from the week and get ready, yes?"

"Y-yes," I agreed, that feeling of overwhelm simmering under the surface. "What should I wear?"

"Something comfortable," he answered quickly, settling back into his seat.

"Really leaning into the crypticness today, hm? First a note, then a surprise ride in a private jet, now a secret date..."

"Sometimes it's better to be surprised. Let me be the one in control for once, hm?"

I didn't know if the quaking I felt in my core in response to that statement was fear or desire. Possibly a heady combination of both, if I was honest.

"And after this weekend, back to the competition?" I pushed.

His gaze heated again. "I love it when you fight me, LB," he said, his voice rough. "After this weekend, you keep fighting me all you want. Just don't walk away."

His voice quieted at the end of his statement, almost as though he didn't intend to speak it loud. Something warm settled in my chest in that moment, something that felt significant and new and precious. Something I was afraid to acknowledge fully.

I pulled my phone from my purse and pulled up Parker's contact, changing his name quickly. I peeked up at him as I did, finding his attention on the window. I joined the plane's open wifi network and sent him a quick message.

> Me: One weekend, then back to it. I'm in.

I attached a screenshot of the change I'd just made. I looked over at him again and caught his indecent smirk as he read my text. His reply was swift.

> Parker: Good girl.

Chapter 22

LB

"Girl, you look cute!" Maya gasped from my bedroom door.

I whirled around in surprise and smiled at her. "You're alive!"

She laughed and nodded, hitching her messenger bag up on her shoulder. "Sure am. Alive and headed out the door in a second. What did you break out your cute jeans for?"

"I have a date. I think," I muttered, turning back to the mirror.

I'd gone for something simple and comfortable, per Parker's suggestion. My good jeans, as Maya had recognized, an over-sized sweater, and flats.

"You *think* you have a date?" she grinned at me. "Girl, you have the best stories. Can't wait to hear this one! But it might have to be over text," she grimaced, "I picked up a couple doubles from a friend."

I grimaced right back at her. "You need a break, hon."

"Tell me about it," she said as she rolled her eyes in exagger-ated agreement. "Enjoy the date, cutie!"

She spun away and was out the door moments later. I had

ARRIVED

no idea what to expect from the day, but I was doing my best to honor Parker's request and let him be in control. As I grabbed my crossbody bag and slung it over my head, I heard a knock at the door. I raced over to it, expecting Maya looking for her keys (an admittedly frequent occurrence).

"Oh!" I gasped, looking up in Parker's bright hazel eyes, "You're not Maya."

He grinned at me. "Not last I checked, no."

"How'd you get in the building?"

"A woman in scrubs held the door for me," he said with a smirk. "I mentioned I was picking someone up for a date and she said, and I quote, 'that bitch better not leave out any details', and waved me up."

I laughed and shook my head. "Sounds like Maya. Did you want to come in?"

I stepped back to let him in, but Parker just crowded me into the wall of my entry and slowly pushed the door closed behind him.

"I've missed you," he murmured, pressing his body flush to mine.

I made a helpless little gasping noise and looked up to meet his gaze, my hands flying up to steady myself against his biceps. "You just saw me yesterday," I breathed.

"Hmmm," he hummed, pressing our foreheads together and leaning into me. "You were in work mode yesterday, all prim and proper. Today, I get the real you."

He tilted his head and pressed his lips gently to mine. Our kisses so far had been fiery, passionate things, full of heat and vigor. They lit me up inside and melted all the best parts of me. But that kiss? It was slow, languorous. He took his time before gently parting my lips with his tongue and delving inside, the weight of his body warm and hard against me, hands cupping my face. That kiss made a mockery of my

175

defenses and laid my heart bare to him, just begging to be scooped up.

"God," he breathed when our mouths parted, "I love the way you taste."

He leaned back slightly to look at me, a smile on his lips. He swiped his thumbs across my cheekbones and searched my face for a moment.

"I can't get enough of you, spitfire," he whispered.

I went up on my tiptoes and threaded my arms around his neck, tugging his lips back to mine. He groaned in appreciation and ran his hands slowly down my curves, hooking around the backs of my thighs and lifting me up. I wrapped my legs around his waist as he leaned into the wall, my body suspended. He kept one hand on my ass, supporting me and kneading the flesh, and the other found its way under my shirt to halfway up my back.

This time, as we slowly parted, I couldn't stop the grin. Parker met my energy and grinned right back.

"The feeling is mutual," I murmured, stroking my hands through his hair. *And, just for today, I'm not going to examine why those words are some of the scariest I've ever uttered.*

"Ready to go?" he asked, leaning in to place a peck on my lips again.

I nodded and shrugged my shoulder, jostling my bag. "Got my bag, good to go."

"Perfect," he said, stepping back from the wall and opening the door with one hand.

"Parker!" I laughed, still perched in his arms. "Put me down!"

"Nope," he said, letting us out of my apartment and making sure the door closed and locked. "I'm in control, remember?"

I sighed and rested my head on his shoulder. He chuckled and rubbed my back.

"It'll be a good day," he promised.

I simply nodded and held on, letting him carry me all the way down to his waiting SUV. I blinked at the car and driver as he gently set me down.

"It's the weekend."

"Yes, I know," he chuckled, opening the rear passenger door for me.

"But why does Athena let you use their car service on the weekend?"

The driver gave Parker a knowing look over his shoulder before focusing on the task at hand. Parker climbed in after me and closed the door, then reached over and buckled me in. We were off just as he did the same for himself.

"Ralph has been my driver for just about two decades," Parker said. "And he and this vehicle are not a perk from Athena."

I just blinked dumbly at him as he picked up my hand, caressing the knuckles with his thumb.

"My family has money," he explained, giving me a rueful look. "I've done everything I can to build my own wealth, but the kind of money we come from is hard to ignore."

"Okay," I said, slowly. "So, you have a car service and a dedicated driver. That's fancy."

He nodded, a delighted twinkle in his eye. "And a jet with a pilot and crew."

My jaw literally dropped. "The plane yesterday?!"

He nodded again, once.

"That's *yours*?!"

"Indeed, it is."

"Holy shit," I mumbled, eyes wide.

From the front seat, Ralph chuckled.

"Can we go back to a minute ago when you didn't know I

had a plane?" Parker asked, turning my face toward him with a gentle hand.

I shook my head. "It's impossible to forget the tiny little detail that you own a *fucking jet*, Parker."

"I see," he said, swiping a thumb across my cheekbone again. "Is it going to break your brain further to know I'm taking you out on my boat today?"

I could only stare at him for a moment before I had to look away from the perfection of his face. I gazed out the window, trying to reconcile how I was feeling. Apparently, Parker was rich. And not just "they live on the nice side of town" rich, like the fancy people back home. No, Parker was I-own-a-vehicle-trifecta-and-can-be-totally-casual-about-it *loaded*.

I glanced over at him again, finding his eyes on me. He was waiting patiently for me to process. I scoffed and shook my head.

"It's not fair."

He cocked his head at me quizzically. "What's not fair?"

"You."

"What about me?"

"You're gorgeous, and kind, and fucking huge," I said, motioning to his lap.

Ralph coughed, and I cringed. "Sorry, Ralph!"

He waved me off with another chuckle.

"And you're, like, a millionaire or something." I looked up at his amused expression and heaved a sigh. "It's not fair for just one person to have all that luck. You've gotta leave some for the rest of us!"

He smirked and shook his head. "Sorry, sweet thing, no can do. I need all the luck I can get."

I snorted. "Oh yeah? Why? Need another million dollars?"

He growled playfully at me and I pretended it didn't make

my panties wet. He leaned in close to whisper directly into my ear.

"Actually, spitfire, I need you," he teased, before placing a warm, soft kiss on my throat.

Tingles radiated out from the spot and I leaned into him, breathing in his scent, all salty air and man.

"I bet you say that to all the girls," I murmured back, giving him a teasing look, "when you take them out to your boat and impress them with your fancy self."

"The only girl I've brought out to see *Moira Leigh* is my sister," he said, a soft smile cast my way.

"Oh," I breathed, processing that. I didn't think for a moment he was lying, but the weight of those words and what they could imply sat heavy in my chest. "Who's Moira?"

"My grandmother," he said. "The boat was my grandfather's. He bought it when they were both young and it's been in the family ever since. He named it after her."

"That's beautiful, Parker."

He nodded. "It is. Grandfather gave me the boat in his will, made sure I got it directly. He used to bring me out here every weekend and sometimes during the week if I needed a break from...everything."

There was something in his words that suggested a story was lurking, but I didn't press. Parker had always given me space, and I would certainly return the favor.

"He taught you how to...uh...go boating?"

Parker's chuckle filled every corner of the car. "He taught me how to sail, yes, spitfire."

A sailboat. I'd never been on a sailboat before. There wasn't much call for them in Pike Road, Alabama, and I'd never had the funds to pay for a ride on one since I'd moved to the Bay. The ocean had always seemed like this great, blue, ethereal thing to me. I wasn't sure of my place in the world on dry land, much less amongst the shimmering waters of the Bay.

Ralph pulled up to the marina ramp and parked, then rounded the SUV to get something from the back. Parker opened the door for us and slipped out, offering me his hand as I stepped from the vehicle. I took it gratefully, and he threaded our fingers together and refused to let go. And he received no complaints from me about that.

"Thanks, Ralph," he said to his driver, taking the picnic basket he held out.

"Of course, Mr. Brooks. Enjoy your sail."

"We will," he replied with a smile, tugging me closer and releasing my hand to throw his arm around my shoulders.

I gave Ralph a smile and wave before allowing Parker to steer me down the ramp and out onto the dock. We were surrounded by beautiful boats of all sizes–some small speed-boats and others large yachts. It was like a foreign land, being this close to something I had only seen from the city.

"She's just in that slip up there," he said, motioning with a picnic basket to a boat just a few slips down.

When we drew near, I gasped in appreciation. "My good-ness, Parker, it's gorgeous."

"She's a beauty alright," he said with a cheeky grin, drawing me forward.

A young man jumped off the side of the boat with a respectful smile and nod. "Hi there, Mr. Brooks. She's all ready for you."

"Thanks, Sam."

"Will you be wanting a deckhand today, sir?"

Parker glanced down at me and winked. "Nah, I've got one." He squeezed me closer to him and I giggled, throwing my arm around his waist.

"Good deal, sir. I'll just help you untie and set off."

"Perfect. Let me get this lovely lady settled and we'll be good to go."

At that, Parker set the basket down on the dock, then hoisted me up as though I weighed naught more than a fly and set me down on the boat.

"Head on over near the boat's wheel, spitfire. I'll be there soon."

I moved down per his direction and watched as he and Sam moved seamlessly through the motions of preparing us to leave. It was clear they were both well practiced in their tasks and in working together, each moving with a surety and trust in the other that was apparent. After scant minutes, Sam stepped back and gave a small wave as Parker settled behind the wheel. He turned to look at me over his shoulder with a grin.

"Ready?"

"Born ready, sugar. Show me the real you."

His answering grin made my knees feel like jelly, and I wondered for a brief moment if he'd ever stop having that effect on me. *God, I hope not.*

As we left the marina for open water, I watched in awe at the city and land we left behind. I'd never seen this view of the Bay before. And as impressed as I was by the landscape before us, I had a hard time keeping my eyes off of Parker. He commanded the helm with a calm confidence that had me feeling some kind of way. The corded muscles in his forearms bunched as he turned the wheel, his biceps straining the soft material of his fitted tee. He looked just as casual as I did today, in a simple black t-shirt and jeans, with a zip up jacket tossed by the picnic basket at my feet.

"You look so at home up there," I called from my perch behind him.

He glanced back at me and motioned me forward. I went willingly, slipping in front of him as he made room for me in the cage of his arms. He wrapped one arm around my upper chest from behind.

"Lean against me," he urged, releasing me when I obeyed and returning his grip to the wheel. "Let me show you my kingdom."

I sighed happily and snuggled against him, loving the feeling of being caged in by his arms and warmed through from the heat of his body.

"Can you swim?" he asked, as though it had been an intrusive thought.

"I can," I nodded. "There was a swimmin' hole the kids all played at in the summer, though God knows what was in it. It wasn't big or deep, and it was brown and muddy as all heck, but we made the most of it."

I could feel him smile against my hair. "I like picturing you in a swimmin' hole, spitfire. I bet you looked real cute, even if you were muddy."

I snorted a laugh and shook my head. "You hold on to that mental picture. I promise it wasn't idyllic. We were poor kids with little to occupy us but our imaginations. There were no bikinis or bathing suits, just a bunch of rowdy heathens in their underwear."

He stepped closer and released the wheel with one hand to wrap it around my waist, his palm flat against my stomach.

"You went swimming with boys in your underwear?" he asked, a growl in his voice.

I laughed outright, playfully swatting at his hand as it flexed against me to hold me in place. "I was ten, Parker! It wasn't what you're thinking. We were scrawny little things, finding somewhere to have fun. By the time any of us knew what a crush felt like, we were too old to enjoy the swimmin' hole."

He hummed a noncommittal response and pressed me tighter against him, his thumb stroking gently under my ribs and his pinky dipping to find the skin bared above my jeans. The sheer size of his hand on me made me feel small and dainty, like he could surround and consume me all at once. I was surprised by how much I liked that notion and squeezed my thighs together in response to the wetness I felt gathering.

Parker bent his head down and kissed the side of my neck, hugging me against him. "I'm going to drop the sails here in a bit and we can have lunch."

"Sounds perfect," I answered absently, running one hand up behind me to wrap around behind his neck, stroking through his longish hair.

I wasn't sure what heaven looked like, exactly, but I suspected it looked and felt and smelled a lot like being wrapped up in Parker Brooks while drifting on the ocean. *This is it, Laura Beth. You've peaked.*

"What's going through that brilliant mind of yours, Laura Beth?" Parker asked, his voice in my ear before he peppered more kisses along my neck and cheek.

"Did you know you're perfect?" I sighed. "Perfect Parker. It's kind of hard to believe."

"Oh? Why's that?" he asked, before shifting to give attention to my other side.

I squeezed the base of his neck in appreciation, holding him to me, and he hummed a pleased sound that traveled along my skin to tease my nipples to attention.

"Boys like you are only real in fairytales," I explained. "They rescue the princess so she doesn't have to worry about anything ever again, sweeping her off her feet and straight to the palace she deserves."

"Hmmm, sounds nice." He stood straight once more to focus on sailing, his hand never leaving its place on my stomach.

"Sure, but...I never believed those stories," I continued. "Life doesn't work like that. There's no magic wand to swipe your worries away, and most men you might think are princes are really villains in disguise. Even as a kid, I knew enough about life to know that happily ever afters weren't real. Weddings aren't the end of any story. Relationships are work, and no amount of doing the right thing can build you a ladder out of poverty if you're in it deep enough."

I dropped my hand from his neck and turned around in his hold to face him, wrapping my arms around his waist as his hand stroked and soothed along my back.

"Life isn't a fairytale, Parker." I looked up at him to find his gaze on mine. "There's no magic wand, no true love's kiss. It's hard work and dedication and sacrifice and compromise, over and over again until you retire or die."

"Gettin' a little bleak, there, sweet thing."

I nodded. "I know. But that's the thing—my outlook on life and dating has been pretty bleak for a long time. I got to witness epic love between my parents, but they still struggled to make ends meet until I started sending them money—they didn't know a single moment of relaxation for years. And my sister found her soulmate before she hit puberty. She wanted to be a nurse, but as their relationship got more serious, Dex's dreams of owning his own business became more important and she stayed home to raise the kids."

I shook my head, then continued, "They're ridiculously happy, all of them. But their lives look nothing like the life I wanted as a kid, nothing like the life I envision for myself even now." I searched his gaze. "I've dated off and on for years, but not once did I feel like love and the future I envisioned could coexist in my reality. Not one single time." I traced a finger along his jawline, appreciating the rough scratch of his stubble against my skin. "But, now, perfect Parker," I teased, "here you are."

He dropped his hand slightly to the hem of my sweater,

then snuck it under the fabric to press to the bare skin of my back.

"And what has meeting me done to how you look at the world?"

"I thought perfect was a myth they told us to push us toward something we could never achieve, so we'd never stop trying," I said. I rested a palm against his cheek and he leaned into the touch, hugging me to him as he did. "Now, I'm starting to think perfect just might be real. And I'm looking right at him." *And I'm scared shitless of what that means for me.*

Parker released the wheel altogether and cupped my face in his hands, his eyes boring into mine with hot intensity.

"You've changed my outlook on something too, Laura Beth."

"I have?"

"Mmhm," he nodded. "I thought the love story my grandfather told me about him and my grandmother was something fantastical and only real through the haze of poor memory. You're so lucky to have seen it in your family, but I've never seen two people in love like he claimed they were, never witnessed something that deep and beautiful firsthand." He stroked his thumbs along my cheekbones and studied me. "But when I look at you, spitfire....there's nothing I want to believe in more. Nothing."

I surged up onto my tiptoes and pressed my lips to his. I didn't know what was ahead for us, but I thought in that moment that I wanted it. Wanted him. Wanted every second he'd give me through this truce and maybe beyond, and that thought scared me as much as it made my heart soar.

Parker moaned into my mouth and squatted slightly to wrap his arms around me and lift me up. I coiled my legs around his waist and devoured his mouth, digging my fingers into his luscious dark hair and letting myself drown in the overwhelming presence and feeling of him. His fingers dug into my flesh as he gripped my ass, and I silently wished they'd bruise. I wanted a reminder of him to follow me into the week, to keep this magical experience on the water close. I could feel his arousal between us, pressing against the juncture of my thighs, and I almost moaned at the sensation.

"You are everything," he breathed against my lips. "Everything I didn't hope could exist. Everything I was too afraid to want." He panted a bit as he held me fiercely to him. "Tell me you feel that, too?" he asked, a vulnerability in his voice that sliced to the heart of me and nestled in deep. "Tell me it's not just me."

"It's not just you, Parker," I whispered, cupping his face in my hands and meeting his gaze. "I'm right here with you."

"Stay with me, then?" he breathed. "Please?"

The open want and hope and longing in his gaze was more than I could take. I melted against him and crushed our lips together again, holding him as if I'd never let go. And as I did, I worried deep down that I may never want to. That I may just be tempted to let this man keep me, deal and promotion and future be damned.

Chapter 23

LB

After we poured our souls out to each other and made out for a while, Parker had opened up his picnic basket to reveal champagne, a charcuterie board with all the fixin's, and chocolate-covered strawberries. We had eaten our fill and cruised around a bit on the open ocean before returning to the Bay as the sun hung heavy in the sky.

"We have reservations at seven," Parker announced as he maneuvered the *Moira Leigh* toward his slip. "Why don't you go check out the bedroom below deck. I'll be down in a few."

The wink he gave me as he spoke suggested mischief afoot, and I grinned. As Parker and Sam called to one another and worked to coordinate the docking, I slipped down the stairs and wandered through the living area of the boat. It was more modern than I had imagined it would be, clearly updated since Parker's grandfather had originally purchased it. I walked slowly into the bedroom and couldn't stop my smile.

There, waiting for me on the bed, were three boxes. I reached out and lightly touched the one on the left, instantly recognizing the iconic color that symbolized one of my favorite jewelry stores. The next box had a bow partially obscuring the name "Louboutin," but I had no doubt about what was concealed within.

Just before I could open the third box to explore the goodies, I heard Parker come up behind me. He looped his arms around my waist and stooped to rest his chin on my shoulder.

"So, what do you think?" he asked, and I could hear the grin in his voice.

"I think you might enjoy spoiling me, Mr. Brooks," I teased.

He groaned and buried his face against my neck. "My cock really likes it when you call me that," he mumbled against my skin.

I laughed and nuzzled back against him, feeling the evidence of his statement against the top of my ass. "Better than...sir?"

I could feel said cock twitch against me, and I cackled, enjoying my effect on him far too much.

"I can't wait to get you to my apartment, spitfire," he growled in my ear, before nipping my earlobe. "You can call me that again while you're on your knees for me."

"Yes, please," I breathed, desire raw in my voice. My panties were a lost cause at this point, and I really hoped the last box on the bed contained lingerie.

"I hate to leave you wanting, but I have to go change, too," he said with a rueful smirk. "I'll be in the galley, but you can use the bedroom and bathroom to get ready. You'll find makeup in the bathroom if you want it."

I wrinkled my nose. "Oh, that's okay. It's not great to share that kind of thing."

Parker raised an eyebrow at me. "It's all new, spitfire. Bought it for you."

I gaped at him, then rushed to peek into the bathroom. "How did you know what I used?!"

He shrugged when I glanced back at him, that boyish grin I

was starting to love—*oh, shit, you did not just think that*—on his lips. "I've been left alone with your luggage a few too many times, spitfire. And I pay attention."

"Well, that's cute *and* stalkery, so I'm conflicted on how to respond."

He laughed. "A 'thank you' would work, you know."

"Yeah, not sure you deserve one, though," I teased, wrinkling my nose at him. "Creep factor might outweigh the gratitude."

He pinched, then swatted, my ass as I yelped and tried to dance out of reach. "You're lucky we have a reservation. Get that fine ass ready!"

I giggled and danced away. "Okay, okay!"

He paused partway down the hall and looked back at me. "Save the blue one for last," he instructed. "I want to see you open it. And help you put it on."

I could feel my heart and gaze going gooey in response, and I simply nodded to save myself from the embarrassment of my voice cracking during my reply. He flashed me one last perfect smile, and I shut the bedroom door.

Feeling light as a feather, I ignored the gorgeous packages on the bed and slipped into the bathroom to freshen up in the tiny shower. I kept it quick, twisting my hair up in a towel to keep it dry. After I stepped out, I used the selection of face creams and makeup on the bathroom counter. I fluffed my hair and smiled briefly at my reflection, appreciating the soft smoky eye and bold red lip I'd chosen. I may have had the soles of a particularly gorgeous pair of stilettos in mind when I picked it out.

I let myself back into the bedroom, towel wrapped tight around me. I opened the big black box nearest me and gasped in delight at the soft, delicate lace awaiting me beneath the lid. Nestled in tissue branded "La Perla" was a black balconette bra and lacy matching thong. I'd never seen underwear that pretty, or fabric that luxe, in my life. I quickly dropped my towel and shimmied into the skimpy garments, loving the soft glide of them against my skin. I peeked over at myself in the mirror and grinned. I don't know that I'd ever felt that confident in just my underthings, but I sure loved the feeling.

I eyed the Louboutin box. I had the overwhelming urge to put on the surely gorgeous shoes that were inside and take a moment to appreciate myself in nothing but lingerie and a pair of fuck-me pumps. Giving in, I snatched up the box and nearly squealed in delight at the stunning black patent leather peep-toe heels that awaited inside. They had a unique scalloped edge at the heel and gave me a solid 5" boost in height. I slipped them on, surprised at how well they fit, and peered at my reflection in the full-length mirror on the back of the bedroom door.

Well, fuck me, Laura Beth. You look like sex on legs.

I smiled at myself and examined the angles, nearly ready to give up on dinner altogether and let Parker ravish me on the boat instead. But my thoughts flashed to that little blue box, and I knew I had to get going. I went back over and dug under the tissue to find a simple red cocktail dress.

The designer label told me this dress may have cost more than my rent this month, and I blinked a few times as I stared at it in my hands. I'd never even shopped in stores that carried designer merchandise, and here I was—decked head to toe and wearing things that cost more than my rent, loan payments, and monthly grocery budget, combined.

I slipped into the red dress and smoothed it over my hips, appreciating the buttery feel of the fabric. It was a simple sleeveless cut with a low scoop neck and a fitted bodice that hugged me perfectly. At my knees, it flared into a flouncy skirt that hung slightly higher in the front. It was sexy and sophisticated, and I felt every inch the billionaire's date.

Just as I reached back to zip it up, Parker tapped lightly on the door and let himself in. He froze when he saw me, eyes blazing as he took me in.

"Goddamn, spitfire," he breathed, "you are a fucking vision in red."

I smiled at him and swished my hips back and forth, enjoying the flounce of the skirt. "You like?"

"Oh, I like," he growled, prowling around to come behind me.

He settled his hands on my hips as he watched me in the mirror, his expression fierce. Slowly, he trailed his fingers toward the zipper, which started just at the top of my ass. He pinched the material at the bottom gently in his fingers, then slowly pulled the zipper up, his fingertips trailing along my skin as he did. I felt goosebumps rise across my body, and I couldn't help but shiver.

He stepped up against me after he finished clasping the hook at the top of the zipper, running his palms across my shoulders and down my arms.

"Look at you, Laura Beth," he said reverently. "You are simply exquisite."

Before I could gather myself enough to say anything in return, he leaned toward the bed and snagged the blue box. He opened it quickly behind me, where I couldn't see.

"Now, for the icing," he announced, casting a quick smirk my way via the mirror as he fiddled with something.

He brought his hands up and over my head, then settled something cool and sparkly at the base of my throat. I gasped in surprise as I caught sight of the pendant in the mirror, my fingers settling on it gently to keep it in place while he clasped it.

"I saw it and immediately thought of you and your beautiful bluebell eyes, spitfire. I don't know what Monday will bring after our truce, but I wanted you to have something to keep with you. Something to remind you of sun on the waves and swim-min' holes full of mud and the feeling you have when you're exactly where you need to be."

His warm hands settled on my shoulders and stroked my upper arms. He squeezed his hands gently, watching my face as he continued.

"I hope you wear it every day," he murmured. "And every day, I hope you remember where you came from and all you've accomplished to get where you are. You have so much ahead of you, spitfire. Don't forget to enjoy the journey on the way, hm?"

"Stop and smell the bluebells," I breathed, my fingers still resting on the circular pendant at my throat.

I dropped my hand and gasped again. On one edge of the circle rested six gorgeous sapphires on a stem. They looked just like the bluebells back home, with a near perfect color match for my eyes. I whirled around and flung my arms around Parker, holding him tight.

"Thank you," I whispered, overcome.

He wrapped strong arms around me, enveloping me in his scent and strength. The mere presence of this man was enough to steal a woman's breath, but like this? To feel him curve his large frame around me wholly and completely? It was enough to transport me to another plane. One where I was safe, secure, and cherished. One where the thought that I just might be falling for this man didn't feel scary. It felt right. It felt...inevitable.

Parker held me for a few minutes, his arms strong around me and his hands soothing as he rubbed my back. If we'd stayed that way any longer, I have no doubt the long, slow touches would've soon turned into something significantly less innocent.

With a reluctant sigh, Parker released me and stepped back, his hands still resting on my waist.

"You ready, beautiful?" he asked.

"Ready for what, exactly?"

"Well, you told me about your dream date during our first conversation. And I thought it was high time someone took you on it." He smiled, reaching out to tuck a stray lock of hair behind my ear.

My heart made a funny little thump in my chest, as though it was tripping over itself in its rush to fall for Parker Brooks.

"Dinner and dancing?" I asked, my voice wavering.

"The very same," he confirmed. "Come on, spitfire. Let's make the most of tonight."

———

As it turned out, Parker had indeed provided me with the absolute best date of my life. He'd started the night by taking me to a delightfully cozy restaurant that offered a bespoke six course tasting menu for only a handful of guests every night. To my astonishment, he'd reserved the whole place just for us.

"I wanted you to myself, Laura Beth," he'd said in response to my surprised reaction, and I swear I nearly melted into the floor.

After what I will always remember as the single best meal of my life, he swept me off again to a little hole in the wall Latin bar. Hidden behind a random red door in an otherwise nondescript alley, the basement venue was pulsing with energy. I wasn't sure what to expect from Parker in that environment, but he'd just winked at me and pulled me into the middle of the dance floor.

"Do you dance, Mr. Brooks?" I'd asked with a teasing look.

"Necessary education for all good little rich boys, Ms. Calhoun," he'd answered with a wink.

He'd then all but dominated me on the dance floor, leading me through seamless and very sexy renditions of the salsa, cha

cha, and tango. We'd paused only for a few drinks and some water, laughing with and clinging to each other in turn.

Then, he'd whisked me just down the street to a dive bar with sticky floors and music that was far too loud. I'd ordered a PBR tall boy and nearly chugged it, much to his delight, and we'd laughed together as we watched the characters that patronized the tiny establishment.

When the night had finally started to settle, we'd emerged from the bar to find Ralph and the SUV waiting at the curb.

"Ralph! Does this man ever give you a night off?!" I'd asked, casting a teasingly accusatory look at Parker.

"He's tried a few times, Ms. Calhoun, but I don't let him," he'd responded with a wink, before gently closing the door behind us.

Now, I was staring at Parker from across the elevator, on our way up to his place in the city. Because he had a place in the city. One that was in addition to the Palo Alto apartment he'd told me about before. *Of course he does, Laura Beth. He's a freaking billionaire.* I might've been freaking out more over Parker's wealth if the revelation of his second, more expensive, ritzier home hadn't come up after an entire day of being treated like a billionaire's girlfriend. And if he didn't look so goddamn good in the black on black suit he'd been wearing all evening. *Did his tailor make a mold of his body? That thing fits like a second skin.*

His hazel eyes were swimming with lust, drink, and no small amount of desire. I wasn't sure why we'd put so much space between us, exactly...but I had the suspicion that if I crossed the chasm I'd be devoured. *Sounds like a good time, Laura Beth. Get on that shit.*

Before I could heed my conscience, the elevator door slid open to reveal Parker's penthouse. It was enormous, with a sweeping open floor plan that emphasized the wall of floor to ceiling windows straight ahead. The floors were a warm, rich hardwood that provided contrast to the white walls and ceilings. I caught a glimpse of what was clearly a chef's kitchen, all done in white with a dark countertop and a massive range, before the twinkling lights of the city and the deep black of the bay beyond stole my attention.

"Oh my god," I breathed, moving toward the windows as though compelled by the stunning view. "Parker, this is..."

My voice trailed off to nothing as I took in the sparkling city and imagined how grand it would look in full daylight. I could feel and hear Parker a few paces behind me, letting me lead. I turned abruptly and pushed right up into his space.

"This place is gorgeous." I reached up to wind my arms around his neck, my fingers twining in his hair. "But you... Parker Brooks, you are incredible."

Parker wound his arms around my waist and leaned his forehead down to rest against mine.

"I have news for you, Laura Beth Calhoun," he breathed.

He was so close I could almost taste his words. His breath fanned over my lips, and I wanted nothing more than to surround myself with him.

"What's that?" I whispered, breathy and unashamed of my want, of the flush I felt in my cheeks.

"You deserve incredible," he said simply, as though he couldn't destroy me with three little words. His hand came up to grip the side of my neck, his thumb stroking along my jaw and cheek. "Every little thing you've dreamed up and let yourself believe you can't have, my beautiful Southern belle...you deserve every last one of them. And so much more."

I could feel the emotions welling up, sliding like prickly syrup through my chest. As my lips parted in a soft sob, Parker invaded my space, pressing his mouth to mine. I moaned, desperate to feel him everywhere. I gave in to his kiss, clutching him to me. As I rose on my tiptoes to get ever closer, he moved to lift me into his arms. I pushed back from him quickly.

"Parker, my dress," I gasped, short of breath. "I can't wrap my legs around you in this thing."

He stepped back into my space, lips millimeters from mine. "I can fix that."

He kissed me again, tongue driving into my mouth, and I grasped his shirt in my hands. I could feel his fingers at the nape of my neck, then trailing after my zipper and down my spine as he slid it open. When he reached my ass, he smoothed both hands under the material of my dress to grab two generous handfuls.

I moaned into his mouth, peeling the dress off my arms and shoving it down to my waist while keeping my lips pressed to his. Parker ended the kiss, forehead still on mine, hands still holding my ass, and chest heaving. I took a small step back, slipping from his grasp, and his fingers flexed before he let me go. I let the dress slip off my hips and pool at my feet, then gingerly stepped out from it. Just as I had in the boat, I wore nothing but the black lingerie and heels Parker had given me.

He stared at me as I walked slowly toward him, his gaze darkening with every step. I could see his cock standing at attention behind his zipped slacks, tenting the fabric. When I was nearly in front of him, he reached for me, but I dropped to my knees. I rested my hands on his hips, eyeing the bulge directly in front of my face.

"What are you doing, spitfire?" he growled, threading his fingers into my hair and gripping tightly.

"I believe you mentioned wanting to see me on my knees for you," I murmured, looking up at him behind my lashes.

"Fuck," he breathed, nostrils flaring. He swallowed roughly, then nodded. "I did indeed. I thought I mentioned tasting your honey again first."

I shook my head slowly, unbuttoning his slacks as I did.

"No?" he demanded, still holding my hair.

"No, sir," I answered, feeling heat flare through my body as his cock flexed in reaction to my words.

He released me, and I pushed his slacks off his hips, biting my lip as I revealed more of him. The man was an Adonis, all lean, chiseled muscle. I surged up and boldly licked that delicious V-line above his boxer briefs, inhaling the scent of his sweat-damp skin as I did.

"Fucking hell," Parker gasped, swaying on his feet as I kissed and licked a thorough exploration of that perfect valley.

I pulled on the waistband of his underwear, then paused, looking back up at him once more. He reached down and cupped my face in his hand, brushing his thumb along my cheekbone.

"May I, sir?" I asked, tugging gently on his waistband.

Those nostrils flared again, and he nodded, watching me intently. I pulled the elastic down and freed his straining cock, inhaling sharply at seeing it up close. Lightly kissing the tip before pushing his underwear down all the way, I enjoyed the way it bobbed, and he groaned in response. I quickly helped him out of his shoes and socks, then discarded his pants and underwear while he dropped his suit jacket and started unbuttoning his shirt.

Resettling on my knees in front of him, I reached up and wrapped my fingers around his base. His skin was smooth and silky over thick hardness, the head reaching red and angry toward his navel. I leaned in and licked a broad stripe from his balls all the way up, closing my mouth around his head when I reached it.

"Fuck, spitfire," he choked out, "that's so good."

I moaned appreciation of his praise and he cursed, fingers threading once more into my hair. Keeping one hand on him as I took as much of him into my mouth as I could, my tongue swirled around and worked his flesh. I backed off slowly, circling his crown with my tongue and paying special attention to the tight little line on the underside. Parker's hand flexed involuntarily as he moaned, his noises of appreciation urging me on. I enthusiastically took more of him into my mouth, hollowing my cheeks as I squeezed his base.

"Christ, beautiful, you look so good on your knees for me," Parker groaned. "I fucking knew you would."

I stroked him from base to tip, looking up at him as best I could with the angle and the tears that had begun. He bit his lip and cursed again, cock flexing against my throat. A look of awe joined the heat in his eyes as he stared at me, one hand fisted in my hair and the other cupped against my cheek. I worked my throat and swallowed, watching his eyes close in ecstasy as his hips thrust again involuntarily. I could feel the warmth and heat of him, could taste his pleasure and precum on my tongue. It was a heady feeling, having this powerful man at my mercy, even though I was the one on my knees.

"So close," he gasped, "spitfire, I'm right there."

Needing no further encouragement, I bobbed my head up and down on his cock, working the base once more, and sucked.

"Fuck," he breathed, "fucking hell, just like that."

His hips thrust again and I could feel him thicken against my tongue. His hand tugged gently on my hair, telling me he was on the edge, but I ignored him, intent to feel him flood my mouth. He groaned again, fingers flexing against my scalp as his cock erupted and his motion stuttered. I swallowed his cum greedily, gently sucking and licking him through his orgasm. As the pulsing stopped, I sat back on my heels and looked up at him once more. I could feel the saliva, tears, and cum on my face, and he reached out to cup my cheek.

"Such a good girl," he murmured. "You're a vision on your knees for me, spitfire."

I licked my lips and enjoyed the flash in his eyes and the twitch of his cock in response.

"Come with me." He took my hand in his and steadied me as I got to my feet. "I fucking love seeing you in the things I bought for you, Laura Beth."

"I love wearing them for you," I replied easily, meaning every word. Dinner and dancing tonight were fun, but getting on my knees in the lingerie, heels, and jewelry he'd draped me in had been the highlight of the evening. So far.

He led me to a palatial bathroom and flipped on the shower. "My turn to take care of you."

Chapter 24

LB

Not letting me focus on myself in the mirror, Parker turned me to face him and the shower. Reaching around to unhook my bra, he slowly slid it off my shoulders, tossing it aside. He pushed me back to lean against the bathroom counter, then kneeled down onto one knee to slip my shoes off.

I bit my lip as I watched him kneel for me, feeling powerful and yet helpless in his hands. Powerful that I had this gorgeous, successful man in such a position, but completely aware of my helplessness to resist him in the moment.

Standing, Parker pressed a soft kiss to my lips and molded himself against me, sinking his fingers into my hair. I held him to me, my fingers flexing against his back, losing myself in the taste of him and his cum, in the feeling of his returned hardness pressing into me. With a heavy-lidded smile, Parker leaned down to slide my thong off and helped me step out of it.

"Let me take care of you, beautiful," he murmured, as he led me to the shower and settled me under the spray.

I closed my eyes and leaned my head back, letting the water sluice away the sweat and tears. Parker stepped close and ran his fingers through my hair, then worked shampoo in with gentle, massaging strokes. My fingers held his hips to ground me, and I sighed in contentment, feeling more cherished than I ever had. His touch was gentle, almost reverent, as he methodically massaged the shampoo into my scalp, then delicately scrubbed it through my long hair. He stood closer than necessary the entire time, crowding me with his body and warming me with his heat, the scent of his bath products surrounding me while the fire of his touch turned me into little more than a malleable doll at his mercy.

After he had thoroughly washed and conditioned my hair, he soaped and caressed every inch of my skin with his body wash and a soft washcloth. He lingered over my legs, paying special attention to my ankles, calves, and inner thighs, carefully following every swipe of the cloth with soft fingertips. Goosebumps raised on my body despite the warmth, my nipples standing at attention. When he had thoroughly rinsed the suds from my skin, he turned me so my back was to the wall and slowly lowered to his knees before me.

I gave a ragged breath at the sight of him like that, hands on my hips and hazel eyes blazing with want. He was the most handsome thing I'd ever seen, and I ached to have more of his touch.

"My turn," he murmured, before turning his attention between my thighs.

He pulled gently on my hips to bring me forward, then ran his open hand up my body to push my torso back against the wall. He lifted one leg up onto his shoulder, then the next, before leaning forward and burying his face between my thighs.

I held onto his hair, steadying myself as he licked a slow, tortuous path up and around my opening, sending bolts of heat through my body as he did. My skin was already flushed, sensitive, and heavy from the lust that had poured through me in the living room. Even the lightest touch had me trembling.

"Oh, god, Parker," I gasped, biting my lip as his tongue lazily slid around my clit.

He hummed in answer and I inhaled a sharp breath, feeling the sound more than I could hear him over the pulse of the shower and echoes of my own panting breaths. He licked across my slit again, then delved his tongue inside me, stroking along my walls. I could feel my whole body tensing in pleasure, my thighs squeezing around his head as he focused once more on that sensitive bundle of nerves. He circled my clit slowly with barely any pressure, then surged forward to suck it into his mouth, teeth scraping gently along my flesh. I whimpered, my fingers flexing in his hair, as I felt a rush of pleasure that sent heat all the way to my toes.

"Right there, ohmygod, don't stop, please, don't stop," I babbled, thrusting my hips forward to press him closer to me.

My wish was his command, and he doubled down on my clit, circling and stroking it with his tongue before sucking gently in pulses over and over. I could feel the pleasure building in me like a balloon, gathering in my core and expanding out. He was a man obsessed, barely pausing to breathe before diving into me again, intent on my satisfaction. He released my clit and licked my opening again, sucking one sex-swollen side of my pussy into his mouth, then the other. I moaned, unable to hold it back, and he growled in approval.

He steadied me against the wall and reached one hand up to palm my breast, then tease my nipple. I gave a desperate, mewling noise and he hummed again. Refocused on my clit, he stroked lightly with his tongue as he teased and plucked my nipple with firm fingers. I could feel my muscles tensing all over, the crest of my orgasm just out of reach, and the tension in my body almost vibrating through me from head to toe. Parker increased the pressure of his tongue just slightly, tweaking my nipple as he did, and I flew off into space. I could barely hear myself moaning through wave after wave, my fingers tightening in Parker's hair as he licked me steadily through my orgasm. Just as it ended, he changed his pace and pressure, and immediately sent me tumbling over the edge again, taking me by surprise and ripping a gasping scream from my lungs. Parker growled in appreciation and praise, licking me through it, as I twitched against him.

I shuddered against the wall and started to go boneless, slipping to the side. Parker slowly ducked first one shoulder, then the next, out from under me, setting me on my feet. He smiled up at me from his position on his knees in front of me, then leaned forward to trail kisses from my hip bones up my stomach. He stood slowly as he went, pulling one nipple into his mouth to tease it with his lips and teeth. Despite my blissed-out state, I arched into him to give him better access, shuddering in pleasure as he rewarded me with a growl and a nip. I gasped at the pain, but a helpless moan of ecstasy followed it as heat flashed through me again.

Parker released my nipple and kissed a trail to the other breast, taking my flesh into his mouth with a deep rumble of satisfaction. His fingers teased and tweaked my free nipple as he licked and nipped the other side into a frenzy, until I was squirming against the wall and making desperate little sounds that filled the shower. He finally released my tits and kissed his way to my neck, lightly scraping his teeth along my skin before sucking it firmly into his mouth. I gasped, knowing he was leaving a mark, but in that moment, I couldn't bring myself to be mad about it. I clutched him to me and shivered, my eyes rolling back as he licked over the spot, and I felt a hot, weighty bead of pleasure settle in my core. He smirked against my skin and I smiled a little, my eyes heavy as I leaned my head back against the shower wall.

He placed a hand on my cheek and turned my face to his,

pressing his lips to mine. I opened for him as I wrapped my arms around him, and he trailed one hand down the front of my body. As he slid his tongue into my mouth, he pushed his fingers into my wet, aching pussy. I gasped into his mouth, but his hand was relentless. Curving his fingers up to hit that perfect spot at the front of my inner walls, he massaged slowly. My breathing went ragged as I clung to him, my legs trembling as he swirled firm circles against my G-spot.

"Ohmygod, Parker," I breathed against his mouth, "fuck-rightthere, rightthere, right...there, don'tstopdon'tstopdon'tstop..."

"That's right, spitfire," he murmured, his fingers never slowing, "tell me how I light you up."

"You do, Parker, right there, don't stop," I mumbled.

I was amazed at the intensity of the orgasm that was building, even after the two he'd already given me. Pleasure was radiating through me, driving me to that peak.

"Come on, Laura Beth," Parker breathed in my ear, his lips teasing my flesh. "Come for me, beautiful. Such a good girl."

His thumb brushed my clit, and I went off again, pleasure sparking behind my eyes, my nerve endings lighting up and sending a fiery blast straight through me. I moaned against Parker as he stroked me through it, holding me up with his body and whispering praises into my ear.

Coming down, I could feel his hard length pressed against me, and my greedy cunt ached to be filled.

"What do you need, spitfire?" he asked, forehead pressed to mine once more. Wrapping my arms around his neck, I hitched a leg around Parker's hips. He lifted me into his arms, holding my ass cheeks in his large hands and pressing me back against the wall.

"You," I answered, looking into his eyes, "please."

He gave me a heated look and kissed me deeply, his cock teasing at my opening.

"I got tested a couple weeks ago." He searched my gaze. "I'm clean."

I gave him a lazy smile. "So am I."

He kissed me again, languid and indulgent.

"Do you want me inside you bare?" he growled in my ear. "Want me to fill that perfect pussy with my cum?"

I shivered as goosebumps flashed across my skin and leaned back so I could meet his hazel gaze.

"Yes, please, sir. I need you to fill me up."

He closed his eyes and groaned in reply, reaching down to line himself up. Parker pushed in slowly, and I moaned at the stretch. He dropped his head to my shoulder, breathing heavily as he bottomed out.

"So goddamn tight," he muttered, "you fit me so fucking well."

His hips pulled back, and he pushed in unhurriedly again, pressing my body more firmly against the wall as he did.

"I'm going to fuck you hard now, spitfire," he rasped, and I could feel my pussy tighten around him in response. "But I'm going to need you to ask nicely."

He pulled out slowly, then paused, looking at me with an expectant expression.

"Please," I begged, chest heaving as I clutched him to me, "please, fuck me."

He grunted in approval and slammed into me. I could hear my screams echoing around the shower as he set a punishing pace, snapping his hips against mine. The sounds filling the tiled space were obscene—both of us panting, my moans, his grunts, and the wet, slapping sounds of our bodies coming together in an intimate and brutal dance. He reached down and grabbed my knee, then hooked his arm under it and planted his hand on the wall, holding me securely. The new angle sent him even deeper, and I cried out at the intensity of the sensation, the fine line between pleasure and pain disintegrating entirely as I writhed in his hold.

"Oh, fuck," I gasped, holding onto his shoulders as need burned through me. "Oh, god, that's so deep."

Parker looked down, watching his cock disappear inside me, an intense possession in his eyes.

"Look how well you take me, spitfire," he gritted out, pace and force unrelenting. "This pussy was made for my cock."

"Yes, sir," I moaned in response, trembling once more.

Every hard thrust sent the thick head of his cock over my G-spot and I could feel a fourth orgasm gathering deep in my core. Parker bent and sucked one nipple into his mouth and I arched into him, scrambling to hold on as he continued pounding into me. My orgasm came barreling up, surprising me as it crashed to the surface in slow, rolling waves that were equal parts agony and sheer perfection. My whole body tensed and I moaned long and low in Parker's ear as I came, curling myself around him as my pussy tightened and fluttered around his length, desperately seeking him deeper as I fell completely apart.

"Fuck, yes, that's a good girl," he gasped, holding me as he slowed his pace through my orgasm. "So fucking perfect when you come for me."

He wrapped his arms around me as my body sagged and brought me back under the showerhead. I gave a soft gasp of surprise at the sudden cascade of warmth, having nearly forgotten where we were, lost as I was to the effect Parker had on me. With gentle hands, he alternated holding me to him and rinsing me again before turning off the water. I remained curled around him, my face buried against his chest. He had both hands on my ass, his still-hard cock brushing against me as he led us out of the bathroom.

"I'm not done with you yet, Laura Beth."

I straightened slowly and blinked at him in surprise. *I'm not sure I can come anymore, even if my pussy did throb with those words.*

"I promised you five," he reminded me, a wicked gleam in his eyes. "And I always keep my promises, spitfire."

Laying me out on the expansive bed, he climbed up after me and pressed our bodies flush together, facing each other while on our sides. Reaching his hand down to hook my knee up over his hip, he leaned in to capture my lips in a bruising kiss. In this position, my pussy pressed to his cock, the heat of him distracting as he brushed the most sensitive parts of me with every movement. I squeezed him closer with one leg, pulling him to me as I lost myself in his lips, his tongue, his touch. In that moment, all that existed were the two of us and this insatiable passion we had been nurturing together since those first moments on the plane. He shifted, causing the head of his cock to press against my clit, and I moaned and ground into him. He groaned his approval and rolled us, putting himself on top of me.

He paused as he settled between my legs, looking down at me with fire and something else, something far softer, in his eyes. "I love seeing you like this," he said, eyes tracing the exposed curves of my body. "I fucking love that I'm the one that put you in this state."

I could feel the flush rising in my cheeks and flaring across my chest. He gave a wicked smile as he watched it spread, then leaned down to kiss my collarbone and then my cheek.

"And I love the way you take me," he whispered as he lined himself up and slid into me to the hilt in one smooth thrust.

I moaned, surprised but so very satisfied at the intrusion.

"So good," he whispered, "so perfect."

His hips thrust slowly, and I dropped my head back in pleasure, eyes closing.

"Eyes on me, spitfire."

I snapped my head back up, my pussy tightening around him and making him groan.

"I want to watch you fall apart for me," he growled, eyes hot on mine as he moved in and out of me.

I shivered under the intensity of his gaze, something warm building in my chest that made my skin feel too tight and my throat close in emotion. I'd have to be blind to miss the warmth in Parker's eyes, the emotion that was simmering there, just under the surface, nearly brimming over. This man didn't just want my body. He wanted every last piece of me; every single thing I could give, he'd take. I could feel the tears burning my eyes, the little drops that betrayed the depth of my feeling for this man. This human who had accomplished and experienced so much, yet, as I had gathered in our soul-baring conversations on his boat, let so few in. This brilliant, beautiful, perfect man wanted *all* of me.

I blinked rapidly to stop the tears from rolling from the corners of my eyes. Parker reached down between our bodies to press a thumb to my clit. I struggled to keep my focus on Parker as my body arched violently, and his eyes widened in response to my reaction. His gaze softened as he watched, transfixed, as my body tensed and my orgasm crept up. He had a look of wonder in his eyes as he slowly made love to me. Because that's what was happening here. Parker Brooks, my would-be rival and the best man I'd ever met, and I were making love.

With a savage intensity that made me cry out and throw my head back against the bed, an orgasm ravaged through me.

"That's it, Laura Beth, so gorgeous, so good," Parker praised, his hips stuttering as my orgasm coaxed his own out of him.

He groaned as he filled me with his cum, my body tingling and trembling through the aftershocks. He hung his head, breathing hard, then gently let himself settle against me. I gripped his body against me, blinking rapidly as I tried to stave off the tears that fought to fall. The depth of my feeling for this man was more than I had ever experienced, and I had no idea what I was going to do about it.

He sighed contentedly and pressed a kiss to my collarbone.

"You're like nothing else, Laura Beth." He looked up at me, and the love I saw in his eyes simultaneously made me want to crawl into him forever and run away crying.

"So are you, Parker" I managed to say, my voice cracking.

He studied me for a moment. "You freaking out on me, spitfire?"

The question was gentle, but the concern and wariness in his eyes was real. I hitched a ragged breath and blinked some more, looking away.

"Maybe a little?" I managed, wiping at my eyes.

He rolled off of me and pulled me back against his chest, tucking my body into his. We fit together like we were made to, and that only wrecked my heart a little more.

"I know this is a lot," he murmured, one arm around my waist and a leg tucked over mine. "And I know you have a plan. But I'm not here to derail it or do anything to stop it."

He took a deep breath, and I wished I couldn't hear the fear in his voice. I wished I wasn't the reason it was there. I squeezed my eyes shut and couldn't stop the tears that escaped. He pressed a gentle kiss to my hair, his tenderness slowly tearing me apart.

"But, Laura Beth...plans can change," he continued.

I tried not to stiffen, but his answering sigh was a sign I had failed.

"They can, spitfire," he pressed. "When something worth changing them for comes along, they can change. And that new future could be even brighter than the one you'd planned."

I choked back a sob. "How do you know that?"

"I know it's possible, beautiful," he soothed, his voice full of so much emotion. Sadness, fear, trepidation, and little hope–I hated that I'd done that to him, especially after the day and night we had. "And as for how you can know, well...," he sighed again and tightened his hold on me briefly, then let me go completely. "I suppose you'll have to have a little faith. In someone other than yourself."

I rolled over to look at him and instantly wished I hadn't. I could see I was hurting him, but I also knew that I had a plan for a reason. Everything I had done was with purpose, and I had always been wary of the idea of "the one". I'd seen what finding "the one" had done for my mother and sister, the lives it had locked them into when they were young and hadn't yet fully formed their dreams. I knew that someone without a plan could end up supporting someone else's dreams, their own discarded.

"I don't know how to do that," I whispered.

Parker rubbed a hand over his face and gave a dejected nod. He sighed again, sounding defeated.

"I'm going to go clean up." He glanced at me with an unreadable expression. "I'll be right back."

He went into the bathroom, closing the door behind him. I knew what he was doing. He was giving me a choice: I could stay in this bed, with him, and wake up to something unknown. Or, I could get up, throw on my expensive new clothes, and run away like I had the first time he'd turned me inside out. One choice meant throwing my carefully plotted life away for a man I barely knew. The other meant continuing down the path I'd forged for myself with my own blood, sweat, and tears.

It took me all of 90 seconds to bolt out of the bed, snatch up my dress, and slip from his penthouse before he returned. And I hated myself for it.

Chapter 25

Parker

I reached my hand out from under the covers to feel blindly for my phone, grasping the device and muting the blaring notifications. Rolling onto my back, I scrubbed my face roughly and read through my messages.

> Twinkie: Higher Grounds Cafe at 11?
>
> Twinkie: ....Hello?
>
> Twinkie: Hey asshole! Answer me!
>
> Twinkie: I'm choosing to take your silence as agreement. I'll see you at the restaurant.
>
> Twinkie: PS, I told Ralph to drag your ass out of bed if you're not in the car in 15. Better get a move on ;)

I groaned, too tired to deal with my sister's particular brand of affection. I thumbs up'ed her message as acknowledgement and flicked back to the rest of my messages, looking for anything from the one other person I wanted to hear from. Even an emoji reaction would do.

After I had left the bedroom last night, I heard LB hurriedly dressing before the apartment door quietly closed behind her. I didn't bother trying to stop her, accepting her mind had been made up. I wasn't about to force a woman to stay in my bed who didn't want to be there.

Although, I had called down to the building's concierge and asked for someone to escort her home. I wasn't about to let her take a rideshare in the middle of the night.

And while I had fought my every impulse to not head straight back over to her apartment and demand we talk through what had made her run, I had caved to the need to text her to make sure she made it home despite double checking with the driver.

> Me: LB, just tell me you're okay.
>
> Me: Please.

She had her read receipts on, so I knew she saw the message and was choosing to ignore my pleading. I stared at the sent messages, willing a reply to come through. Sighing at the sense-lessness, I tossed my phone across the bed and headed to scrub off the night before.

As if a shower could wash away the impression LB had made on me. The futility of that idea made me scoff. She had wormed her way under my skin and had carved off a piece of my heart. If she would shatter it completely was yet to be seen.

"Fuck, took you long enough, brother!" Preston waved from a small table in the corner as I entered the cafe.

Sliding into the chair opposite her, I took a long sip of water, mentally preparing for the conversation we were about to have.

212

"Oh, shit," she coughed. "What happened to you, big?"

I exhaled sharply, feeling the impact of her question and knowing eyes.

What had happened to me? How do I begin to unpack that question?

"It was a rough night, sis. Tell me you ordered coffee?"

Nodding, she reached out and squeezed my hand. "Should be here any minute. Start talking," she urged. "You had your date with LB yesterday, yeah, Operation Treat Her Right? What happened?"

"We had a great date," I started. I quickly corrected myself. "No, it was fucking perfect, Preston. I took her out on the water for the afternoon, and she absolutely loved it. I gave her the necklace you helped me pick out, and dinner was flawless. We went to that Latin bar you suggested, and I've never seen a woman have so much fun."

"I'm not hearing the problem, Parker," she questioned. "What has you looking like I kicked your puppy?"

I dropped my head in my hands and sighed. "She fucking ran, Pres."

"Oh," Preston stated.

At that exact moment, the bubbly server bounced up to our table and slid two coffees between us.

"Alright, folks! We've got those two oat milk lattes. Can I go ahead and get some food started for you?"

Seeing me in such a state, Preston went straight into protective mode and thrust the menus at the poor guy.

"We'll just take two orders of avocado toast. Thanks so much!" she clipped out, clearly sending the message she wanted him to fuck right off.

Sputtering, the startled server nodded, apparently taking the signal, and rushed off towards the kitchen.

Sitting back in her seat, Preston sighed. "Alright, you're

going to have to rewind and explain what happened between your dream date and Cinderella running home at midnight."

"Not funny, twinkie," I ground out.

"I'm not making jokes. You're leaving some big chunks of information out of the story, and it doesn't make sense."

"I took LB back to my place in the city, and things were going great. More than great. Pres, I swear everything was green lights. It was the most fucking incredible experience of my life."

"Until it wasn't?" she gently asked.

"Until it wasn't. I didn't even know it was possible to crash that quickly from such a high. It was like a switch flipped, and she iced me out."

Preston chewed over my words. "Did she tell you what was wrong?"

"I could tell she was freaking out. I tried to tell her I didn't want to mess with her plans and we could figure things out, but I knew she wasn't listening." Staring at the ceiling, I breathed deeply. "Pres, she walked out. For the second time. What is it about me and people I love leaving?"

Leaning across the table, Preston squeezed my arm. "First of all, LB's not Mother so don't think that for one second. And secondly, you didn't answer my question. Did you even bother asking her what she was feeling before you tried to mansplain how your entire relationship was going to play out?" She shook her head. "For fucks sake, brother. For someone so smart, you sure are dense."

I gaped at her, unsure how anyone could think this form of verbal abuse could be construed as support.

She continued, "Parker, she didn't need you to tell her how to think at that moment. She was obviously experiencing some big feelings and she's gonna need some time to sort through those."

I stared Preston down. "And I'm supposed to do what? Just sit here while she works them out?"

Crossing her arms, she nodded solemnly. "That's exactly what you do, Parker. If you really want this to work, you can't force her into it. She has to be ready."

I shook my head. "You know that really fucking sucks right? I know she felt the same way I did. There's no way it was one-sided."

"Sorry, brother. Sometimes you have to let the head catch up to what the heart already knows. She'll eventually find her way to you if you're meant to be together."

I stared out the cafe window, watching the pedestrians go about their morning and wondering where LB was and how she was feeling. "Remind me to call Raj next time I need advice. You're cruel."

Preston scoffed and pinched my forearm. "I'm not. I'm just the only one to tell you that you can't have exactly what you want on the exact timeframe you want it. This is out of your control, big."

Meeting her eyes, I grumbled. "My comment stands."

The server from earlier appeared, setting dishes between the two of us and breaking our stare down.

"Perfect! Here are those avocado toasts! Are you two all set or is there anything else I can grab you?" he asked.

Smiling sweetly, Preston shook her head. "We're perfectly fine, thank you."

She grabbed her utensils and pointed her knife at me. "Now, brother. After we eat, I'll let you take me over to the shopping center with your credit card, and I'll help distract you from stewing in your misery all day."

I shoved a bite of avocado toast into my mouth and mulled over my sister's advice. Was I really supposed to just sit back while LB decided where we went from here without trying to get her to see things like I did? Why was I so unsure if she would arrive at the same conclusion I had?

I am completely lost for Laura Beth Calhoun.

Chapter 26

LB

I was hiding.

That was the truth, and I could at least admit it. It wasn't like there was any excuse I could tell anyone, including myself, that I would believe.

It was Monday morning, and the idea of facing Ana at the office after my date was too much to bear. So, I took the coward's way out and shot her a text letting her know I was working from the coworking space–Connexions–all the venture capitalists in the Bay frequented.

It was a plausible enough alibi, as the space was the place to see and be seen by anyone working in the Bay. Before being assigned to court Gaspar Technologies and my frequent trips to Boise, I had tried to make a point of working from the shared workspace at least once or twice a week to make connections with others in the investing and startup community.

The space was built in a converted, restored bus depot, and it was always swarming with people. Private offices lined one wall of the building, and the rest of the open space was filled with long, open coworking tables. The expansive, arched glass ceiling flooded the space with light, and at the center of the main floor sat a buzzing cafe.

Sipping my coffee, I stared out the windows and tried to piece together a recounting of my date with Parker that my sister would find acceptable. I had four unanswered texts from Sara Jean from the day before, and I knew I only had until the end of the day to respond. She would make my momma call and force me to answer the phone. The woman played dirty.

I had shot Sara Jean a text when I got back to my apartment in the early hours of Sunday morning, letting her know I had made it home safely before collapsing into bed and crying myself to sleep. And when I had finally managed to drag myself out from under the covers later that morning, I feigned a headache to get out of answering the phone when she had called me back.

There was a time limit on how long I could evade my sister, but I didn't know how I was going to explain my reaction to what was objectively the best date of my life. When she found out Parker was a billionaire with a capital B, her head might actually explode. And if I went so far as to explain how he'd listened to me during our first conversation, then spoiled and pampered me in an effort to recreate what I had shared as my dream date, only for me to run out on him without a word? I could practically hear her screaming at me already. She'd already mentioned multiple times that she thought Parker and I were end game, and, in the Calhoun family, women did not walk away from their would-be future spouses. It simply was not done.

But what was more, Sara Jean didn't, and couldn't, relate to my situation. When she'd met Dex as a kid, she didn't have any big life decisions to make. She wasn't standing at a fork in the road, and she hadn't been forced to make a choice between staying the course or taking a new, uncharted path. She had always accepted that she would stay in Pike Road, marry young, and have babies, just like Momma and the other women in the family had done before her. Meeting the man she wanted to fulfill that destiny with was just another box checked off her list.

I, on the other hand, had no intentions of prioritizing love. Was it something I had assumed I'd get around to eventually? Sure. But I also knew that I had watched countless women decide to set aside their aspirations for a man, and I was determined not to lose focus on what I was building. What I had been working towards for close to a decade. I was determined not to be some kept woman, nothing more than a trophy wife for a successful husband. And the thought of sacrificing my career hopes and dreams for a house and kids at this stage? It made me physically ill. There was so much I had yet to accomplish, and I wasn't comfortable putting it aside just because my family and conventional society told me I should.

My truce with Parker over the weekend had muddied the waters and addled my brain. I had thought I had the resolve to enjoy a date with a handsome, charming man, but the allure had been too great and my heart far too weak. From the very beginning, I was on the back foot. While Parker may have agreed to a ceasefire when it came to the deal between us, he was fighting with everything he had in the battle for my heart.

"Hi! Sorry to bother you. Is anyone sitting here?" a woman asked as she smiled and gestured to the seat across from me.

"No, no go ahead," I replied absently, shaking my head.

Refocusing my thoughts back to the email I was drafting, I added the finishing touches to the update to Nate. I felt as good about it as I could, sharing how well the dinner in Boise had gone and my plans to make introductions with several researchers for Dr. Gaspar. What I left out from the update were our conversations over dinner about what a joint investment with Athena could look like. Was it chicken-hearted to avoid the inevitable confrontation over my recommended approach? Absolutely. But there was only so much stress I could handle for one week, and I had hit my limit on Sunday. I hit send on the email before I could change my mind.

Leaning back from my laptop with an admittedly dramatic sigh, I glanced up to find a familiar face across the room and wheezed. *Fucking Fate, you rat bastard.*

Lo and behold, there was Parker, smiling warmly and nodding to the barista at the cafe's counter, waiting for his order. In all the times I'd come here before, we had never crossed paths. I knew that with certainty, because Parker's wasn't a face one could ever consider forgettable.

Okay, LB. Time to put on your big girl panties. You expected this. You knew seeing him again would be weird. You planned for this.

After another good cry on Sunday, I had gone on a run and gave myself a firm talking to. I was resolved to get back on level footing with Parker. He may have swept me off of my feet over the weekend, but it was a new day, and my feet were back on solid ground. What we needed to do, I'd determined, was move as far away from the emotional, heartfelt intimacy we'd experienced on Saturday as possible. We had incredible chemistry between us, that couldn't be denied, but that didn't mean we had to bring our emotions to the table every time. If we had only kept it casual, fed into the desire but not the heart, this wouldn't be so difficult.

I watched from my table as Parker grabbed his coffee order and ducked into one of the coworking space's private offices. He slid the blinds closed, and a plan to reestablish some normalcy between us took shape in my mind.

Truce over, Parker Brooks.

Chapter 27

Parker

I glanced at my phone yet again, my mind wandering away from the conversation happening in the conference call blaring from my laptop. *She hasn't texted you in the two minutes since you checked last, dumbass.* I sighed at myself, annoyed that I had allowed myself to be reduced to this.

"Parker, anything to add?" Van's voice boomed out of my laptop speakers, and I internally groaned.

I had needed a change of pace this morning, something to break up my usual routine so I could attempt to distract myself from the constant thoughts of LB. So far, the attempt had proved futile.

"No, sir," I answered, not entirely sure what I was responding to.

Van could tell, as he gave me a pointed eyebrow raise and a look that suggested I get my shit together. I nodded back at him, letting him know I received his message. He turned the call back over to the team in the office, and I tried to refocus and play catch up. I was one of only a few people joining the call remotely, so Van's pointed callout had been both an attempt to ensure those of us on the phone were included and a smack upside the head for being distracted from the conversation. I had muted myself and was sorely tempted to turn off my video, but knew I'd hear about it from him if I did.

Just as I was feeling engaged in the conversation, the door to the private office opened gently. I looked up to wave the person away, given I had booked the space for the day, but froze when I saw who it was. LB stood just inside the doorway, facing me, while she gently closed the door behind her.

"LB, what–" I started.

She shook her head and held a finger up to her lips, telling me in no uncertain terms to be quiet. I glanced down at my laptop and saw Van's eyes flicking to the screen where the call attendees were projected, checking in on me. If I went off camera now, he'd likely call me out. I didn't want to look away and risk another random prompt from my hawk-eyed boss, so I stayed put. I could see LB drawing closer in my peripheral vision, and I could feel her move through the room as though attuned to her completely. When she was nearly next to me at the small conference table, she dropped to her knees.

"LB, what are you doing?" I hissed, trying not to move my lips and draw Van's attention.

"Shhh," was her only reply as she crawled under the table.

I could feel her growing closer, and my cock was swelling already at the thought of her on her knees like that again. Memories of Saturday night flooded my mind, and I fought hard to keep any sign of the desire that surged through me off my face. Just as I was about to take advantage of Van's attention returning to the people in the room with him, someone asked about one of my other accounts. I quickly unmuted myself to respond.

"No change in status, there. Clients are happy and their next quarterly earnings report is due next week for review."

I saw Van nod in approval as I went back on mute. Relief

swept through me—he'd been ready to catch me in another mistake, but now that I had been engaged enough, he'd likely give me a break. And that break could not come soon enough, because LB's hands were running up my thighs. I hurriedly clicked off my camera and looked down in time to see her fingers close on my waistband and start unfastening my slacks.

"Seriously, LB, we need to—"

She pushed her face forward so I could see it, and I groaned. She was fucking gorgeous all the time, but there was something about her in that position—poised before me with her big blue eyes peering at me through thick lashes—that was my complete undoing.

"Fucking hell, spitfire, what are you doing to me?" I muttered, reaching down to stroke her cheek.

She flinched oh so slightly away from my touch, and my heart cracked a little more. I let my hand fall away as she fought back the panic that had flashed briefly in her eyes. Ignoring the incident entirely, she pulled my zipper down and reached through the fly of my boxer briefs to wrap her small, smooth hand around my cock. She gasped a little, eyes flying up to mine.

"Yeah, spitfire. I'm hard. Ready for you," I muttered, my voice like gravel. "You going to tell me what you're doing?"

Her hand squeezed around me and I inhaled a sharp breath, vaguely hearing Lex and Van talking about plans for an announcement of some kind at a charity event we had coming up. But LB stole my attention entirely when she surged forward and took my dick into her mouth. Just as she swirled her tongue around my swollen, dripping cock, I heard my name again.

"—Parker. We'll connect later this week."

I flicked myself off mute for long enough to answer Lex, "Sounds good."

I must've said the right thing, because conversation

continued as normal and none of the people in the room threw me any shady looks. Good thing, because LB had swallowed more of me down, cheeks hollowed as she bobbed on my cock.

"Fuck's sake, spitfire," I ground out, my whole body tense, "the mouth on you."

She hummed a bit, then looked up at me through her lashes again, a taunting gleam in her eye. Holding my gaze, she sucked harder and dug her fingertips into my thighs, making me feel her everywhere.

"Is this payback for dinner last week, LB?" I asked, almost afraid of her answer.

If LB was back to playing games, it was going to tear another little piece of me apart. I knew the clock had run out on our "truce," but I had been ready to lay the white flag at her feet Saturday night. I'd been ready to do so from the start, if I was honest.

Her gaze flicked to mine again, and my dick left her mouth with an audible pop.

"Whatever do you mean, Parker?" she asked with exaggerated innocence, smirking at me briefly before slowly licking a stripe from my balls to my tip.

My heart froze at her flippancy, but I could see something in her eyes that looked like fear and sadness. Whatever had transpired between us to cause her to run on Saturday was clearly affecting us both. Vaguely, I could hear the conversation on the conference call continuing. Van's voice boomed once more, calling on someone else, and I let my attention drift back to the siren on her knees before me.

"If you're here to punish me, spitfire, this is an odd way to do it," I rasped. I kept my hands clear of her, not wanting to see her flinch away from my affection once more.

She was relentless in her pursuit of my pleasure, teasing with her lips, tongue, and hand as she worked me over. I could hear Van giving everyone a quick pep talk for the week, a signal that the call was almost over. But I had a feeling LB was only going to stay if she thought she was getting one over on me, so I didn't close my laptop.

As I watched, her cheeks heated, tears marking tracks down her face as she took me as deep as she could. I almost missed her little squirm, but as soon as I saw it, I smirked down at her.

"Are you getting wet, spitfire?" I asked, my voice low. "Is sucking my cock making you gush in anticipation?"

She gasped and gave a little whimper that had my balls drawing up tight, bringing me right to the edge.

"I shouldn't be the only one enjoying this," I murmured, flexing my hips ever so slightly to drive into her mouth.

Her eyes rolled back, and she moaned again, dropping one hand to her lap.

"That's it, spitfire," I encouraged. "Touch yourself. I want to see you come while you choke on my cock."

The look she gave me was filled with a helpless kind of lust that had my head swimming and my skin feeling too tight. I had no idea if the call had ended yet, and I honestly couldn't care less. I had LB's complete attention, and that's how I wanted it to stay.

"Give me your hand," I demanded. She always responded immediately when I told her what to do in the bedroom, and I had a feeling any softness from me in this moment would send her running again.

She tentatively offered her hand, and I leaned forward to suck two fingers into my mouth. She moaned around my cock, her eyes falling closed as she paused, a shiver running through her. I released her hand after a moment, her fingers glistening with my saliva.

"Put those wet fingers in your pretty pink pussy, spitfire," I ordered, flexing my hips to push further into her mouth.

She whimpered and slipped her hand under her skirt. I couldn't tell exactly what she was doing, but her eyes fluttered closed in pleasure as her fingers disappeared. I reached out to steady her head in my hands.

"I'm going to fuck your mouth now, LB, and you're going to come for me."

Her eyes flashed to mine, swimming in lust and pleasure, and I took that as both acknowledgement and permission. I began thrusting in earnest, groaning at the tight, hot, wet feel of her mouth and throat.

"That's it, beautiful," I crooned, my orgasm building rapidly. "Take that cock. Take it all."

The sounds she made were sending electricity straight to my balls, and I felt that telltale tingle telling me I was right on the edge. From the way her body was flushed and stiffening, I knew she was right there with me.

"That's it," I ground out. "Come for me now, spitfire. Shatter for me."

I watched as her orgasm rolled through her, a moan escaping and providing just the right vibration to push me over after her. I stifled a loud groan as I pumped cum into her mouth, my thrusts getting shallow and erratic as I erupted.

When we had both finished, breathing hard, I tucked myself back into my pants and fastened my belt. I closed my laptop, noting that I was the only one still in the meeting as I did. LB was still on her knees, flushed and beautifully disheveled. She was watching me with this disappointed look that suggested that the scene had not gone at all how she expected it would.

I leaned back in my chair, my legs still bracketing her body, and looked deep into her eyes.

"Are you ready to talk to me, LB?" I asked gently. "Ready to tell me why you ran?"

She blinked those bluebell eyes and looked away, swallowing roughly.

"You don't have to be ready," I murmured. "I won't push you. But I do want to know when you are." I ran a hand through my hair and sighed heavily. "I want to know all of you, LB, if you'll let me in."

Her answering expression was panic and pain wrapped in twisted agony. I remembered Preston's words from yesterday and I thought for a moment she might be right. Maybe I just needed to give LB space to figure out what she wanted to tell me and when. Because I could tell with a single glance that pushing her right now would only drive her away.

I pushed my chair back and picked up my laptop and water bottle, nestling them into my backpack.

"I'm here for you when you're ready to talk, LB," I reassured, turning back to her.

She hadn't moved, and the broken expression she was giving me was deepening that fissure in my chest.

"But, until then," I took a deep breath, steeling myself, "it's probably best if we keep things professional."

Hurt and panic flashed in her eyes, even though she'd been the one to ice me out on all personal channels since Saturday. Hadn't stopped her from emailing about Gaspar, though. She scrambled to her feet, frantic eyes searching mine.

"I gave you my number for work, originally," I continued. "I think it's a good idea to go back to using it for that, for now." I gave her a soft, encouraging smile. "Just until you're ready."

She drew a shuddering breath and wrapped her arms around herself, looking away.

"You okay?" I pressed, not wanting to leave her in this state.

She swiped at her tear-stained cheeks and sniffled. "No, Parker. But I don't imagine you are, either."

"Fair assessment," I confirmed. "I'm going to go. You can stay here as long as you want. I reserved the room all day."

She nodded absently, looking anywhere but at me. "Thank you."

I stepped up into her space and opened my arms, offering her a hug. She gave a strangled sob and fell into me, her shoulders shaking as she fought tears.

"I'll be here when you're ready, baby," I breathed into her hair, holding her against me for a moment.

I pulled back, reluctant, and moved toward the door. I paused with my hand on the door handle, looking back at her.

"You deserve everything you want, Laura Beth." Her gaze met mine, and I gave her an encouraging smile. "And I really do mean everything."

I turned away from her tortured look, walked out, and closed the door behind me.

Chapter 28

LB

I've heard people say they were spiraling before, and I thought it knew what it meant. News flash: I had no fucking idea. But, as Parker closed the door behind him, that's exactly what I did. I spiraled.

The moment the door shut, the sobs broke free. I clapped a hand to my mouth to contain them, but there was no holding back the flood of emotion that experience had unleashed. I had only intended to tease him, distract him while he was on a call, to prove that we could do something casual and both come out unscathed. But it was a naive, childish thing to have believed that could be true. I was lying to myself when I thought I could get on my knees for Parker and not feel the effect of him deep in my soul.

I lowered myself gently into one of the chairs at the table and buried my head in my hands as I cried out the emotions that had been gathering for the last day and a half. I was confused, scared, and hurt, unsure of what to do next. And that was truly unfamiliar territory. I was the girl with the plan. I was rarely unsure.

As my crying settled, my phone buzzed in the pocket of my skirt. I tugged it free, looking down to find another text from my sister.

> Sara Jean: You better be dead or hospitalized, missy. There are no other acceptable reasons for avoiding me.

Two minutes later, the phone buzzed again, this time with a call. I snatched it up.

"Hello?" I sniffed, fully expecting to hear Sara Jean's voice on the line.

"LB, why the hell did I just get a call from Gaspar Technologies thanking me for my openness to a joint deal with Athena Ventures?" Nate demanded, voice hard.

My scrambling was both mental and physical. I jumped to my feet, as though that would help me deal with the fallout of my actions, and tried to come up with a way to diffuse the situation.

"Nate, hi. Uh, I'm surprised they called."

"Well, that makes two of us, LB," he snapped back at me. "Do you want to explain why Dr. Gaspar seems to think we're willing to come to the table in a non-exclusive deal?"

"Sir, I truly think it's the best option–"

"That wasn't my question, Ms. Calhoun," he barked, his tone brokering no objection. "I asked if you wanted to explain the situation, not your opinion on it."

I pressed my eyes closed and took a deep breath, screaming in frustration internally. "I made the call I thought was best for the client, sir."

There was a tense silence on the other end of the call, then I heard him blow out a breath. "I see. Despite my direct orders?"

"Yes, sir."

"You didn't think it might be worth it to call me and talk

through the options, get my take on how to move forward?" he pressed.

"I–uh, well," I fumbled for a response. *You should've done that, Laura Beth. Why didn't you do that?!* "Sir, I–"

"Let me ask you this, LB. Do you want a future at P&L?"

I blinked rapidly, feeling like I was standing on a foundation of sand. Everything was slipping away, out of my control. "Yes, sir, of course I do. I–"

"And you know our policy for associates seeking a senior associate promotion, yes?"

"I–yes, sir, of course. We have to close our first solo in addition to meeting all criteria for the senior associate role."

"And if you don't close your first solo?" he asked, tone icy.

"I–sir, please, I am only intending to–"

"Answer the question, LB."

I froze, staring at the wall opposite as though it had the answers. I gestured wildly in frustration and pressed the heel of my free hand to my forehead, trying to steady myself. "There is no future for associates who cannot close a solo," I recited. "If I fail with Gaspar, my services will no longer be required at P&L."

"That's correct," he said, voice clipped. "And what do you think that means for your future in this industry?"

I felt the blood rush out of my face at the implication. "Nothing good," I said meekly.

"Now, I asked you to step up, take a leadership role in these negotiations, and get Gaspar over the line in an exclusive agreement. What are you going to do from here?"

"Renegotiate an exclusive for P&L," I replied, my voice wooden.

"I certainly hope so," Nate snapped. "Don't disappoint me again, LB."

I closed my eyes and swallowed roughly. "I'll certainly do my best, sir."

But he had already disconnected, and as I pulled my phone from my ear, I realized he'd gotten the last word.

"Shit, shit, SHIT!" I cried out, slamming my phone down on the table and collapsing roughly into the chair. "You have got to be fucking kidding me."

I scrubbed my hands over my face and sat there, staring at the wall, as I tried to figure out my next move. There were no good options. None that moved Gaspar Technologies forward in the best way, and none that would mean me keeping my job. Everything that had transpired with Dr. Gaspar so far had made it clear that an exclusive deal would not be an easy sell, if I could even sell it at all.

My phone vibrated on the table.

> Sara Jean: Okay, I'm officially worried. You okay?

I picked up the phone and called her.

"Oh, my god. She lives!" she crowed.

"Yes, I'm alive, but I am not okay. My entire life is falling apart, and that is not an exaggeration, and as much as I love you, I do not have the time or energy to get into it right now, so. Can we please consider the situation addressed so I can get back to trying to fix the absolute clusterfuck I have made of my life?"

There was a long pause. Then, "Laura Beth, honey, you've got this. I love you. You call me when you need me, you hear? You do not have to do this–whatever this is–alone."

I let out a shaky breath, my eyes misting all over again. "Thank you," I whispered.

"I mean it, hun. If there's anyone who can navigate a clusterfuck and come out on top, it's you. Believe in you."

"I'll try," I muttered.

"Do better than try. Love you."

"Love you, too."

As she hung up, I dropped my head into my hands once more. I had one hell of a web to untangle if I was going to get my life back on track. First, I had to figure out how to convince Dr. Gaspar to prioritize P&L over Athena. My gut twisted as I thought it, as it meant going behind Parker's back. But it also wasn't the right call for the business, and those two things combined felt like the kind of low I had always aspired never to be. I knew hostile business practices were commonplace, particularly in this industry, but I had never wanted to stoop to using them. And yet, if I didn't achieve what Nate wanted, when and how he wanted it, I was going to be out of a job. Not just at P&L, as he had emphasized, but in the VC industry in the Bay in general. And losing my place here meant going back to Pike Road.

For the first time in my life, a small voice popped into my head to ask if going back would really be so bad. In my sheer shock that the question was even a thought, I actually considered it. Would it be awful to find myself surrounded by my family and the community that had raised me? The idea didn't strike the fear into me it used to, but the thought of having it as my only option made my skin itch. I could go home, yes. But I couldn't stay. I needed to have something to return to the Bay for. Something to return to. And that meant I had to fight for this job tooth and nail. It was the only thing securely tethering me to this city and the life I wanted to build for myself.

Resolute, I snagged a tissue from the box on the table and did my best to clean the tear-streaked makeup from my face. As I went to leave the room, I paused at the door and looked back at the chair Parker had been in when I'd come in. I could still taste him, and it both warmed my belly and cooled my blood to think of what had gone on between us. He had said he'd wait until I was ready, and I had to trust him in that. And, some small part of me (one that sounded an awful lot like the part asking me if home was such a bad thing) wanted desperately for him to still feel that way after this deal was said and done.

Chapter 29

Parker

On Wednesday, I was back in the office. I hadn't heard from LB, professionally or otherwise, and that fact left a heaviness in my gut that I couldn't ignore. I was doing my best to push through, but random things would distract me and draw my attention back to some moment LB and I had shared, which only made my discomfort with the whole situation deeper.

I looked up from the spot I was absently studying to find Van's eyes on me from across the conference table. I was in our senior leadership team meeting, discussing updates for our full client portfolio.

"Well, Parker?" Van prompted.

Shit, I have no idea what he's asking about. Better wing it.

"Thanks, Van. All is well on the Gaspar Technologies front," I said, taking a wild guess that the topic was about my most eccentric current project.

"Thank you for sharing with the class, but the topic of discussion was the upcoming gala with Feed the Bay. Are you bringing a client?"

Of course, I'd missed the conversation. How could I focus

on this team standup when all that filled my head were thoughts of LB naked on her knees, in my shower, and in my bed?

"Right," I said, rubbing one eyebrow in thinly veiled frustration at myself. "The topics are related, as I think August would be a good add for the guest list."

"I agree, which is why we have him, Nathaniel Livingston, and–" Van glanced down at his notes for a moment.

I sighed. "LB Calhoun."

"Yes, LB Calhoun," he nodded crisply. "All on the guest list. Anyone else to add?"

"No, sir," I said, giving a brief smile.

Lex and Van shared a look.

"I think we've caught up on everything else," Lex announced, dismissing the room. "Parker, stay a moment."

Ah, fuck. It was fair of her to call me out, honestly. I'd been scattered and distant in most conversations all week. The rest of the team quickly filed out, a few tossing me encouraging smiles as they went. Once the room was clear, Van stood, buttoned his suit jacket, and strode over to shut the door.

"Have I been sent to the principal's office?" I asked, hoping my typical levity would diffuse the tension.

Lex gave me a droll look. While Van was a ruthless boss and mentor, Lex suffered absolutely zero shit. She had a reputation for being one of the toughest, most successful, and most respected business leaders in the Bay. She was also whip smart and could see through me in a heartbeat.

"Parker, what's been going on the last couple of weeks?" she asked.

I knew she didn't mean with work. I knew it, but I wasn't sure I was ready to cop to it. "Happy to resend my weekly status, if that would be helpful."

"Cut the shit, kid," Van barked. "Don't play dense. We all know you're not."

He flicked a switch on the wall and the glass separating the conference room from the office went opaque. I gave him a grateful look and sighed, slouching onto the table.

"I'm sorry, both of you. I've been distracted the last few weeks."

Lex gave me a pointed eyebrow raise that said, "Yes, we know, go on." Verbose for a single eyebrow, but the woman was talented.

I tilted my head in acknowledgement, considering how to frame this. "I've gotten a bit involved personally with the associate from P&L, and, well...she's in my head."

"Personally," Lex said. It wasn't a question, just a statement.

"Yes, personally. Professionally, she's brilliant. Has great instincts, listens, takes initiative, and has a real knack for understanding the motivations of her clients."

"All the markers of someone who could be wildly successful in this business," Lex confirmed, her expression thoughtful.

"Exactly. It's been great to watch her take charge on this account." I sighed, "But it's her first solo."

Lex's upper lip lifted into a small sneer on one side. It was the kind of physical reaction she rarely showed to most, but the relationship between the three of us was unique. I might work for them, but in the eyes of the Bay, we were on a level playing field. Lex had always treated me as such, and I only ever saw her lose control of her carefully constructed persona when the topic was P&L.

"They still doing that archaic shit?" Van asked, blunt as ever.

"Apparently. She's been worried that she's going to fail and lose her job. Doesn't help that she's not from around here and doesn't have deep connections in the Bay."

"She has you," Lex said, as though it was obvious.

I blinked at her. "I don't think she realizes that."

"Have you told her?" Van chimed in, giving me an "I bet you haven't" look.

He was right. "You know what, I haven't. Not so blatantly."

"Should probably get on that," he muttered, looking down at his nails as though he needed distraction from the banality of this conversation.

"Back to the deal," Lex said, saving us both. "This is taking longer than usual to close, especially for you. Does that have to do with LB too?"

"Yes and no," I answered. "She's largely been leading negotiations and leading them well. But August is eccentric on a good day. Half the time he wants to get to know us as humans as opposed to sticking to business. Plus, it seems like LB doesn't have much support from P&L–it's really up to her to structure and drive the joint deal. I'm supporting where I can in the best interests of Athena and Gaspar Tech, but I don't see how we could've accelerated things given the doctor's peculiarities."

"I'm surprised Nate is allowing her to pursue a joint deal," Lex mused.

"Do you think he knows?" Van drawled.

I hadn't even considered that LB wasn't keeping Nate informed, but based on the expressions on both of their faces, I should've.

"Oh, shit," I murmured. "Would he really let her go if she delivered a joint proposal?"

"Unfortunately, yes," Lex confirmed, without hesitation.

I mulled that over for a moment. At the end of the day, we were going to pursue the best deal for the client, because it was the right thing to do. Ego didn't play a factor. It was part of why Lex had the reputation she did–she was relentless in her pursuit of advantageous deal terms for the businesses she supported, even if it meant doing things unconventionally.

"I don't know how you're going to untangle the personal

aspects of this, Parker," Lex continued, "but on the professional side, I assume you know the best move if things go sideways with P&L."

"I do. We'll set August and his company up for success, Lex."

"I know you will. The gala would be a nice moment for an announcement, given the alignment between August's goals and the vision of Feed the Bay. I imagine he'll make some valuable connections," she said.

"I'm sure he will. You said August, Nate, and LB are all on the list?"

Van was the one to answer. "Given your updates about pursuing a joint deal, we thought it best to extend the olive branch. And Feed the Bay was happy to add another billionaire to the guest list."

Lex gave him an admonishing look, but he just canted an eyebrow in response. The two of them were close, and Van was fiercely protective of those in his inner circle. Lex's family had done her more harm than good based on the limited information I knew, and I was pretty sure Van would never forgive Nate for it. Not that I could blame him.

"It will be a successful event," Lex said firmly. "Parker, we'll leave it to you to communicate with the doctor and LB about attending. I'll handle Nate."

Van grumbled at that, but I just nodded.

"Thank you, Lex. Van."

We all stood, moving toward the conference room door. Lex put a hand on my shoulder before I could open it.

"A word of advice, Parker?"

"Please." I'd take any advice she thought I needed.

"Be gentle with your girl. P&L is as cutthroat as they come, and Nate still thinks my father's methods are to be revered. He will be putting immense pressure on her. She's driven?"

"Incredibly so. First person in her family to get an undergraduate degree," I said, hearing the pride in my voice.

She smiled softly and nodded, dropping her hand from my shoulder. "He'll know that, and he'll use it to get what he wants. Like my father, Nate sees people for the value they can bring him. And there's nothing a Livingston male values more than money."

I blew out a breath, both grateful for her transparency and concerned for LB.

"Thank you, Lex. For everything."

"You deserve good things, Parker."

I swung the door open, and she breezed through, followed quickly by Van. Before I could follow them out, Van turned on his heel and gave me an intense glare.

"She'll never be as frank about that family as she needs to be, so I'll tell you this: Nate is going to tell that girl to go behind your back. I guarantee it." He clapped a strong hand to my shoulder, squeezing firmly before letting go. "Do with that information what you will."

"Thank you," I murmured, following him down the hall toward my desk.

From everything they had shared, I knew LB was going to be in a tough position. It was only a matter of time before Nate learned of our collaboration, and I had no doubt LB would be hearing about it. If she caved to his pressure and tried to back into an exclusive, I knew August would resist. *There's no good answer to this one, Brooks. Just gotta make the best of it, whatever happens.*

Now, I had to strategize how to get August and LB to the gala. One as my guest, and the other as my date. *Yeah, sure, that should be easy.*

I eyed my phone. Maybe the best path forward was leaving

it open to interpretation. I picked up the phone and started typing a new text message.

> Me: LB, there's a gala a week from Saturday for Feed the Bay. I'll be inviting August; would love for you to join us.

The ball was in her court. Again.

Chapter 30

LB

As my plane descended into Boise on Friday morning, I felt out of place. The memories of Parker bundling me into his private jet to fly us home to the Bay after he had taken care of me all night filled my mind. We had so many shared experiences tied up in flights, airports, and this idyllic Idaho town–it felt like he was everywhere I looked.

When I saw Boise for the first time, I was enchanted. It was just big enough to feel like a city, but small enough to not overwhelm a small-town girl like me. Now, after everything that had transpired with Parker, I felt like my paradigm had shifted. Boise looked so small to me, and the enchantment I'd felt at having freedom on my first real solo work trip had well and truly worn away.

After Nate's scathing call, I'd had no choice but to go back to the drawing board for Gaspar Technologies–this time, on my own. I worked all week to put together a proposal that was as close as possible to Dr. Gaspar's ideal state, without requiring Athena to come to the table. We didn't have the same local connections in the Bay that Athena did, which I knew would be a challenge. Regardless, I had to try. There was nothing left for me except to do my best.

It had felt like a betrayal to schedule this in-person meeting with Dr. Gaspar without coordinating with Parker. I had seriously considered reaching out, but knew it would only put things at risk. Plus, there was a small part of me that worried Parker would prioritize Athena and drop this thing simmering between us like a hot potato to get the win. It's what Nate would want me to do, and he and Parker's boss were both trained by their dad, the ruthless owner of P&L Capital.

Nate had largely given me the cold shoulder this week, ignoring my emails and declining to meet with me before my trip. His only contribution had been to text me this morning. I glanced at my phone, wishing I could go back in time and ignore the message.

Mr. Livingston: Tick tock, LB. Get it done.

Really helpful, boss. I pressed my fingers to my temples, willing some of the tension to bleed away. Meeting with Dr. Gaspar today was my Hail Mary–either I'd walk away with some measure of confidence in P&L's success, or I'd know we were destined to fail.

———

"LB, it's good to see you. I thought for today's meeting you might want to tour the greenhouses while we chat? It's so dull sitting in these conference rooms, don't you think?" Dr. Gaspar asked by way of greeting me.

"Oh, um sure. I suppose I can talk you through my agenda and send over the deck for you to review after our meeting."

Clapping his hands together, he leaped to his feet and

headed to the door. Turning back towards me, he paused and quirked a brow. "I was surprised to get your last-minute meeting request and to find your shadow, Mr. Brooks, not with you."

"I, uh..." I started and stopped, feebly trying to find the right response. "I felt this conversation was best had between the two of us."

Nodding, he held the door for me and gestured down the long corridor. "Right, then. Just this way."

As we walked down the office building's fluorescent-lit hallway, I took several deep breaths before launching into my rehearsed spiel.

"So Dr. Gaspar," I began before he held a hand up for me to stop.

"LB, don't you think we've moved past the formalities? After all, we have gotten to know one another quite well over the past few months. I really must insist you call me August," he said as he smiled warmly at me, the small wrinkles around his eyes creasing.

His characterization of our relationship as familiar only twisted my stomach into more knots. This man was trusting me with his company's future, and I was being forced to look after P&L's bottom line.

I returned his smile before going on. "Yes, of course August. As I was saying, after reviewing the deal terms and proposal shared by Athena Ventures in greater detail, I do have to recommend we enter into an exclusive partnership instead."

Dr. Gaspar came to a stop at the glass double doors, turning to face me completely and crossing his arms. His lips thinned into a tight line as he studied my expression.

"Where is this coming from, LB? Last week, you were pitching me on working with both P&L and Athena. What about the community network Parker shared at dinner?"

I motioned for him to open the greenhouse doors, desperate

to get out of this windowless prison, and charged ahead in what was a complete reversal of opinion.

"Yes, Athena does indeed have fantastic connections in the Bay, but P&L is most excited about introducing your tech to several of the agrichemical and biotech companies we have deep relationships with. They are always interested in the latest R&D to expand their portfolios," I said as I followed him into the enormous, plant-filled space.

With his arms clasped behind his back, Dr. Gaspar paced down the row of hydroponic crops, and I held my breath in anticipation of his reaction.

"This is a different approach than before."

I nodded. "Yes, it is. But it is also the fastest path to market. And you won't need to worry about hiring, as those companies employ small armies of scientists. Only the best will work on your tech," I replied resolutely.

Spinning on his heel, he turned back to face me, more stoic than before. He watched me carefully, like a poker player assessing his opponents, before giving me a sharp nod and leading me back towards the doors we entered from.

"Right, LB. Well, you've certainly given me plenty to consider. I trust you'll share all the finer details in the revised proposal you'll be sending over. If I have any questions, I assume you'll be at the Feed the Bay gala next Saturday?" he asked as we walked back towards reception.

"Oh, um yes of course." Tugging my bag back up my shoulder, I extended my hand in goodbye.

I guess that means I have to attend.

Parker had texted me earlier in the week, letting me know he had invited Dr. Gaspar, but I had hoped the doctor would decline. It would have certainly made declining Parker's invitation that much easier. Now that our deal with Gaspar Technologies was on the line, I had no choice but to go.

"I'll be seeing you then, LB. Thank you for the visit."

"Thank you, August. Please feel free to call me with any questions while reviewing the updated proposal," I encouraged. "P&L wants this partnership."

He gave my hand a single firm shake before nodding in agreement and leaving me alone in the reception area. I exhaled a deep breath and opened my phone to order a rideshare back to the airport.

For the first time that I could recall, I wasn't sure what I had waiting for me back in the Bay.

Chapter 31

LB

Ana shouted through the bathroom door. "You coming out from in there, or am I going to have to come in there and drag you out?"

I chuckled. "Hold your horses, lady! I gotta let this lotion dry before climbing into my dress."

Standing in my lingerie, I stared into the mirror. Inspecting Ana's handiwork, I checked to make sure I didn't need to do any final touch ups to my makeup. She'd offered to come over and help me get ready for the Feed the Bay gala, and I was grateful for the support.

She'd chosen to go light on my makeup, emphasizing the blue of my eyes with a light dusting of bronze eyeshadow, lashings of mascara, and a subtle pink blush. I had to admit I seemed far more sophisticated than my usual 5-minute makeup look made me appear.

Happy I was dry enough, I grabbed the dress off the hanger and slid it over my head before opening the door.

"Hello, Miss Calhoun! You look like a certain Kate in that yellow silk number!" Ana exclaimed from her perch on my bed.

I smiled timidly and glided my hands down the smooth, pale

fabric. The floor-length gown was sleeveless, with a deep v-neckline, crisscrossing straps, and an open back. I felt beautiful in the dress and appreciated Ana's enthusiasm, but I also knew deep down the only person's opinion that mattered to me was Parker's.

I thought back to the adoration I had seen in his eyes on the night he had given me a different dress on his boat, and my chest tightened in sadness. *Would he ever look at me like that again? Would any man?*

After my meeting with Dr. Gaspar, I had agreed to attend the gala with Parker. Not as a date, but as colleagues. The distinction mattered to me. I wanted to remain focused on closing the deal for P&L and getting Nate off my back.

Ana threw back another sip of champagne. "So, have you heard from Parker since last week?"

Sitting at my vanity, I started to work on my hair. "Yeah, he messaged me on Wednesday. I guess word got back to Athena that we had proposed a new offer to Gaspar."

"Shit, was he pissed?"

If only. Mad was easy, mad was simple, mad I could understand.

I shook my head. "No. Here, have a look and see for yourself," I suggested as I tossed her my phone.

Ana scrolled through my messages and read the thread aloud.

> Parker: I heard about the revised proposal.

> Parker: I'm sorry LB, I know how hard you worked on the joint-partnership agreement, and it couldn't have been easy having that conversation with August. How are things with Nate?

> Parker: I'm here if you want to talk, about work or anything else.

Tossing the phone to the bed, Ana sighed heavily. "LB, honey. I'm so sorry. This is such a tough position. If there's anything you need, you just let me know, alright?"

I met her eyes in the mirror and gave a weak smile. "Thanks, hun. Having you here to help me get ready is more than enough."

She scoffed. "Are you kidding me? Drinking someone else's booze and getting to do makeup on a modelesque face like yours? It's hardly a chore."

I chuckled and refocused on pinning up the last section of my hair when there was a knock at the front door.

"LB!" Maya called from the living room. "There's a man here insisting you have to sign for some delivery."

Ana and I shot each other puzzled glances before heading to the door. Sure enough, there waited a suit-clad messenger, standing at the door with a small box and card. Maya looked between the man and me before shrugging and heading back to her room. "I'll leave this to you two."

"Miss Calhoun? These are for you," he explained as he handed over the items and turned to leave.

"Oh, um, okay, well thank you then," I muttered as I stared down at the seal on the card.

The initials PB were embossed in wax. My fingers traced the seal absentmindedly, as I wondered which Parker had written this note. The charming businessman, or the heartbreakingly beautiful man who had given me a piece of himself.

I opened the note and read:

Laura Beth, you have touched me like no other

has. You deserve a jewel as rare and beautiful as you. xx

My hand found my mouth as I tried to process the words on the page. *What did I do to deserve this man?*

With shaking hands, I set the note aside and opened the black velvet box. Looking inside, I gasped at its contents.

In it sat the most exquisite necklace I had ever laid eyes on. The lariat style showcased flawless round diamonds set in yellow gold, with a single string ending in a large, pear-shaped yellow diamond at the center.

"Oh my god, LB," Ana whispered from behind me. "It's stunning."

I was too dumbfounded by the generous gift to speak, so Ana took the box from my hands and set it on the table. "Here, let me help you."

She gently grabbed my shoulders and steered me to face the floor length entryway mirror. Taking the necklace from the box, she raised her arms over my head and settled the jewels around my neck, securing the clasp.

I let out a small gasp as I traced the delicate path of diamonds down towards my cleavage where my fingers landed on the sparkling yellow gemstone.

Ana squeezed my shoulders in support and caught my eyes in the mirror.

"He cares for you, LB. That much is obvious."

I dipped my chin in agreement, still mute from too much emotion.

"Things will sort themselves out babe, you'll see. You just gotta have faith." Twisting me back around to face her, she dug through my clutch sitting on the table and pulled out a lipstick bullet.

"One final touch," she said as she handed me the tube and watched me apply the color to my lips.

After inspecting my application, she grinned, obviously happy with the final result. "Now go get out of here before your carriage turns into a pumpkin or some shit!" Swatting my butt, she cackled loudly.

I knew she didn't mean anything by the comparison, but I couldn't help feeling a bit like Cinderella in that moment. I was a small-town girl, not meant for things like gowns or jewels or galas. And while I wasn't looking for my prince charming, I had a nagging suspicion that he had already found me.

Chapter 32

Parker

The Feed the Bay Gala was a veritable who's who of South Bay. Held in the local art museum, the attendees ranged from local educators to the Bay's upper echelon. Naturally, both my father and mother were in attendance. While that would normally be a reason for me to avoid the event at all costs, the thought of seeing LB overrode any distaste I had for them.

"Parker, there you are," Van called, striding toward me with August hot on his heels.

I smiled at them both, offering a hand first to August, then to my boss. "Gentlemen! Wonderful to see you. August, so pleased you could make it tonight."

"Yes, well," he huffed, pulling his glasses off to swipe at them with the handkerchief tucked in his lapel, "I certainly couldn't have turned down such a generous offer. I've never ridden in a private jet before."

I arched a brow at Van. I hadn't realized we'd sent Athena's jet to collect the good doctor.

"The commercial flight availability was limited," he said gruffly. "We're just glad we could find an alternative, August. There are several people here we'd love to introduce you to."

"Yes, yes, so you've said. Bar first, though, yes?"

Van gave a throaty chuckle. "Sure. Lead the way."

August headed toward the bar in the far corner, while Van paused momentarily, his gaze meeting mine. "Lex is making the announcement in about thirty minutes."

I blew out a heavy breath. "Right, thank you."

"I'll introduce August to some contacts, but I expect you to finish the courting once the dust settles."

"Of course, boss. Thank you."

He nodded once, then strode away evenly. I'd never seen the man hurry. I didn't think he knew how–he was too used to the world waiting for him. Sure enough, August had paused to glance over his shoulder, checking on his progress. Van's stride didn't falter, and August matched his pace the rest of the way to the bar. I huffed a chuckle and turned my attention back to the entry, hoping to catch sight of LB before she slipped away into the crowd.

"Parker!"

I smiled and turned towards my sister as Preston rushed over, my mother trailing after. My smile flickered, but I managed to keep it up. "Preston!"

She gave me a quick hug, then a pointed look. She was desperate to lose her maternal shadow, I could tell. I'd call it a twin thing, but the reality was that most people wanted to get out of my mother's orbit as quickly as they could.

"Hello, son," my mother said, offering her hand for a kiss.

I lightly gripped her fingers in mine, giving them a squeeze before releasing them without so much as a fake kiss. "Mother."

Her brows arched slightly, but I held no remorse for the slight.

"Is your husband well?"

She sighed dramatically. I caught sight of Preston's expression and struggled to keep a straight face. She looked like she simultaneously wanted to disappear into the floor and gut punch our mother.

"He's not," Mother replied, stiffly. "He's entered hospice care. It won't be long now."

"I'm very sorry to hear that. He seemed like a decent man."

While none of my mother's husbands were winners, exactly, this one had seemed to at least possess a moral compass.

"He was. I mean is. Very decent," she muttered, distracted, as she cast her eyes over the crowd.

"Hunting already, Mother?" Preston drawled. "How very uncouth."

Mother gave her a sharp look. "Don't you start, missy."

"Oh, Mother, when will you learn? I started decades ago. I've just never stopped."

She took our exasperated parent's arm and moved to lead her away.

"Good luck tonight, Parker," Preston called as she steered my mother in the opposite direction.

My sister gave me a meaningful look, one I knew meant "go get her". That wasn't twin intuition, it was just Preston. She knew how much LB meant to me, and she'd support us until the end, no matter what the future held. But she didn't want our parents meddling in my life any more than I did, so she kept her mouth shut. I'm also sure Mother had put up a fuss until Pres agreed to bring her over, but now she was going to manage her away, as she always did.

"Thank you, twinkie," I whispered.

She extended her free hand and squeezed mine for a moment before turning her attention back to our mother.

"Alright, Mother. Let's go find Daddy. I'm up for some family drama tonight."

"Oh, Preston, no," Mother protested, shaking her head. "Introduce me to someone new!"

"I don't know anyone who would be age appropriate," I could hear her say in response as they disappeared into the crowd.

I scoffed an incredulous laugh and shook my head at my mother's sheer audacity, turning once more to the entry. I'd kept an eye on it through that painful exchange, but there had been no sign of LB. Then, a mass of people shifted, and a flash of burnished gold caught my eye.

I knew immediately that it had been silly to worry about missing LB's entrance. It was as though a supernatural force moved through the crowd, parting a clear path for her right toward me. The lights of the venue were warm on her blonde hair and the yellow silk gown she wore, making her look as though she was spun of gold. I could feel my breath catch in my chest as she paused atop the small staircase that led down to the main floor, where I waited. People flowed around her, respecting that invisible force field, and I was frozen.

As though she could feel my eyes on her–*of course she can... god, I hope she can*–she turned her head to meet my gaze. A rush of unreadable emotions crossed her face before she straightened her shoulders and gave me a professional smile. It was as though I could see her don her LB persona, the real her slipping away behind her mask.

She moved quickly through the crowd, the force field effect no longer at play now that she was in work mode. She had such gravity of spirit as she was. One day, I hoped she'd see that.

"Parker," she said as she reached me.

I realized belatedly that I hadn't moved toward her. I had just stood, transfixed, caught up in her. I blinked myself back to reality and gave her a warm smile.

"LB," I greeted, pulling her into a hug that was just this side of professional. "You look absolutely stunning, spitfire."

I murmured the praise under my breath, so only she could

hear. I was rewarded with the slight pinkening of her cheeks behind her makeup, which I glimpsed as she released me and straightened.

"Thank you, Parker," she said softly.

Her hand flew to my gift at her throat, and I desperately wanted to reach out and run my fingers along the chain, then cup them around the yellow diamond. But in the interest of propriety, I refrained.

"It's perfect on you," I said, gently, nodding at her sparkle.

"It's far too much," she murmured, hands falling away and fidgeting. She took a deep breath and looked back up at me. "But thank you. It really is gorgeous."

I shook my head slowly. "It has nothing on you, Laura Beth. It looked fine on the stand, but on you..." I let my gaze travel her body, appreciating the slight goosebumps I saw rise on her arms, "on you, it's art."

She flushed again, looking desperate for something to say, and I gave her an out.

"August is here." I motioned at the bar in the corner. "He and my boss, Van Costa, are making the rounds."

She nodded. "I see. Has he...said anything?"

I tilted my head at her. "He didn't tell–"

"LB, there you are," a gruff voice interrupted.

I looked up and saw none other than Nathaniel Livingston striding toward us. We had never met, but I'd seen enough photos in print, online, and in Lex's office to know him on sight.

"Mr. Livingston," I said, extending my hand. "Parker Brooks. It's good to meet you, finally."

He offered me a firm shake and an assessing look, then gave me a single nod. "Brooks, yes. You're part of Alexandra's team."

"I work for Lex's business partner, Van," I confirmed. "I've had the pleasure of working with LB, here, on Gaspar Technologies."

"Have you?" he asked coolly, giving LB an arched eyebrow.

I could feel her shrink. She held her own physically, her stance strong and shoulders back, but I could see the minute changes in her expression and feel the shift in her energy under his scrutiny.

"And how has working with the enemy been for you, boy?"

I barked a laugh, much to both of their surprise. "I wouldn't know, Nate," I drawled, knowing the immediate informality would grate on his nerves. His jaw clenched, indicating my assessment was accurate. "We're just shrewd business people who saw potential in the same company. As long as Gaspar Technologies grows, we all win. Doesn't sound like much need for competition or declarations of war to me."

"I couldn't agree more," Van called from over my shoulder.

Now it's a party. I turned to him with a smile. "Boss! And August, welcome back."

"LB!" August said with enthusiasm. "You look lovely, dear. So good to see you."

He gave her hand a warm, vigorous shake–just one–and beamed.

"You, too, August." She rewarded him with the first genuine smile I'd seen from her all evening. "It's an honor to be here."

"So it is!" He agreed with a nod, then turned his attention to Nate.

"Ah, Nathaniel," he said, the energy in his tone dimming. "I wasn't sure if you'd be here."

"Well, we were so pleased to hear of a potential collaboration with P&L," Van cut in, his hawkish look trained on Nate, "we couldn't miss an opportunity to celebrate the success of Gaspar Technologies together."

August nodded, his eyes wandering away from our small gathering. "Yes, well, it's a shame–"

The lights dimmed twice in quick succession, signaling the

start of the brief presentation portion of the night's agenda. I stole a glance at LB and saw her gaze trained on August as he looked resolutely at the stage, waiting for what we all knew was coming. At the panic on her face from what he had started to say, I realized she hadn't gotten the update. I wanted to throttle August for taking the coward's way out, for that was surely what had happened here.

"Ladies and gentlemen, welcome to the fifteenth annual Feed the Bay charity gala." Lex's voice boomed out over the hall's speaker system, and everyone turn to where she stood at the podium in the center of the room.

A chorus of cheers went up from the audience, all eyes trained on her. All eyes but mine, which were zeroed in on LB. She had stiffened, looking between August and Lex with concern written on her features.

"As a member of the board of Feed the Bay, it is my privilege to be one of your hosts for the evening. For those of you who don't know me, I'm Lex Livingston, founder and general partner of Athena Ventures."

There was another round of cheers. I watched Nate's expression fall into a slight frown of confusion as he looked around, clearly unaware of his sister's stellar reputation in this town.

"She's royalty here," I explained quietly. He shot me an incredulous look and I shrugged. "She has a stellar reputation, Nate. A true pillar of the community."

He scoffed, then turned it into a cough when August shot him a death glare. Nate's expression settled into something that looked like a cross between frustrated and bewildered. I glanced over at LB to get her reaction, but her eyes were trained on Lex. When they widened in shock, I realized I needed to pay more attention to the speech.

"...We're so thrilled to have the opportunity to partner

closely with Dr. August Gaspar and Gaspar Technologies to bring his revolutionary technology to market here in the Bay and globally. We are honored to have been chosen as an exclusive investment partner and look forward to what we will accomplish together, and with all of you."

There were more cheers and applause, but I ignored them as I watched the blood drain out of LB's face. She looked to Nate, who had turned slowly to face her, brow furrowed and lips drawn down in a scowl. My chest constricted at the panic and horror in her expression. She turned to me, wide-eyed.

"LB, I thought you knew," I said in a rush.

She shook her head, clearly stunned, and I threw a death glare of my own at August's back. He was being fawned over by more attendees in the wake of Lex's announcement. I caught Van's eye, silently asking him to stay with August. He gave me a slight nod, then looked behind me and thrust his chin in that direction.

I whirled around to find LB alone, staring into space with glassy eyes. Nate had already disappeared into the fray. She took a shuddering breath as I hurried toward her. Her eyes snapped up to mine.

Ah, fuck. She's going to run.

Chapter 33

LB

No, no, no, this isn't happening.

    Nate's harshly spoken words were ringing in my ears. The moment Lex Livingston had finished her announcement, he'd turned on me with fire in his gaze.

"There are few valid reasons to go to the office on a Sunday, Ms. Calhoun," he had ground out through gritted teeth, his eyes flashing. "But I suppose you've just given me one. Be there at 8am." He straightened his tie needlessly, looking down his nose at me. "Bring a box."

He had turned on his heel and strode away, and my world dropped right out from beneath me. *I...I just got fired.* I shook myself internally, trying to get my brain back online. *I'm going to get fired tomorrow. I don't–I can't–*

I sensed someone coming closer and looked up to see Parker moving toward me. That was enough to jolt me back to action, and I spun on my heel and dashed for the exit.

My brain was a plastic bag in an angry storm, my thoughts flying incoherently around my head. I thought of my early days in college, the excitement I felt to be learning things surrounded by equally driven peers. I saw the light in Dr. Gaspar's eyes as he shared his tech and the impact it could make on the world, the fierce conviction that he could improve people's lives. I saw Parker at the wheel of his sailboat, the sun on his face making his hazel eyes flash as he grinned at me, completely at home. He was always completely at home wherever he was.

I am never at home.

I dodged around partygoers, weaving my way toward the exit as quickly as I could. Vaguely aware of Parker on my heels, I refused to turn, slow, or falter. I felt like I was drowning, like the world was caving in on me. *Is this what claustrophobia feels like?* My world was narrowing down to one tiny speck on the map in Alabama, a little town with a great high school football team and little else to claim as its own.

The sobs were working their way up my throat, but I fought them down. I was so far beyond behaving professionally at this point, fleeing like some lost princess wannabe, but I was not about to add to my humiliation by breaking down in tears on my exit. I drew a shuddering breath and tried to clear my head, but the visions wouldn't stop flashing through my mind.

Sara Jean, telling me I was going to marry Parker.

Nate, welcoming me to his team on my first day, challenging me to exceed his expectations and promising to help me do just that.

Maya, laughing at a random late night TV show we caught together once when our schedules miraculously aligned.

Parker, bracing over me in bed with a look of what could only be described as love in his eyes.

I squeezed my eyes shut against it all, trying to stop the flood of memories. *That's what you stand to lose, Laura Beth. All of that.* A crack grew in my chest and radiated out, tearing through me. If I didn't have this job and I couldn't work in VC anymore because P&L declared me persona non grata, the life that I knew would be over.

"LB, please!" Parker's anguished voice finally cut through my thoughts.

I whirled around, surprised to find us both on the sidewalk in front of the Art Museum. I had run the same path I'd walked earlier when I'd arrived, headed out to the bus stop on the corner. There were only a handful of people around, and I wished there were more. I wished I could use them as an excuse to lock up the emotion that wanted to burst out of me.

"Laura Beth, I'm sorry," Parker called, his hands out in a calming motion as though I was a wild animal he needed to tame. "I'm so sorry you found out like that. I'm sorry this didn't go the way you wanted. I'm sorry Nate is an absolute Neanderthal and didn't support you like he should have."

I blinked at him and shook my head. "None of this is yours to apologize for, Parker!"

"I know!" He ran his hands through his hair roughly. "Spitfire, I know. But I feel for you. I know how hard you work, and I know how much all of what just went down must have hurt. And for your hurt, for your pain, Laura Beth, for that I'm so, so sorry."

"I–" I gasped on the sob that forced its way through, pressing a hand to my chest. "Thank you," I whispered.

I didn't think I could manage to say anything else.

"Please, stay," he pleaded, reaching a hand out to me. He was still standing several feet away, as though he was worried he'd spook me if he got to close. His instincts were spot on.

"Please," he begged, and I felt his need like an itch on my skin. "It doesn't have to be you against the world, spitfire, please. It can be us. You and me. You don't have to do this alone."

"This isn't your problem to solve, Parker!" I cried.

"I know, Laura Beth, I know," he said gently. "But I want to help you solve it. I want to be there for you and ease the hurt. Will you let me? Will you let me help you fix this?"

"How–" I clenched my hands into fists and squeezed my eyes shut, feeling like a conduit for more emotion than was humanly possible. "How am I supposed to fix this? All I've worked for my whole life is just...gone. It's gone. GONE!" I screamed.

I stared off into the distance; the tension running from my body in a quick whoosh. I shook my head and looked away, blinking back the tears that burned and threatened to fall.

"I have to go," I whispered, my voice cracking. "I have to be at P&L at 8am with a fucking box so Nate can fire me properly, and I have to go."

"Spitfire, please, stay with me tonight. Let me–"

I turned to him. I felt numb, like all the emotion that had just torn through me had left me hollow and empty. "You told me to only use your number for business until I was ready."

He opened his mouth, looked away, and closed it. "I did."

"I'm not ready, Parker," I muttered. I watched his expression fall, concern still prominent in his gaze. "Enjoy the gala."

"Please," he begged, voice gentle.

In any other circumstance, his broken voice would've given me pause, made me consider the impact I was having on those around me. But my world was crashing down around my ears, and I didn't have the capacity to feel anything. In the face of my pain, I was hollow.

"Bye, Parker." I turned away. "And don't send a car after me. I won't get into it."

"Laura Beth!"

Hearing that name on his lips, again, broke something in me. The Bay didn't know me as Laura Beth. No one outside of my family and friends in Pike Road called me by my full name. And when he had said it before this moment, it had always filled me with a sense of lightness and joy. A feeling of contentment that someone here in the Bay was holding space for the parts of me I couldn't take completely out of Alabama. That someone here saw me for all I was. But now that I was losing this job, which meant losing the Bay...hearing that name on his lips felt more like a death sentence than a balm.

I whirled on him, anger flaring in me even though I knew it was misplaced. "It's L *fucking* B, Parker! L! B!"

I spun back toward the bus stop and didn't stop. I could hear his voice, but I tuned out his words, drowning once more in my panic as I went. *You've done it now, Laura Beth. You've fucking done it now.*

Chapter 34

LB

S unday dawned bright and gorgeous, and I couldn't even enjoy it. It was as though the weather was making a mockery of my misery. I scowled out the window at the bright sunshine and blue sky the entire time I got ready. Even dressing felt like a futile activity, so I completely ignored my usual work clothes. I didn't need them, anyway.

I tugged on a pair of jeans and a soft, old band t-shirt I'd stolen from my momma's closet years ago. It was so worn the seams were barely holding, but it was the closest I could get to a hug from Momma, so on it went. I pulled a light jacket on top, shoved my feet into my Chucks, and marched out the door and into the offensive sunshine.

After I had stumbled home in tears last night, I had taken myself into the shower and sobbed for a good hour. The water had definitely run cold, but I just shivered under it, unwilling to leave the water because it felt like accepting my fate. Eventually, the adrenaline dropped and my brain kicked in, reminding me that dramatics wouldn't get me anywhere. I had pulled myself from the spray, dried off, and fallen into bed in nothing but a t-shirt and underwear. When my alarm had gone off at

6:30am, I was sorely tempted to ignore it entirely. But then my phone had buzzed.

> Mr. Livingston: See you at 8.

As though I could forget that little appointment he'd set for us the night before. In a fit of pique, I had thrown a middle finger at my phone and chucked it across the bed. Ten minutes later, I dragged myself from the covers and started my visual assault of the sky.

As I walked to the office from the bus stop, I thought of the many mornings I had spent just like this. I tried to remember how I'd felt about going to work. I knew I had always felt driven to succeed, to achieve that next milestone, but had I ever felt truly excited about *what* I did? The why was easy. I'd always had a clear picture of that in my head. But the what? I couldn't remember if I had been excited about it or if I'd been indifferent.

I had wanted to stop in at my favorite coffee shop, but then I remembered I didn't have an income anymore. I sighed and walked right past it, the anxiety over my future churning in my gut as I did. *This is going to suck.*

I steeled my nerves as I approached the office building and scanned my badge one last time, letting myself up to Nate's office. His door was slightly ajar when I got there, and I tapped lightly.

"Come in, LB," he called.

I stepped in and almost froze in the doorway. Nate was sitting on the couch in front of his desk, dressed in jeans and a polo shirt. I had never seen the man in anything less formal than a suit and tie.

"Uh, good morning." I stood awkwardly in front of the couch.

266

"Sit." He waved to the armchair to his left.

"Sure," I said, taking the seat. "Thanks."

He arched a brow at me. "Is it really a good morning, LB?"

I snorted a laugh and shook my head. "No, Nate, it's not. It's a terribly shitty morning, for me, but the weather didn't get the memo, so. Here we are."

He laughed, and I realized I'd never heard that sound before.

"You should do that more often."

He looked at me with raised brows. "Do what?"

"Laugh. Makes you way more approachable."

He leaned forward to rest his elbows on his knees, studying my face intently.

"Who are you, and what have you done with LB?" he asked, a teasing tone in his voice.

I didn't know who this version of Nate was, but I wasn't about to look a gift horse in the mouth.

"Well, she was a people pleaser," I answered. "Terribly scared of doing or saying the wrong thing. But I know I'm fired, so there's not much to lose. May as well speak my mind."

"You should always speak it, LB."

"Laura Beth," I corrected. "I don't know that LB is going to survive this early life crisis of mine. Call me Laura Beth."

He gave me a little smile and nodded. "Laura Beth it is."

He studied me for a moment more, then slapped a hand on his knee and stood, walking over to his desk.

"I have a severance package here for you."

He picked up a folder and a pen and brought both over to me, setting them on the coffee table in front of me. I looked up at him in surprise.

"A package, sir?"

He grinned. "It's Nate. And, yes. A package. You can take a peek at the details in a minute."

"Okay," I muttered, waiting for him to give me more context.

"LB–Laura Beth," he said, "I'm sorry I didn't support you as I should have."

I stared at him wide-eyed, stunned.

"This isn't how this situation should have gone down, and I know I'm responsible for that," he continued. "I pressured you to act in a way that you felt was wrong for the client and for you, and that's not the kind of leader I want to be."

"Oh, I...uh, thank you." I tried to gather my rapidly scattered thoughts. "I really appreciate you saying that."

He nodded. "You have a lot of potential, Laura Beth. You have solid instincts and an impressive understanding of the people you work with. You pegged the things that were most important to Dr. Gaspar from the beginning. I just didn't listen."

He studied me for another moment, eyes seeking something in mine.

"I'm going to give you some advice."

"Okay," I agreed, quickly, knowing he was going to give it to me regardless.

"Take some time away from the Bay. Go home for a bit, be with your family. And ask yourself what it is you want to do with the talent you have and the skills you've developed."

He gave me a pointed look, and I looked back in mild confusion. "I'm not sure I understand, Nate."

"I don't think venture capitalism is the right fit for you, Laura Beth," he said bluntly. "I think your talents would be better served elsewhere, but it's up to you to determine where. That's not something I or anyone else can tell you."

I gaped at him as I processed his words. "But, I thought–"

"Don't take any of what I just said as an indication that you failed in this role, Laura Beth," he said, firmly, his tone brokering no argument. "I meant what I said–you are talented, and you were an asset to this firm the entire time you were here. But I think you'll be an even bigger asset when you find a place that's the right fit. And I look forward to seeing what you accomplish when you find it."

"I–okay. Thank you, I think," I stammered, feeling untethered.

Nate chuckled. "I know, this is a lot. And after a night like you had, I'm sure it's all a bit overwhelming."

"You could say that again."

He smiled and handed me the folder and pen. "Take a look, read it over. Let me know what you think."

"Okay," I said, softly.

"I'm serious, Laura Beth," he pressed. I looked up at him again as he met my gaze. "I'm proud to have been part of your professional journey, and I'm more than happy to be a reference when you decide where you want to go next."

"Wow, Nate....thank you. Sincerely, that means a lot."

"Good," he replied. "I don't offer that to just anyone."

I chuckled, feeling a bit in awe. This was not how I expected our conversation to go. I opened the folder and my eyes bugged out of my head. He was offering me six months of pay.

"Uh, Nate? This says my last day is in two weeks."

"That's correct," he confirmed. "You have additional PTO. Use it, collect your normal paycheck at the end of it, then take the severance while you figure out your next steps. I know this is a lot, but I'm doing you a favor here. You need to land somewhere that your talents will be put to better use."

I nodded absently as I scrawled a signature on the severance letter, handing it back over to him.

"Again, thank you," I said. "This isn't how I saw my experience at P&L ending, but I appreciate your support."

"It could have been a lot worse," he teased. "I could've fired you last night and not had a chance to get my head out of my ass."

I laughed in surprise and gaped at him. "Okay, it's my turn to ask—who are you, and what have you done with Mr. Livingston?!"

He laughed and shook his head. "Let's just say someone gave me a lot to think about at the gala last night."

"Well, when you talk to them next, thank them for me."

He smirked and nodded, and I took that as my cue to leave. I paused at the door and glanced back to give him a wave, which he returned with a rueful look.

His recommendation to bring a box had been dramatic, I decided as I walked by my desk. I had very few things that were truly mine, and I spent a few moments going through the drawers to make sure I had everything. I could fit it all easily in my bag. It felt surreal to pull my badge from my bag and leave it atop my laptop before I turned to leave.

As I walked out, I paused at the front door and looked back at the office that had been my only professional home since graduation. I had learned a lot here, and I had no idea what I was going to do next, but I was grateful for all P&L had given me. *Now to figure out what the hell the future holds.*

Chapter 35

LB

Landing in Montgomery on Monday felt like an out-of-body experience. Every time I'd been home in the last decade, it had been for my family. It had been to hug my momma, welcome my nieces and nephew into the world, or otherwise connect with the people who had helped me grow into the human I was. As the plane drew nearer to the runway, I was reminded that this trip was for me and me alone. Yes, my parents were excited to see me. Yes, Sara Jean had been blowing my phone up nonstop since I texted her the day before to tell her I was coming. But even they knew this visit was going to be different.

The pilot navigated a smooth touchdown, and I turned off airplane mode on my phone. It immediately started buzzing in my hand.

Sara Jean: OMG I SEE YOU TODAY!!!

Sara Jean: Please tell me the instant you land.

Sara Jean: Dex found an app that tracks flight status! You're landing 5 minutes early! Woohoo!

> Sara Jean: I know you landed, brat. I'm here—
> see you soon.

I huffed a laugh, surprised at the emotion that welled up in me in response to her pestering.

> Me: See you soon.

> Sara Jean: 😢

I went to close out of my messages app, but another unread thread caught my eye. Steeling myself with a deep breath, I clicked the thread open. The messages started the night of the gala and ended Sunday night.

> Parker: Did you make it home?

> Parker: Spitfire, please. I just need to know you're okay.

> Parker: Good luck with Nate this morning. I can be there in a heartbeat if you need me.

> Parker: Thinking of you.

My heart squeezed in my chest. My thumbs hovered over my keyboard, but I didn't know what to say. There was still so much I had yet to figure out. I closed the app and pulled my bag out from under the seat in front of me.

The journey from plane to curbside was quick, and Sara Jean was indeed waiting for me in the passenger pickup area outside. The heat and humidity of Alabama hit me like a truck as I walked out of the airport, and I staggered for a moment.

"Laura Beth!" Sara Jean hollered, running toward me with a squeal. "I can't believe you're here!"

She snatched me up without warning, squeezing the life out

of me as she jumped up and down. I couldn't help the laugh that tumbled out of me.

"You're ridiculous!" I cried, clinging to her to stay on my feet.

"So are you!" she fired back with a grin, reaching up to pinch my cheek.

I pushed her hand away and rolled my eyes at her. Teasing aside, it was good to see her. She looked just as she always had—blonde, petite, perky, and so cute it was basically a crime.

"Hey, Dex," I called, waving at her giant of a husband.

"Sweet pea," he said with a nod. "It's been a while."

"Sure has," I murmured, dragging my suitcase toward their waiting car. It was older than I was, and I'd never seen my sister drive anything else.

"Momma is beside herself, Laura Beth. She's been askin' me why you didn't give her any notice for this visit and frettin' that she doesn't have everything she needs for supper."

"It'll be fine, I'm sure," I muttered, handing my bag over to Dex. "She'll make enough to feed an army and we'll be eating leftovers all week."

Dex chuckled and cast me a little smile, knowing the truth of my words.

"You try tellin' her that!" Sara Jean said, throwing her hands up in exasperation.

I didn't know if it was the same in all small-town, Southern families, but all the adult women I knew in Pike Road shared the same favorite pastime: complaining about things they couldn't change, yet rising to the occasion and making it turn out perfectly anyway.

"Momma will be fine, Sara Jean." I rested my hands on her shoulders and gave her an earnest look. "Now get your ass in the car so poor Dex can stop blockin' traffic."

I swatted her and she squealed, swinging her hand behind

273

her to smack me right back. I laughed and winked at Dex as he grinned and rolled his eyes at our shenanigans, letting himself into the front seat as he did. I clambered in the back, per usual, and watched first Montgomery and then the fields surrounding Pike Road pass me by.

Sara Jean talked the entire time, peppering question after question at me. The more she asked, the more my spirits fell. As I tried to explain why I was here so suddenly and for so long—a week was so much more than the one or two nights I'd usually managed—my words got stuck in my throat. *How do you tell the people who love you that you've failed?*

I didn't know the answer to that question, and I wasn't sure I wanted to. So I deflected for the most part, ignored some, and flat out redirected the conversation for the rest. Dex caught my eyes a few times in the rearview mirror, giving me a clear look of "I see you". I tried to convey back, "you do, but don't tell her," but I don't think our silent communication had quite reached that level of sophistication.

"Are you even listenin', Laura Beth?" Sara Jean prodded. She twisted around in the front passenger's seat to face me. "When are you gonna tell us what you're doin' here?"

"When she's good and ready, Sara Jean," Dex said firmly.

Sara Jean whipped around to narrow her eyes at her husband. "Excuse you, did I ask you that question?"

His lips quirked to the side in an amused smirk. "No, ma'am."

She reached over and smacked him with the back of her hand. "Damn right. Stick to drivin', slick, and leave the questions to me."

"Yes, ma'am," he said, a glint in his eye. He caught my gaze in the mirror again and threw me a quick wink.

I chuckled and shook my head, staring out the window as the town flew by. It was always surreal to be back here.

"At least you're dressed kinda normal today," Sara Jean mused, eyeing my t-shirt and yoga pants ensemble.

"Gee, thanks, Stinky," I said. For my last visit, I'd gone straight to the airport after work and had arrived in Pike Road in a fitted black pencil skirt, pink blouse, and black stilettos. I couldn't have been more conspicuous if I'd tried.

She glared at me, hating the nickname, and I stuck my tongue out at her.

"None of that around the kids, girls," Dex rumbled, and I blinked over at him in surprise. "Althea is on a copycat kick."

"Say no more, brother mine," I said sagely. "I will do my best to not disturb the peace."

Sara Jean cackled, "Oh, you've already disturbed it, sister. Pretty sure Momma activated the church phone tree for this one."

"Why?!" I cried, throwing my hands up in the air.

Sara Jean held up a hand and pointed to her thumb. "You're here on a moment's notice," she said. She pointed to her pointer finger. "For an entire week. You've been largely unresponsive for the past month." She pointed to the next finger. "And you forgot Roscoe's birthday."

"I did not!" I gasped, indignant at the thought.

"Sure did," Sara Jean insisted.

"Roscoe's birthday is next week."

"Last week," Dex rumbled.

"Shit," I said, dropping my head in my hands.

"None of that," my sister piped up. "The cursing or the moping. None of that is allowed."

"The bad emotions are just as valid," I mumbled at her from behind my hands.

"No shit, Sherlock, but wallowin' doesn't help a soul! Stop moping!"

I pulled my hands down and glared at her. "And what do you do to handle your big emotions, hm?"

She arched an eyebrow at me and gave me a seriously disturbing look. "Sure you want to know?"

"No," I said quickly, shaking my head. "I definitely do not."

She frowned and rolled her eyes. "Your loss."

"I'm sure," I muttered, shaking my head.

Dex slowed to a stop, and I realized with a start that we were at my parents' house.

"I take it you don't have room at yours?" I asked hopefully, leaning up between their seats.

Sara Jean snorted. "Sure, with the addition from the last remodel we have plenty of space!"

"Okay, okay," I grumbled. "No need for the sarcasm."

"She misses you, little sister," Sara Jean said, her expression kind.

I sighed. "I know she does. I just hate disappointing her."

My big sister looked at me like I was completely insane.

"You live in one of the fanciest places in the whole world all on your own," she said. "She's proud as hell of you, as are we all. Where's this comin' from?"

I groaned, knowing Sara Jean would not ignore it now that she'd caught the scent of blood. "It's been a rough few weeks. But I'd rather tell this story once."

"Come on, then. I convinced Dex to watch the kids tonight so you and I can have a good ol' fashioned girl chat with Momma."

"Really?" I flashed Dex a grateful smile. "Thank you so much."

"Anytime, sweet pea," he said with a nod. He'd been calling me that since I was a kid. I always used to think it was an odd endearment for a high schooler to give his girlfriend's little

276

sister, but then I met his three younger sisters. He called every single one of them, and then his two daughters, sweet pea, too.

Dex parked and we all piled out of the car. I went to get my bag from the trunk, but he leveled me with a hard look and I backed off with my hands up.

"Okay, okay, big brother," I teased, backing away with a smile. "Thank you for your brutish ways."

He grunted and rolled his eyes in response, and I giggled.

"There's my girl!" Momma boomed behind me, making me jump.

"Momma!" I said, losing myself in her embrace.

"You're finally home for longer than two shakes of a lamb's tail," she said, leaning back to look at me. "I'm so glad you're here, baby."

I swallowed thickly and nodded. "Thank you, Momma."

She slung her arm around me and squeezed me to her. "Come on, Laura Beth. I bet you're starving."

———

True to my prediction, Momma had made far too much food for supper. I'd eaten my fill before dragging myself up to my room—still decorated as though I had never left—and flopping onto my old bed. Sara Jean followed shortly after, laying herself right down next to me. We were both flat on our backs, staring up at the ceiling.

"Alright. Talk to me, little sis," she pressed, threading her fingers through mine.

I sighed and squeezed my eyes shut. "I got fired."

Sara Jean's whole body tensed. I knew she was an external processor—all her emotions and thoughts had to be expressed to be understood—so I knew she was tempering herself. Unrestrained Sara Jean would've been jumping to her feet and screaming curses by then.

"Elaborate, please," she said, her voice tight.

"It's a thing at P&L, where I worked," I explained. "They give associates one chance to close a deal on their own, without a more senior sponsor. Do it, and you're promoted. Fail, and you're fired."

She rolled over onto her side and stared at me, incredulous. "That's the stupidest thing I ever heard."

I laughed, nodding. "You're not wrong."

"There will always be other jobs, Laura Beth. What's really got you down?"

It was my turn to look incredulous. "Excuse me? I've worked literally my whole life toward this and you think it's something else that's got me in a state?"

She rolled her eyes and sighed. "Oh, sweet, sweet, Laura Beth. My innocent little sister."

She reached out to pat my head, and I ducked away, groaning. "Ugh! Don't patronize me!"

"Girl, you're a force. Always have been. I have no doubt you'll pick yourself up and find something that you'll love even more. I never thought that whole VC thing was for you. But you're smart, you're talented, and I know you'll be able to move on to something that's a better fit."

"But P&L was the whole reason I was in the Bay. How am I supposed to afford to live there without a job?"

She leaned back and arched an eyebrow at me. "Okay, honey, there's a lot to unpack there. First of all, you're in the Bay to make a name and a life for yourself, not to work at one specific company you stumbled upon out of college."

"Well, I–"

"Uh uh," she held up a hand, "I'm not done. Second, I know you better than I know my damn self. You have savings, yes?"

"Sure, but—"

"Nope, it's still my turn." She sat up, drawing me with her so we were sitting cross-legged, facing one another. "Laura Beth, honey, you've been so set on getting out of Pike Road and being successful, I think you forgot to define what success means for you. Because it's not the same for every person. Success for me looks like marriage and a home full to bursting with unruly, lovable rugrats."

"But you gave up your dream," I said, squeezing her hands.

She looked at me, bewildered. "What dream?"

"Nursing—you told me when we were kids you always wanted to be a nurse. Then you met Dex and all of a sudden it was all about his dream."

She laughed. "Honey, nursing was my *back-up plan*. Once I got old enough to picture a future with Dex, I knew it was what I wanted. He and the life we'd build together were better than anything I could hope for by myself. That path isn't for everyone. Goodness knows we were just babies ourselves when we got married and started havin' babies, just like Momma and Daddy. And I always knew that wasn't the life you wanted, and I was proud of you for chasin' what you did want so doggedly."

I blinked at her, my mind reeling. "You're kind of breaking my brain right now."

She nodded, a soft look in her eyes. "I know. You've never asked me what my version of success was, because I think you might have assumed it was this uniform thing everyone pursued. But it's not. And it's not something static, either. Somedays, it's gettin' out of bed and gettin' all the kids dressed and not screamin' my head off at someone. Other days, it's gettin' up early to have two hours of me time to read before the chaos descends." She squeezed my hands back, a little smirk curving her lips. "You've been drivin' yourself so hard, I think you forgot to check in and see if you still wanted what was at the end of the path you were headed down."

I exhaled a shaky breath, mind swimming.

"I think you might be right about that," I said softly.

Movement by the door made me look up to find Momma smiling at us, a watery look in her eyes.

"Momma, how long you been lurkin' there?" Sara Jean asked, a teasing lilt to her voice.

"Long enough to be damn proud of you girls," she said with a sniffle.

"Come on, Momma." I patted the open space on the bed.

She came over and joined us, perching on the bedside. "Why are you home, baby?"

I took a deep breath, then just ripped off the bandage. "I got fired."

She just nodded. "Sure, honey, but why are you really home?"

I gave her a confused look. She sighed and shared a quick look with Sara Jean.

"Tell me about the boy."

The breath left my lungs and my chest felt tight. That had been happening a lot, when I let my mind turn to Parker. And he was in my head constantly.

"His name is Parker," I said, tears coming to my eyes. "He's smart, and funny, and kind, and gorgeous."

"And he thinks you hung the moon," Sara Jean added, nudging me with her shoulder.

I huffed a laugh. "I don't know about that."

She rolled her eyes, and I got the feeling that she was holding out on me. Before I could prod, Momma drew my attention back.

"Why are you talkin' 'bout him like you've lost him, honey?"

"Because I have," I cried, fighting the tears. "I had to. Everything was tied up in this deal and my promotion, and I couldn't risk my future in the Bay for someone...someone I..."

My voice trailed off. I was about to say "for someone I barely knew," but that felt dishonest. I knew Parker in most of the ways that mattered. I knew he was a good man with a big heart. I knew he cared deeply for the people in his life, and that had somehow come to include me.

Momma fixed me with a look. "So why are you really here?"

"Because I got scared," I whispered. "And I ran away."

Sara Jean wrapped an arm around me and rested her head on my shoulder. "What are you scared of?"

I pressed my eyes closed, my chin quivering. "Losing my way," I sobbed. "I'm scared of failing. Of disappointing you—"

"Honey, we're proud of you and always will be," Momma interjected. "But it's okay if you were scared of disappointing yourself. You've always made a pretty big deal of that plan of yours."

Sara Jean tightened her arm around me. "Change can be scary, Laura Beth, but that doesn't mean it's the wrong path. Maybe you need to change your definition of success and look at all this from a different angle."

I sniffed and wiped my tears away, though it felt futile as more kept cropping up. "But if I'm not LB the VC associate... who am I?"

"Sounds like that's something you get to figure out," Momma said, patting my knee. She had a gentle smile on her face. "Honey, I've known you were destined for big things from the moment you hollered in my arms, little face so determined. You've had a plan ever since you were tiny, and I have never doubted you'd make it come true. I trust you to find your way, wherever your path may lead. I think you should trust in you, too."

I grabbed her hand in mine and squeezed it, smiling through the tears. "Thank you, Momma."

"I agree," Sara Jean piped up. "And I also think you should throw out all your future plans and go chase down that man who so clearly loves you because I am so ready for a brother-in-law."

I laughed and knocked my shoulder against hers. "Sara Jean!"

"What!?" she cried. "I am!"

Momma gave her a patient look and chuckled. "If you want that boy, honey, you go after him. You've got a big heart, but you sure don't love easy. Him breakin' through those walls is no small feat."

I considered her words. Had I been protecting myself from the people around me, scared of making a connection that could derail me from the path I needed to take? *Um, duh. Yes.*

I sighed, rubbing my hands over my face. Maybe it was time to change the trajectory of this conversation.

"Momma, how did you know Daddy was the one?"

"Ooooh, this is gettin' good!" Sara Jean shuffled closer, giving Momma an expectant, excited look. She looked just like a kid on Christmas morning.

Momma's eyes softened and went a little gooey like they always did when she talked about Daddy. "Your Daddy was the best man I'd ever met."

My heart panged, remembering having thought that very thing of Parker on more than one occasion.

"He was kind, and patient. And so driven," she looked off, lost in the memories. "He had such big dreams, for who he was and where he came from. No one else in his family had finished high school. None of them owned a business. He was determined to be the one who made it."

"And he did," Sara Jean quipped, a smile on her face.

Momma winked at her. "He sure did, honey. And even though those early years when he was building up the shop were hard, I was so proud to be there with him through it all. It wasn't easy, havin' young kids and buildin' everything from scratch, but look at us now." She turned those gooey eyes on us, a smile on her face. "Two gorgeous, successful daughters. A business that thrives, most days, and the home of our very own we never thought we'd be able to afford."

In the presence of her soft, proud smile, I felt guilty. I had always judged my parents, my home, dreaming of how I could get out. Dreams I had thought were so much bigger than theirs. Sara Jean's words about success being different for everyone echoed in my head, and I found her knowing gaze on me when I glanced her way.

"But it was the way he made me feel that helped me know he was the one," Momma continued.

"How did he make you feel?" Sara Jean asked eagerly.

"Like I was the only woman in the world he could see," she murmured, remembering. "He still does, to this day. One look, and I know how much he loves me. And I also know, no matter what I say or do, he'll look at me that same way for the rest of our lives."

I could picture Parker's face outside the gala, his expression twisted in fear, grief, and a hint of desperation. The tears pricked at the backs of my eyes again and I sniffled. When I wasn't breaking his heart, Parker looked at me like that, I knew. With love and a little bit of awe.

"Momma, I think I made a mistake," I whispered, voice unsteady.

She nodded. "I know, honey. But that's the beauty in a mistake. When you get to the other side, you can see where you went wrong. And then you can fix it."

Chapter 36

Parker

This had been, without a doubt, the longest week of my life. After the gala, I had canceled brunch with Preston on the off chance that LB would reach out. She hadn't. I could barely remember what else I had done during the week, but Sunday had arrived once more.

> Twinkie: We're having brunch at my place.
> Cami's at home this weekend. 15 minutes.

I pocketed my phone and headed down for the quick walk to Preston's place. I knew she'd sent Cami home to give us privacy, and I was grateful. I wasn't yet sure what I was going to say to my twin, but I knew I needed her insight.

My mind wandered for the short journey, and I was surprised to find myself suddenly at Preston's door. I knocked, this time, instead of letting myself in. The door opened moments later, a confused look on Preston's face.

"Where the hell is your key?"

"Good morning, Preston, how are you? I'm lovely, thanks so much for asking," I mocked, giving her a pointed look.

"Wow, okay. So, I'm super glad I sent Cami away. Get your ass in here, Mr. Snarkypants."

Sighing, I stepped in, making a beeline for the kitchen. She'd laid out a huge brunch spread on the island, along with a pitcher of what I hoped were mimosas. I pointed to it with a raised eyebrow.

"Screwdriver. We ran out of champagne."

"That'll do," I nodded, pouring a hearty glass.

"Okay, who are you and what have you done with my very level-headed, patient brother?" she demanded, folding her arms over her chest.

I waved, "Present."

"You are not Parker. You're Parker's mopey, more frustrating doppelganger."

I rolled my eyes. "Food first, Pres. Then I'll fill you in. And maybe you'll have some advice for what the hell I should do next."

She nodded slowly. "Help yourself, big. Cami was testing new recipes all week, so you know it's going to be delicious."

"Does that mean it's all vegan and gluten free?" I asked, eyeing what looked like french toast casserole.

"I don't even ask anymore. It doesn't matter. Everything she makes is incredible."

I shrugged, because Pres wasn't wrong. We both piled our plates high and took them to the dining table by the window. Preston brought the pitcher with her, and I nodded my thanks for her wisdom.

We ate mostly in silence until my sister simply couldn't take it anymore. Leveling me with a look, she questioned, "Is it LB? Do I need to shank a bitch?"

I choked on my bite of casserole, much to Preston's delight. When I could breathe again, I gave her a pointed look.

"Good lord, you sound like you spent a stint in juvenile

detention, not an elite boarding school. Where do you get these things?" I pointed my fork in her direction. "No, there will be no shanking the woman I love."

It was her turn to choke, this time on a sip of her screw-driver. She gaped at me once she'd recovered.

"I didn't know you were in l-word territory. Have you told her?"

I shook my head. "Haven't had the chance. She's not responding to my messages."

She blinked at me. "You're surprisingly calm about this."

I guffawed. "Not even remotely, but I know she's safe. Found her sister on Instagram and messaged her."

"Wow, Parker. Full stalker mode, got it."

I glared at her. "You have a better idea?"

She returned my glare with interest. "Considering I have no idea what's going on since you literally ran out of the gala last weekend without a word, Parker, no. I don't. Want to clue a sister in here? Help me help you, for fuck's sake."

I sighed, dropping my head into my hands. "Sorry, Pres. This whole situation has just been...not ideal."

"Believe me, I picked up on that. Want to start with the fact that you fell in love and didn't bother to tell me?"

"You think I should tell you before I tell her?"

"Well, I mean, isn't that where we are?"

"Fuck," I muttered. She wasn't wrong, and it just further illustrated how far off track things had gotten.

"What happened at the gala, big? Start there."

I nodded. "Yeah, okay. That works as well as anything, I guess."

I gave her the brief history of the deal, giving just enough context for her to follow along. Once I'd caught her up to the actual gala, she nodded at me with wide eyes.

"Lex's announcement must have been like a gut punch for LB," she winced.

I nodded. "Exactly. I had no idea it was going to happen that way, or I would've warned her. But she'd iced me out by that point."

"I mean, I get it. Clearly this deal and her job mean a lot to her."

I glanced at her.

"Don't look at me like that. You've said it yourself. Just because this all means a lot to her doesn't mean you don't mean a lot to her."

"I don't feel like I mean much of anything to her."

"Oh, stop the poor me act, big. We're way too old for that shit."

"We are not old," I protested.

"You're taking the bait and getting distracted. Go back to the gala. What happened after Lex's announcement?"

I sighed. "She was upset, obviously, and she ran away. I followed her outside and tried to get her to let me help her, but she refused. Pushed me away."

"Physically?" She looked surprised.

I snorted. "No, twinkie. Verbally. Emotionally. Physically would've been welcome, but she kept her distance."

"And you haven't heard from her since."

"Correct. But I know she went to her office the next day to meet with Nate, her boss, because I had overheard Lex dressing him down at the gala when I came back in."

Preston's eyes flashed and she leaned forward eagerly. Lex was her idol. She soaked up every story I told about her without reservation.

"When I got back, I saw Van and August across the room talking to a few of our industry contacts...

I didn't want to be there at the Gala. I wanted to chase after

LB, make sure she got home safe, try again to break through the walls she was putting up. But I knew now wasn't the time—she wasn't ready to hear me, to let me in. My wanting her to be ready would not change the facts.

I turned toward the bar, taking the route on the outskirts of the party to avoid being sucked into conversations I wasn't emotionally capable of faking. As I moved, I caught sight of Nate and Lex, half hidden behind a tall decorative vase filled with greenery. I paused, stepping closer and out of view.

"Alexandra, I really don't have time—"

"You do, Nate. For this, you do. Don't worry, I'll be quick," Lex said. Her tone was firm, straightforward, and dominant. Not a hint of sarcasm or apology.

I heard a sigh and assumed Nate had given her some sign of acquiescence.

"From everything Parker has told me, that girl on your team is talented with a ton of potential. If you let her believe for one moment that she's the reason P&L lost this deal, you're not half the man I thought you could be," she said. "But you sure are our father's son."

There was a brief silence, and I could picture her glaring daggers at him. I'd seen that expression, aimed at others, and it was not for the faint of heart. I heard Nate clear his throat awkwardly and almost felt bad for the man.

"Alexan—"

"It's Lex," she snapped, cutting him off without remorse. "I've told you enough times. When you're ready to give me the same respect and courtesy I extend to you, I'll gladly discuss this and anything else. But until then, Nate, keep your condescension to yourself. And for fuck's sake, do better."

I heard her stalk away and peered around the greenery to catch sight of Nate's expression. I expected him to look thunder-

ous, but under the furrowed brow he was thoughtful, considering–a bit stunned. Maybe there was hope for him yet.

"God, I love her," Preston said reverently, pulling me from the memory. "She is such a fucking badass."

"Indeed she is." I nodded, taking another sip of my screwdriver.

"So what now?"

I looked up at her, eyebrows raised. "Come again?"

"Are you just moping around, waiting for her to come back?"

"Well, I–"

"Because that just sounds lazy."

"Please, Preston, tell me how you really feel."

"Gladly," she said, with a prim nod. "This girl has just had her entire life yanked out from under her. Yes, she sounds a little overly obsessed with work, but, Parker–so are you. Hasn't your entire thing at Athena been a giant 'fuck you' to our parents and your trust fund? An example of how you could make it all on your own?"

"I mean, that's not the only reason I–"

"Sure, keep telling yourself that," she barreled right through my protest. "What if you hadn't made it, hm? What if you'd gotten stopped on your way up, made a poor decision and lost a deal, or, hell, lost one because your idiot of a boss threw you under the bus for his damned ego?"

"Van is not–"

"I'm talking about Nate, jackass. See the parallel?"

I shut my mouth and nodded, letting her continue.

"It sounds like LB doesn't have the support system you did, or even still do. Yes, our parents are deadbeats in the parenting department, but you still have the Brooks name. You've never wanted for anything. But from what you've shared, LB clawed her way out of bumfuck Alabama on her own. She made it to the associate level at one of the biggest firms in the country by herself, completely, with no one to support or mentor her along the way."

She gave me a pointed look.

"And here she is, at a gala that could mean the rest of her future plans blossom before her, and instead she's basically fired on the spot."

I swallowed and leaned back, scraping a hand over the stubble on my jaw.

"No wonder she ran, Parker," she said gently.

"But she has me," I insisted, leaning forward. "Now, she has me."

"But she doesn't know that, big," Preston insisted, her expression as soft as her tone. "You may have shown her an incredible time on dates or whatever you got up to on work trips, but you haven't told her you love her. You haven't told her you're in this as more than just a fling because this deal brought you together."

"I know," I sighed, leaning back. "I know I haven't. She won't let me."

"Boy, wild horses have nothing on your bank account. What the fuck are you waiting for?"

I blinked at her.

"Go get her, dumbass! Use those resources and find your girl! Tell her what you need to!"

Fuck's sake, Brooks, she's right. Of course she was. Preston made it a point to always be right, irritating as that trait was in a sister.

"I'm not saying she hasn't made her own share of mistakes in all this, because she has," she continued. "You both have, clearly. But if you love her, big? You need to get off your ass and make sure she knows that. Because whatever she's deciding for herself and her life right now, she doesn't have all the information she needs to make the right decision."

"You're right."

"I know," she smirked, giving me a knowing look.

"Fuck," I said, scrubbing my hands over my face yet again. "Okay, I guess I'm going to Pike Road."

Preston made a face. "What's on Pike Road?"

I laughed. "It's a town in Alabama. Where Laura Beth is from."

"Whoa, she's *real* country, isn't she?"

I rolled my eyes at her, shaking my head. Just as I went to gather my dishes, my phone buzzed in my pocket. I pulled it out, eyebrows raising.

"Is it her?" Preston asked, seeing my expression slowly morph into a grin.

"Her sister," I answered, turning my phone to her.

My Instagram app was open on our thread, which I'd started on Monday.

> Me: This is Parker. I've been working with and dating your sister, and she disappeared Saturday night. Please just let me know if she's safe.

> SaraJean87: She's home safe, hun. Hang tight.

> Me: Thank you.

–Today–

> SaraJean87: She lands at 3:40pm. Go get her.

Chapter 37

LB

M y stomach twisted into knots as I watched Alabama disappear through my window, despite not being a nervous flier.

There were so many questions I still had to answer about what I wanted for myself and my future. But if there was one thing I knew for certain now, after spending nearly a week with my family, it was this: I wanted Parker Brooks.

My visit to Pike Road had felt therapeutic in its intensity. It was as though I'd never seen my home or my family for who they were. As if I had always viewed them through the distorted lens of my own dreams. And I felt both appreciative and guilty for the new perspective.

What had my grand plans been, really, except for an excuse I gave myself for wanting something different? Sara Jean's words on my first night had stuck with me, and I'd spent the rest of my time in my hometown watching my family live their own versions of success. My aspirations were no more noble than theirs were, and in some ways, I envied the lives they had created for themselves.

I saw my momma smile and laugh with her grandbabies

while she made dinner for my daddy every night. Those kids knew their way around the kitchen better than I did. I mentioned to my older niece, Bellamy, that she chopped onions better than I ever had, and she just grinned at me. Momma, on the other hand, had piped up, "You were always more interested in readin' than learnin' from me."

There was no hurt in her words, and an indulgent smile accompanied them, but I realized she was right. As a kid, I hadn't seen the value in those moments in the kitchen or around the house. But watching everyone move through their daily lives made me realize how true Sara Jean's observations were. Success was different for us all, but if you found someone whose version matched yours? Well, you needed to hold on to that person with everything you had.

It had been a wonderful kind of torture to be surrounded by two couples who loved each other as deeply as my family did. Momma and Daddy were just as gooey around each other as ever, and the saucy banter Sara Jean served up to Dex was met with nothing but patience and warm smiles in return. I pretended to gag behind his back half the time, just to make my sister laugh, but the knowing look in her eyes when she did told me everything I needed to know. I wasn't fooling anyone. As much as I'd insisted that I wanted a career above all else, something had shifted in the time since Nate had assigned me to Gaspar Technologies. And everything had changed since I'd first met Parker on that flight.

I wanted that kind of love.

I glanced at the empty middle seat beside me and smiled to myself, remembering that first meeting. I'd never had a flight go so quickly as that one when we talked the whole time. The instant connection we'd felt was unlike anything I've ever experienced with another human being. And then, in every moment we spent together after, Parker just kept proving to me what kind of man he was. In the way he worked with me on the collaborative deal, the way he saw through me to know more about me and my motivations than I'd ever shared out loud. The way he held me and played my body like it was an instrument that had been made just for him. And the way he played and challenged me, then met my sass with equal fire.

He was my equal. Despite the bucket loads of money, access, and power Parker possessed, I realized he had always treated me like I was his match. My fear of falling into his orbit and becoming nothing more than a supporter to his success was entirely unfounded. In the time that I had known him, he had only wanted to support what I wanted to accomplish. Even at the detriment of his own personal agenda.

He could have easily closed that deal with Gaspar Technologies on day one, I realized. He was the more connected, more experienced professional. And yet, he had invested the time and energy into the collaboration between our two firms, not because he saw it as the only way forward, but because he believed in me and the ideas I brought to the table. All while little ol' me insisted we were enemies. For that, I was both grateful to him and desperately annoyed at myself.

I also knew Nate was right. Venture capital wasn't for me. The idea of profits over the humans involved hadn't sat right with me, and the ruthlessness the industry required didn't bring me joy. I needed to find something that didn't demand I ignore my internal compass.

The idea of waking up on Monday without a job terrified me, but I had to listen to those closest to me: I had to make a bet on myself. I had achieved every last thing I set out to accomplish before this point, and this would be no different.

Grateful for the six months of severance Nate and P&L had provided, I was confident I could land on two feet. If I could figure out what new path I wanted to carve for myself during that time? Even better.

One thing I knew for sure: whatever the next step held for me, I was showing up as Laura Beth. I was proud of what the LB persona had accomplished, but I didn't need her to protect me anymore. I was beginning to see I didn't want to exist in places that wouldn't welcome me as my whole self.

I closed my eyes and took a deep breath, willing my heart to settle in my chest. I still had a layover to navigate and another plane to catch before I could make it back to the Bay, but my pulse was already racing over what I planned to do once I got there. I needed Parker Brooks to know how I felt. I needed him to know he was mine, and I was finally ready to be his. The rest, I had decided, we could figure out. Together.

Chapter 38

Parker

For once, I didn't mind the traffic. Ralph was driving me to the airport, giving me the opportunity to plan how this encounter was going to go. Sara Jean hadn't given me many details, so I didn't know where Laura Beth's thoughts were after her time in Pike Road. All I knew was that, as Preston had suggested, she needed to have all the facts. She needed to know how I felt, how important she was to me, and how willing I was to dig in and figure out whatever came next together.

"I'll drop you off at ticketing, yes?" Ralph's voice broke through my thoughts.

I looked up and caught his gaze in the rearview, giving him a smile. "Thanks, Ralph. That's perfect."

"Just text me when you're ready for me to pick you up."

"Will do," I said, opening my door as he stopped at the curb.

"Parker," he called, and I turned back to him. "I know you don't ask many people for advice, mainly because I don't think you need it. You've always had great instincts."

I slowly folded myself back into my seat, giving Ralph my full attention. It hadn't been an exaggeration when I'd told Laura Beth that he had been driving me for two decades. He'd known me since I was a boy, and I'd taken over his contract from my father as soon as I had enough money to cover a generous raise and an annual bonus.

"I haven't seen you tied up over anyone before, so I know this girl means a lot to you," he continued, turning in his seat to face me. "And as someone who has been married for coming up on thirty years, I have one question for you."

"Let's hear it," I said, giving him a warm smile.

"What do you feel, when she's around?"

His question burrowed deep into my chest, and I took my time to give it full consideration. I hadn't had many reliable father figures in my life, and Ralph was professional to a fault, but I trusted his judgment more than most. If he felt strongly enough to ask me this question, I was going to give it its due.

What did I feel when I was with Laura Beth? When I met her on the plane, I'd felt interest and humor, and no small amount of lust. Once we were collaborating, her motivation and intelligence inspired me and I was excited by the prospect of what she could accomplish. But when I took her out on the *Moira Leigh*, an experience I hadn't shared with many people, it had simply felt...right. Her presence on my boat, in my penthouse, at the gala...it made me feel warm, welcome, content. Emotion, hot and potent, filled my chest.

When I looked back to Ralph, he had a knowing glint in his eyes and a soft smile on his face.

"Home," I answered, my voice cracking. "She feels like home."

"I'm glad," he said, voice gruff. "You deserve a love like that."

I huffed a laugh and pressed knuckles to the corners of my hot eyes. "Thank you, Ralph. I'm grateful for you."

"And I you," he said with a grin. "Now go on."

I smiled and heeded his order, stepping out onto the curb

and straight into the airport. I cut a straight line through the throng and walked up to the first ticketing agent who was free.

"I'd like to buy a ticket."

"Where are you headed, sir?" he asked, eyes on the screen behind the counter.

"Terminal B."

That immediately got his attention, and he looked up at me. "Sir?"

"The woman I love is scheduled to land at terminal B in 45 minutes, and I need to be there when she arrives. I don't care what the ticket says, I just need to get through security."

His eyes widened, then a slow smile spread across his face. "Oh, my gosh. They always said I'd witness at least one of these. Guess it's my lucky day!"

I cocked an eyebrow at him. "I'm almost afraid to ask."

"A dramatic, romantic airport rendezvous!" he said with enthusiasm, typing as he spoke. "You know, like in a romance movie! Anyway, it looks like the first flight of ours is going to cost—"

"I don't care," I interrupted, placing my black card on the counter, along with my ID.

His eyes widened at the exclusive card, then grinned as he snatched both items up. "It's a day of firsts for me, I guess. Say no more, sir. I'll have your boarding pass momentarily."

He hit a key and I heard the printer whirl. He snatched the ticket and my cards and handed them both over. "I can't believe I'm going to miss the best part, but here you go. Go get her."

"Thank you," I said with a grin, tapping my hand on the counter.

I turned and took off toward security, moving swiftly through the crowd. I checked my watch, grateful for once in my life that I was at the airport well ahead of time. If, by some miracle, she landed early, I didn't want to miss the chance to get to her right away.

My friend Fate had decided to be kind today, and I breezed through security and found myself at her gate with minutes to spare. Her plane had just arrived early and was pulling up to the gate. My skin felt hot with anticipation, and I realized with a sense of surprise that I was nervous. It wasn't a familiar feeling, but Laura Beth had a knack for putting me off my game in the best ways.

As the door to the jet bridge opened and people began pouring through, I searched for a head of golden hair atop a tiny frame. Before I could even see her face, I knew she was there. I recognized the way she moved and the confidence she carried.

Like an invisible force connected us, it only took a moment for her to spot me. Her eyes widened, she gasped, and she immediately abandoned her suitcase and started to run. Determined not to stand there, stupefied, like I had at the gala, I rushed forward. People cleared out of the way in surprise, turning to watch as we collided. Laura Beth leaped into my arms and I swept her up, crushing her to me as she wrapped her legs around my waist.

"Oh my god, Parker," she gasped, pressing her cheek to mine. "I'm so glad you're here. I've been thinking about you all week."

I just smiled and breathed her in, feeling that warm, calm feeling that came with being near her filling my bones. "I'm glad I'm here, too, spitfire. I've been worried about you."

"Oh, god, I know," she gushed, leaning back and loosening her legs, sliding back to her own two feet. "And I'm so sorry for that. I just–there's been so much I've been processing and I didn't know what to say, nothing felt right, and I just thought it best to wait until I saw you in person."

She was standing before me, now, holding my hands in hers,

staring up at me with those gorgeous bluebell eyes. Her hair was loose, wild, and there was a flush in her cheeks that I had only seen a handful of times before–on my boat, on the dance floor.

"Parker, I've been in my head for so long, I didn't even realize it," she said, gaze searching mine as she spoke.

She was talking so fast I was worried she was going to pass out, and her drawl was in full force. It made me so happy just to hear her being her authentic self, and I knew I was smiling at her like the lovesick, besotted fool I was.

"I know, spitfire, and it's okay–"

"It's not," she interjected earnestly, squeezing my hands in hers. "It's not okay at all. I had built up this idea in my head of what my future looked like. And then you came along, and it felt like you had derailed it. I never even stopped to question why. Why were you able to make me feel like my plans had all gone to hell in a handbasket?"

She paused, taking a breath, and I gave her a teasing smile.

"Was that a rhetorical question?"

She laughed, bright and quick, and shook her head.

"It wasn't, no," she said, as though that revelation was a surprise. "It was one I needed to ask myself a long time ago. I was so worried about the power you had over me, I never asked myself why you had that power in the first place."

I gently pulled one hand from hers to cup her cheek, stroking a thumb along her cheekbone. "You have all the power, Laura Beth. You always have."

She nodded, tears gathering in her eyes.

"I know that now," she whispered. "I watched it play out, with my momma and my sister, while I was home. Really watched, for the first time, to see what love looked like in practice."

She took a deep breath, leaning into my touch. "I never should've feared what being with you would mean for my future, Parker. I let myself create this...this story that I could only have you or my career, not both. And that's all it was, a story. A silly story I told myself out of fear of doing something unknown, something off-plan. But I'm not afraid anymore, Parker. Not of you, and not of what's between us."

I brought my other hand up to hold her face in my palms and she stepped closer, wrapping her arms around my waist.

"You look like you have something to say to me, spitfire," I whispered, drinking her in with my gaze.

She nodded, eyes shining. "I do, Parker. It's something I should've said in your penthouse that night, instead of running like a coward."

"We all have our moments," I murmured with a small shrug and the slightest of smirks.

She grinned, and her arms tightened around me. She took a steadying breath and anticipation, hot and prickly, filled me. I wanted to remember every little thing about this moment for the rest of my life. I wanted to sear the image of her before me in her oversized high school hoodie and bright pink yoga pants into my brain. I wanted to memorize the look of hope in her eyes so I could paint the door of our future home that same color. I never wanted to forget the flush in her cheeks, the shine of what I desperately hoped were happy tears welling and ready to spill. Whatever she wanted to say to me now would play on repeat in my head for years to come, I knew.

"I love you, Parker," she said, and I felt as though I would burst from the intensity of the feelings that burned through me as I finally heard those words from her lips. "And I want you. And I don't know what our future holds, but–"

"Is it my turn, yet?" I interrupted, raising a brow.

She nodded, chastised, and went to bite her lip, but before she could, I captured her mouth with mine. It was an all-consuming kiss, one I felt in every fiber of my being as she surrendered to me and let me in, lips parting, heart wide open and welcoming. I gave her everything I could in that kiss, poured every ounce of love and longing and forgiveness and hope I possessed into it. She reacted immediately, surging up on her tiptoes and winding her arms around my neck, clinging to me with a newfound ferocity that made my heart soar. *That's right, spitfire, claim what's yours. All of me.*

When we parted, both breathless, I rested my forehead against hers and held her face in my hands once more.

"I love every part of you, Laura Beth Calhoun," I said reverently.

A little laugh sob broke free from her, and she sniffled. I straightened a bit so I could look into her eyes and smiled at the emotion I saw swimming in their depths. I hoped she could see my sincerity in my gaze. I hoped she could tell, just from the way I looked at her, how perfect she was. How cherished, and how loved. I hoped she knew I'd always look at her that way... and that, in a way, I always had.

"I've loved you in so many moments from that day on the plane, so many perfect glimpses of the incredible person you are. But do you know my favorite part about our story, beautiful?"

She shook her head slowly, just a few tears spilling over as she did.

"That it's only just begun," I said earnestly, smiling at her and feeling as light as air. "We have a lifetime to write it together. You and me." I stroked her cheek again. "And I can't wait."

She sob-laughed again. "I can't wait either. I don't know what the hell is going to happen in my life otherwise, but I know I want you. I want us."

"I've been waiting for you to arrive at that conclusion for a while, spitfire."

"I know," she whispered, giving me a little smile. "Sorry I took the scenic route."

I chuckled and pushed a hand into her hair, cradling her head and pulling her up for another searing kiss. Just before I lost myself in her entirely, I realized I could hear clapping. I drew back from her slowly, giving her a conspiratorial look.

"Ready to lose the audience?" I asked, tilting my head toward the exit.

She bit her lip and nodded, cheeks flushing bright red. I reached up with a thumb and pulled her lip free.

"None of that, love. We're in public," I teased, winking as she giggled. "Let's get your bag and get out of here, yeah?"

She nodded. "I'm glad to be home," she said, almost shyly.

"In the Bay?"

I didn't realize what I had hoped she'd say in response until she said it, eyes shining once more.

"No, Parker. With *you*."

Epilogue

LB

"I think that's the last box!" I called as I dropped the moving box onto the floor of the window-lined bedroom.

Every inch of the apartment was gorgeous. The four bedroom, renovated penthouse had original hardwood floors, a chef's kitchen, and stunning natural light. To compare it to my crappy one-bedroom apartment in the city was laughable.

Parker met me in the living room as I dusted off my hands. "Christ, it better be," he panted, as he wiped his brow. "Remind me again why we didn't hire professional movers like I suggested?"

Putting my hands on my hips, I shot him "the look." "Because moving into your first place as a couple is a moment to be remembered, not tasked to somebody else!"

He barked a laugh and pulled me into his sweat-dampened arms. "Yes, ma'am." He nodded against my head. "You're lucky I like you bossy."

"Damn right. The men in this family know their place," I said as I tilted my head up to kiss his cheek.

Parker and I had agreed it made the most sense to move into his downtown Palo Alto apartment. It had been six months since I departed P&L and my new job at the Good Fortune Foundation was based in the South Bay. We also spent every night together, so my apartment in the city made little sense to keep once my lease was up with Maya.

There was also the fact that Preston and Cami had become my closest friends in the time Parker and I had been together–the two women immediately accepting me into their circle. It didn't hurt that they both helped to keep Parker in line and his ego in check.

The new rhythm I had fallen into made the Bay feel more like home than it ever had before. Most Saturdays I joined Cami at the local farmer's market, helping her choose the best looking produce of the season and Sundays were a family brunch. Preston and Parker's apartments were within walking distance of one another, and I never passed up the opportunity to escape over to their place for a girls' night during the week.

My new job was better than I ever could have imagined. It had turned out I didn't need the six-month severance package offered by P&L. After two weeks of letting myself enjoy Parker and the Bay without the demands of a corporate job, I was ready to dive back into job hunting. But much to my surprise, several head hunters were courting me.

I had been lucky enough to find my match in the Good Fortune Foundation–a nonprofit organization focused on addressing food insecurity in rural communities. The foundation was excited by my background in venture capital and lived experience coming from Alabama, and I was able to put all my skills gained at P&L to good use. I led our investment team, determining which technology startups had the most potential to make an impact and which community organizations were deserving of grants from the foundation.

Squeezing me tighter, Parker kissed the top of my head and

pulled away. "There is actually one more box that I need to open now."

"What? The van was empty. I double-checked."

Grinning, Parker reached into his back pocket and began to lower himself to the floor.

My heart stopped as I realized what was happening.

"Park–," I began before he held up his hand.

"Shh. Let me say this, Laura Beth," he said with a wink, and I slammed my lips shut.

Watching this indomitable man get to his knees before me was unlike any other experience before it. The way he looked at me now said a thousand words. His hazel eyes spoke of all the trust we had built, of honesty, and of a love deeper than the ocean.

"Laura Beth Calhoun. The day you waved at me on that flight was the day I became yours. God knows you made me work to earn the right to call you mine, but I wouldn't have traded a single moment along the way."

I laughed and nodded, tears beginning to well.

"I didn't know a love like this was possible for me and now that I've found it, I never want to let you go. You are without question the best thing to have happened to me in this life, and the idea of spending one moment without you is unthinkable."

Tears fell openly now and I sniffled, wiping my eyes.

"Marry me, spitfire. Be my partner. Be my challenger. And let me be your biggest supporter and the place you come home to. If that's in the Bay or in Pike Road, in a mansion or a house down by the river, I don't care, as long as I get to call you mine."

Parker reached up to take my hand, turning it over and sliding the most stunning ring I had ever seen onto my finger.

"It was my grandmother's ring, designed by my grandfather. He left it to me and told me to save it for someone special. I asked Sara Jean if you'd like it, and she told me she was gonna marry me if you didn't just to have it. I hope you love it, spitfire."

"You talked to Sara Jean?" I gaped at the enormous emerald stone occupying half my ring finger, trying to make my brain function. "Parker, it's...it's stunning. I...I don't even know what to say."

"How about yes?" he said with a smirk.

Surging forward, I took both his cheeks in my hand. "Yes, yes, of course, Parker!" I laughed through sobs. "I love you so much."

He broke into a dazzling smile before capturing my lips in a searing kiss. Standing, his hands found the back of my legs, and he scooped me up. Wrapping my legs around his hips, he walked us back towards the living room.

"Took you long enough," he muttered as he trailed kisses along my jaw.

Turning, he dropped us both onto the sofa, my legs straddling his.

"Patience is a virtue, Mr. Brooks. I was just processing."

Parker nipped at my earlobe before sucking it into his mouth. "I never claimed to be a virtuous man," he whispered.

Lifting his hips, Parker let me slide his sweatpants down, freeing his already hardening cock. I quickly discarded my leggings and tank, desperate for the feel of our bodies together.

I wrapped my hands around his neck and into the hair at the nape of his neck. I met his glittering eyes and smiled. "I love you, Parker Brooks," I mouthed as I lowered myself onto him.

His lips parted on a soft groan. "And I, you, Laura Beth."

Fully seated, I began to ride him, never breaking eye contact. As I moved, my muscles fluttered around his length, already building towards release.

One of Parker's hands found my ass, fingers digging into the soft flesh, as he helped to guide my movements, working my hips in a languid rhythm while he watched. His gaze was a physical presence, capable of traveling down my chest and stomach, caressing my thighs and stopping at where our bodies joined.

Stealing his attention, I glided my fingers through my soft folds and drew small circles around my clit. The pressure climbed, and my orgasm hovered just out of reach.

Parker arched his brow. "Is my fiancée going to come for me?"

I bit my bottom lip and nodded, my hips slowing to find an excruciatingly delicious motion. My pleasure wound tighter and tighter through me, the intensity almost overwhelming.

Parker cupped my cheek and swiped his fingers over my mouth, freeing my lip. "You're so fucking beautiful. And you're mine." Eyes locked on my mouth, he pressed his thumb into my open mouth, and I sucked it eagerly. "Let go Laura Beth, I've got you."

His words pushed me over the edge, my back arching, and I buried my head into Parker's neck. Still grinding my hips, my pussy clenching around him, Parker's release followed mine.

I stayed there, nestled against his chest, as the wave receded and I fought to catch my breath. All the while, Parker's hands skated up and down my low back in soothing motions.

I loved this man, and now I was officially going to spend the rest of my days with him. While neither of those things was part of the picture a year ago, thinking about it now, I was so fucking glad Parker Brooks walked into my life and changed that plan. Because I couldn't imagine life without him.

I pressed a kiss to his throat and a thought dawned on me. "You did talk to my momma and daddy before proposing, right?"

Parker barked a laugh, and I felt him twitch inside me. "Really, spitfire? My cock is still buried in you."

"I just need to know because if Sara Jean knows, Momma's gonna find out, and you do not want to be on the receiving end of her fury when she finds out her baby girl got engaged without her knowin' first."

Parker smoothed his hands up my sides and cupped my cheeks, pulling me back to look at him. "Your momma and daddy gave their blessing and couldn't be more excited. Why don't you go have a shower, and we can video call them when you're out."

He gave me a chaste kiss. "I love you, spitfire."

"I love you, too."

———

Not ready to say farewell to LB and Parker? We weren't, either. Get a bonus scene featuring a flight back to Pike Road that includes an extra spicy scene just for you. Visit the url below to sign up for our mailing list and start reading!

GET THE BONUS SCENE
https://BookHip.com/QVVHZVM

Excerpt from Reserved
South Bay Billionaires Book #2
Chapter 1: Van

"Did you order from the trolley?"

I looked up from my monitor to see Miles Davenport, my business partner's executive assistant, leaning in the doorway. I furrowed my brow in annoyance and his eyebrows flew up.

"I don't think so, Mr. Grumpypants," he snapped, holding a finger out in admonishment. "I am not here for your particular brand of alphahole today. Just answer the question and I'll leave you alone."

I scoffed at his over-the-top antics. "No."

He rolled his eyes heavily, as was his habit, and muttered under his breath as he turned to leave. "Heaven forbid I try to help a man out." He threw a hand up in the air in a haughty wave and called back to me without turning. "Sorry I care about you missing lunch, boss man! Won't happen again."

My chat pinged on my screen, drawing my attention.

> Lex: Stop antagonizing Miles.

How dare she.

Me: I did no such thing.

Lex: I could hear him bickering with you from my office.

I pressed two fingers to my temple in exasperation.

Me: It's not my fault you hired an unprofessional assistant.

Her reply was swift, and I could tell she was amused. Because of course, she was. The woman knew me too well.

Lex: That man keeps this place afloat and you know it. Apologize, publicly, even if he is being dramatic. We don't need any dissension in the ranks.

Isn't that the fucking truth. Athena Ventures, the venture capital firm Lex had founded and brought me on to help her build and run, had a stellar reputation in the Bay. But we were also under the microscope for a few reasons, including the fact that her father's global investment firm had opened its first venture capital firm right down the street. The competitive relationship between the family was well documented and had been getting some press thanks to a few highly public recent events, so Lex was on high alert about ensuring things stayed as level as possible for our team. We didn't need the manufactured, and frankly unnecessary, tension to cause any challenges for our people.

I had no desire to get out of my chair, abandon my progress on the pile of work in my inbox, and chase Miles down for an apology he would immediately know was performative, but if Lex was asking...I'd do it. *He knows it, too, the little shit. Probably set me up.*

Chapter 1: Van

> Me: Fine.

I stood up abruptly and pulled my suit jacket from the closet behind my desk, settling it back on my shoulders as I strode for the door. Suits weren't a requirement in the VC world–in fact, they were often seen as overkill amongst the casual tech startups we often worked with. But I had worked hard to earn the kind of salary and savings that could outfit me in custom Italian craftsmanship. And, after my humble beginnings back home in New Jersey, I was damn well going to enjoy the luxuries I could now afford.

I felt the team's eyes on me as I passed, and I gave a nod to those bold enough to make eye contact. I had a reputation in this town, and this industry, for being ruthless but respectable, and I wore that like armor every day–even here.

"Miles," I called, approaching him. I immediately noticed that he'd paused to chat with a junior associate in the busiest area of the office, right in the middle of the open collection of desks where our junior and operations team members sat.

"Yes, Mr. Costa?" he replied, turning to me with an accusatory eyebrow raise. His eyes flashed and the corner of his mouth quirked ever so slightly up.

Little shit-stirrer, I was right. I gave him a tight smile, refusing to call him out for his performance in front of our staff.

"I believe there was a miscommunication."

"Oh, was there?" He gave me an overly innocent look, batting his lashes. "Please, do tell."

"My short reply was not in response to anything you did," I said. "I was merely concentrating on my work and found context switching difficult in the moment."

"Apology accepted," he responded primly, knowing full well that I had in no way apologized.

"Good," I gritted out, even though "thank you" might have been the more polite response.

I could tell he was fighting back a laugh, and I rolled my eyes to the ceiling and sighed. I was already out here, with an audience. I may as well make Lex happy and try to seem more human for the troops, as she was always asking me to.

"You mentioned a trolley?" I asked, immediately regretting the question when Miles's eyes lit up in delight.

The man was nothing if not conniving, and I had no doubt he was going to play this situation to his advantage. Even if only to get maximum entertainment out of it.

"That's right," he smirked. "Jax, the mail boy, started ordering from there last week."

"He says they have the healthiest lunch options," the young junior associate Miles had been chatting with piped up. "He's getting in shape for an upcoming shoot or something. You know, for his modeling side gig."

I raised an eyebrow at her, surprised she was indulging in office gossip with me, of all people. Miles grinned, clearly thinking the same.

"Right, you are, Rebecca! And, well, it's all delicious, so he's got the whole Pit ordering from her now," he continued, gesturing at the many desks around us.

"Her?" I asked, glancing around.

"Cami," Rebecca said brightly, "the trolley girl."

Just as I was about to ask for more information about this trolley girl, I caught sight of her. She was on the far side of the office, having delivered food to the row of offices opposite mine first. She had her back to us as she chatted animatedly with Jax, our resident mail boy/model. She was average height, maybe 5' 6", with luscious dark brown hair that cascaded down her back. It was long enough to wrap around my fist, I observed. She looked at home amongst the more casually-dressed members of our team, with her well-worn high-rise jeans beautifully framing an ass I'd love to sink my teeth into.

I blinked at myself, surprised at my train of thought. About to turn back to Miles and excuse myself, I heard the woman–Cami–laugh. She angled her body toward Jax as she did, throwing her head back to send her hair dancing across her over-sized white linen shirt and filling the room with the most melodic sound. It hit me in my chest and my gut, my whole body tightening in response. *She is exquisite.*

She was. She laid a friendly hand on Jax's arm before moving back to continue pushing her cart, and I heard a rumble start in my chest. If that overgrown surfer boy was doing anything other than paying for his lunch, I'd–

"You alright, there, sir?" Miles interrupted my wildly inappropriate, but completely justified, train of thought.

I whipped my gaze toward him to find a look of surprise etched onto his features. *Ah, shit. He heard that.*

I cleared my throat gruffly. "Fine, Miles. I'm fine."

"Mmhm," he taunted, that infuriating smirk reappearing. "I can see that."

I fought my eye-roll and turned back toward my office. It just so happened that Cami was headed that way, as well. It was clear she'd been here a few times, as she greeted most people with a friendly smile and a hello, many of them by name. I followed after her, slowly, thinking through my options. Jax saw me passing and raised a hand to catch my attention, opening his mouth to no doubt call my name, but I shut him down with a look. His jaw snapped shut and he slumped back against the desk he'd been standing near, leaning on it in defeat instead of hurrying after me. The kid was a character, I'd give him that, but if he tried to get between me and the angel in front of me right now, I'd tear his head clean off.

"Excuse me, I don't think we've met," a sweet voice called.

I looked up and realized both Cami and I had reached my office, which was ultimately a dead end for her.

"I haven't had the pleasure." I offered her a hand.

Her eyebrows rose but she accepted my hand, the soft press of her calloused fingers sending shockwaves across my skin. Her handshake was gentle but not weak, and her hand slipped from mine slowly.

I was mesmerized by the play of light in her warm brown eyes. "Van."

"Cami," she replied, a bright smile taking over her features, rivaling the sun. "Of Camellia's Kitchen," she continued, gesturing to the happy floral logo on the side of her trolley.

"*Bellissima*," I murmured and was rewarded with a gentle rush of pink to her cheeks.

"Um, thank you." She tucked a strand of hair behind her ear. "Do you have an order today, Van?"

"No." I looked down at the orderly pile of sandwiches, salads, and bowls she had with her. "Is everything accounted for?"

"I have a sundried tomato pesto veggie sandwich or a quinoa bowl if you want one of those?" She offered both, one in each hand, with a hopeful glint in her deep eyes.

"The quinoa." I went to fish my wallet out of my pocket.

"Oh no, it's okay," she protested, waving away the card I was retrieving. "Jax always over orders, they're already paid for. He told me to find them a home."

I grunted, both surprised and not, and accepted the bowl she handed over with a nod.

"This is my favorite," she whispered, conspiratorially, "it's got pickled onion and this absolutely gorgeous kale I found at the market this week."

"Do you make them?" I asked, finding myself desperate to keep her talking, just so I could keep her with me.

She nodded enthusiastically, "Sure do, every single one. It's a small business but fulfilling work."

"Well, Jax apparently has only good things to say. I'm looking forward to trying it."

Her smile turned sheepish, almost self-deprecating, and she gave a little shrug. I could feel frustration rising in me. Not at her, but at whoever had made her feel like she had to reject praise or soften her shine. I wanted to buff and burnish her—mind, body, and spirit—until she glowed more powerfully than the sun.

"Have dinner with me," I blurted, unable to hold back any longer.

She gasped quietly, her eyes widening. I could see her pulse thunder in the hollow of her neck, could see the effect I was having on her. We were standing close enough that my six feet, five inches loomed over her, and I loved the way she looked as she craned her neck to meet my gaze.

"Um, well," she muttered, taking a tentative step back and starting to turn her trolley. "It was, uh, nice to meet you, Van."

"Tonight," I pressed, intent on seeing her again.

Her gaze flew to mine again and that flush crept back up her cheeks. "You sure are a forward one, aren't you?"

"I'm a man who knows what he wants, Cami." I flashed a grin. "And I'm unafraid to pursue her."

Her mouth dropped open a bit, her breathing a bit heavier than it had been a few moments ago. Her reactions were absolutely stunning, and I was glad that my suit coat and the quinoa bowl in my hands obstructed her view of exactly how much I was enjoying the conversation.

She blinked at me and shook her head a bit as though she was gathering her wits. But I didn't want her to gather them. I wanted them to stay scattered so I could slowly, deliberately gather them back up myself and piece her back together like the work of art she was. And then shatter her all over again. And again.

"I'm flattered, Van, really," she recovered, her natural inclination to be cheery warring with the way my words had affected her. "But you're a stranger to me."

"Fair." I nodded, perversely pleased that she wasn't throwing herself at my feet just because I'd asked her out. I wanted her to be safe. "I'll just have to help you get to know me. Won't I, *bella?*"

I so desperately wanted to stroke the backs of my fingers along her cheek, neck, and down to the delicious swell of her breast I could see above her neckline, but I offered my hand instead. She assumed, as I knew she would, that I was going in for a handshake. Instead, I turned her hand in mine and brought the back of it to my lips, pressing a chaste, but lingering, kiss to her warm flesh. I heard her breath stutter and saw her smile as I slowly released her, stepping to my office door.

"*Buongiorno, bella,*' I said, reveling in the heat I saw flash in her eyes. "It's been a pleasure."

"Um, thank you, Van," she replied, trying to find her footing. "Have a good one."

She began to push her trolley back toward the Pit, casting a glance over her shoulder with a tentative smile as she did.

"See you tomorrow, Cami," I called, enjoying the way her eyes widened far too much.

This is going to be fun, fiore mio. *I can't wait.*

PREORDER RESERVED NOW

https://books2read.com/reserved

Acknowledgments

Okay, y'all, that was fun! This was our very first book and, boy, did we have a blast writing Parker and LB's story. We learned a lot about them—and ourselves—in the process, and we can't wait for you to join us with Van and Cami in Reserved, South Bay Billionaires #2.

Writing this book feels like it's been both years and weeks in the making. We've been friends and colleagues for a while now, but it wasn't until the summer of 2023 that we discovered we shared a mutual dream to write for a living. It only took us a couple of days to go from "hey, we should write a book together" to owning an LLC, establishing a website, and setting up umpteen social media accounts. And from there, everything just came together.

Not that it wasn't hard work—it was, a shit ton of it—but it was seamless hard work. And we were both wholeheartedly in it. We hope it shows. We may be baby authors, but we tried to take great care with Parker and Laura Beth.

It wouldn't have been possible to bring you this story without the love and support we received from some special people. First, shout out to the husbands for saying "heck yes!" when we had the idea to start a self-publishing business—you're our MVPs. Second, to those we call our early benefactors—thank you for funding our first writing retreat, where we finalized *Arrived* and took a gigantic step toward making this shared dream a reality. And to our alpha and beta readers—Dawn, Jake, Matt, Apple, Lara, Nicole, Sydney—thank you for handling our first book with care and helping us write the very best story we could.

For those who encouraged us by asking for stories like ours in book groups, sharing billionaire stories on social media, and being avid fans of this genre, we salute you. You're why we're here, and you're awesome.

This was just the first of many books we plan to write for you all. If you want updates on the next four in this series or the four in the–ahem, *cough* dark mafia *cough*–series to come after that, you should join our Facebook reader group, Ashley Jacobs & S. S. Rich's Billionaire Babes.

'Til next time!

xo

ashley & s

About the Authors

Ashley Jacobs is a debut contemporary romance author. She loves to write alpha billionaires and the strong women they fall for. She lives in the United States with her golden retriever husband and goldendoodles. When she isn't spending time with fictional characters, she is busy hunting for the perfect croissant.

An avid reader from an early age, S. S. Rich grew up on old school sci fi and fantasy. Now, she enjoys creating strong female characters and the growly alphaholes who melt for them. Getting to do it with her bestie is the icing on the cake. When she's not writing, you can find S. chasing her children and dogs, enjoying the Pacific Northwest, obsessing over special edition book boxes, or feeding her wanderlust.

Find out more and sign up for our newsletter at shelfindulgences.com.

Made in the USA
Las Vegas, NV
09 May 2024

89716980R20194